ALSO BY W. M. AKERS

Westside

WESTSIDE SAINTS

WESTSIDE SAINTS

A NOVEL

W. M. AKERS

HARPER Voyager
An Imprint of HarperCollins*Publishers*

WESTSIDE SAINTS. Copyright © 2020 by William M. Akers Jr. All rights reserved. Printed in the United States of America. No part of this book may be used or reproduced in any manner whatsoever without written permission except in the case of brief quotations embodied in critical articles and reviews. For information, address HarperCollins Publishers, 195 Broadway, New York, NY 10007.

HarperCollins books may be purchased for educational, business, or sales promotional use. For information, please email the Special Markets Department at SPsales@harpercollins.com.

Harper Voyager and design are trademarks of HarperCollins Publishers LLC.

FIRST EDITION

Designed by Paula Russell Szafranski

Map by James Sinclair

Library of Congress Cataloging-in-Publication Data has been applied for.

ISBN 978-0-06-285404-9

20 21 22 23 24 LSC 10 9 8 7 6 5 4 3 2 1

For August,

born on the Westside

of our apartment

WESTSIDE SAINTS

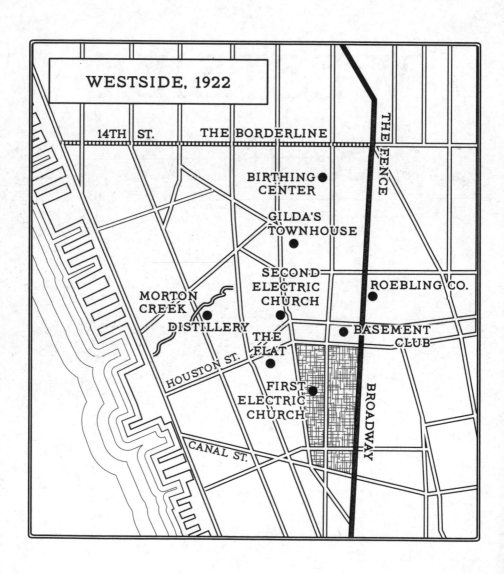

WESTSIDE, 1922

14TH ST. THE BORDERLINE

THE FENCE

BIRTHING
CENTER

GILDA'S
TOWNHOUSE

SECOND
ELECTRIC
CHURCH

ROEBLING CO.

MORTON
CREEK

DISTILLERY

BASEMENT
CLUB

THE
FLAT

HOUSTON ST.

FIRST
ELECTRIC
CHURCH

BROADWAY

CANAL ST.

ONE

On a night of hard frost, in the ruins of a burnt church, I found a body in the snow.

Its hand poked through the powder, gripping a crumbling stone altar. When I touched the wrist, a fistful of white tumbled away, exposing a derby hat and a tuft of thin orange hair spotted with blood.

"Find it?" called the woman I traveled with.

I wiped my hand on my black dress, which had seen much worse than the residue of a corpse, and walked back to her.

"There's nothing here," I said, and left the dead man behind. It was no feat. I'd been walking away from corpses all winter long. This was March 1922, when our bodies refused to stay buried.

Ten days prior, I was spitting off the ledge of Berk's Third Floor. Owned by one of the rare Westsiders as short and uncompromising as myself, Berk's was a shabby saloon on the Westside half of the stem whose eastern walls and roof had, some years back, simply melted away.

The exposure to the elements made it a pleasant summertime beer garden. In the winter it remained popular only with the committed few: those antisocial types who would happily freeze for a peek over the top of the fence and the chance to drink illegal liquor in full view of the Eastside throng. The people on the far side of

Broadway were fat, happy, honorable, and safe, but when they cast their sober eyes up at us, all we saw was thirst. We raised our glasses to say that though west of the fence we had no electricity, no heat, and no conveniences, that though there were no guns on our side of the island but countless murders just the same, that though we lived in what they called hell, we had liquor, and some nights that made it okay.

On the other nights, we spit.

It was at least twenty feet from the lip of the saloon to the fence, but that didn't stop us trying to expectorate clear over the barrier to the Eastside. Long nights were passed in drunken argument about the proper angle to launch one's missile, the ideal texture for flight, and the correct place to stand in order to harness the wind. No one had ever seen anyone clear the fence, but every drinker there insisted that once, just once, they had made it.

My mouth was drying and my projectiles were growing feeble when Bex Red appeared at my side, wrapped in every layer of fabric she owned. Born in Florida, but a fixture on the Westside art scene since before the fence was raised, Bex had never embraced the brutality of the New York cold. Sharp blue eyes peeked out through a slit in the scarves that swaddled her head, yet her voice was unmuffled by the cloth.

"Every time I see you, Gilda, you've managed to find a worse bar," she said.

We sat at my table, a few inches from the edge, and I sloshed some gin into a chipped cup. It ran like sludge, and the glass was cold enough to cling to her lips, but she lifted a scarf and drained it. She dug her mittened hand into a coat pocket and pulled out a carefully folded square of thick homemade paper marked up with ninety-nine shades of blue.

"This is every blue I can mix," she said, "and that's every blue there is, from the not-quite-black of deep river water to this washed-out near white that's too fragile even for a robin's egg."

"They all look blue to me."

"You have always lacked an artist's temperament."

"Thank you."

"Any of these look right?" she said with a theatrical sigh. I ran my finger down the page, squinting until my eyes crossed.

"Blue 72, maybe. Or it could be 74."

"This was my whole afternoon, you know. Do I get paid for the time?"

"You get paid when I get paid."

"Are you going to get paid?"

"Probably not." I put the color chart away.

"Well, while we're on the subject of wasted time . . ."

From deep in her coats she drew a worn paper envelope as soft as an old dollar bill. Inside were three portraits: two I would force myself to look at, and one I could not stand to see. The first showed a man with a gut as round and heavy as a pumpkin, shirtless at a table, a forkful of sausage and cabbage poised before wet red lips. The other was of a woman, handsome but joyless, waiting in line at an Eastside bank.

"These are good," I said.

"Better than last week?"

"Last week's were fine."

"But you like these more."

"Perhaps. They are so, so ordinary."

She swirled her cup, scowling at its emptiness. I tilted the bottle in her direction, but she refused.

"It's not healthy, drinking this filth," she said.

"Beats the cold."

She pulled her layers tighter, then leaned across the table and gave me an entirely unworkable hug. I stared as she walked away and wished I knew how to leave by her side. But I had one more appointment to keep.

A party of slummers poured through the door, nearly knocking Bex to the floor, and flung themselves at the bar crying for gin. Berk slid them a couple of bottles, exacting an outrageous price in return, and they occupied the table beside mine, laughing like only Eastsiders can.

"Isn't it the most marvelous pit?" asked their leader, an over-grown boy in a cashmere overcoat whose slick curls stuck out below the brim of his hat. "Berk's a troll, but she has her uses. I've been coming here for ages, you know, and she loves me like a son."

I eyed the leg of his chair, which teetered beside the drop. If I smacked it, there was a strong chance he would fall to his death. Warmed by that happy thought, I returned the drawings to the envelope, taking care not to see the one that remained inside, and poured myself another drink.

I was watching snow swirl across the hardwood floor, savoring the mawkish burn of Berk's red gin, when the bells of Grace Church sang ten o'clock, and Judy Byrd kicked open the stairwell door.

"I come to preach the electric resurrection," she bellowed, and those familiar with her ministry pulled their glasses close to their chests.

A black woman whose tight curls were just smoked with gray, Judy vaulted onto the oak bar without apparent strain and did not turn her head at Berk's perfunctory cry that she get the hell down. She wore a homespun orange dress and a tightly knotted kerchief, and spoke with a heavy Haitian accent that I knew to be an affectation. She clutched an ancient broom whose few remaining bristles stuck out at odd angles, hoisting it over her head like an executioner showing off his ax.

"What business have I, an honest woman, a god-fearing woman, what business have I skulking in the worst gin mills the Westside has to offer?" she asked the room.

"I think Miss Berk would take exception to that," said the cashmere overcoat. He looked around, waiting for the room to acknowledge his barb, but even his friends were watching Judy. She was well into her reverie, which she would follow, as she always did, down twisting paths of mixed metaphor until it led us all to salvation.

"I tell you why I come here, why I drag my frostbitten feet up those unreliable stairs, why I leap upon this bar the same way we all must leap across the valley of death and into the arms of our savior. I do it for love. I love you drunks, the way you slur like the devil's caught your tongue, the way you stumble like he's hobbled your feet, the way your skin blisters and cracks and turns as red as hellfire, as bloody as the gin in your glass. I love you all, no matter how you try to blot out the light God lit inside you, no matter how greedily you suck the intoxicating sweat that runs off the devil's backside. I love you as Christ loves you, and in his name I will sweep you clean."

She snapped her old broom down on the bar, sending a hail of cigarette butts and stained linen to join the snow on the floor. She ran the length, giggling as she swept empty bottles and dirty glasses crashing to their death.

"By god, boys, she's insane!" cackled one of the slummers, drawing Judy's eye for the first time. With three quick steps, she bounded onto their table. They stopped laughing. The man in the cashmere coat spun around and glared at Berk, who watched the whole scene from a stool at the edge of the room, her face like stone.

"So help me," he said, "if you let this Negro clown spill a drop of my liquor—"

He never completed his threat. With a practiced flick of her wrist, Judy flung their glasses into space—all save that of the leader, whose cup she tipped into his lap, staining his cashmere beyond repair.

He grabbed her by the ankle. She pointed her broom handle at his forehead, a matador preparing to deliver the final blow. He snickered, the way you do when your father has money and you understand the whole world has been set up for your benefit. No one else laughed.

"You'll pay for that liquor," he said. "The coat, too."

"You're the one who'll pay," Judy answered, as readily as a comic taking the straight man's line. "The cost is far more than the dime Miss Berk charges—it's ten million years in a pit of fire, with snakes pricking your pecker until it bursts, over and over again."

"Cut out that noise and buy us another round or I'll throw you into the street."

"God wouldn't let me die."

The man tightened his grip on Judy's leg. I saw no sign that God was preparing to intervene, and so I stepped in. I placed my hand on his soft black glove.

"Let her go," I said.

"What'd I tell you boys," he said to the friends who could no longer meet his eye. "Westside women are hellcats."

"You are outnumbered and badly disliked. This could be an amusing anecdote for your fellows on the Eastside, or it could be a tragedy. What would you prefer?"

He chuckled. His laugh sounded like slime. In a room without a wall, he was backed into a corner, and I really didn't know if he'd give up or lash out. I believe I was ready for either. His friends made the decision for him, cinching their scarves and slinking for the exit. Seeing that he really was outnumbered—even rich boys must learn some arithmetic—he broke his grip on Judy's ankle and followed them out.

Even through the cold, my face felt hot. I drained my drink, grateful it had survived the sermon. Judy jumped down and wrapped me in a welcome embrace.

"Gilda Carr," she said. "My favorite sinner. God truly takes all forms."

"Are we getting the gospel tonight, Judy, or ain't we?" asked one of the men at the bar.

"Give 'em a show," I said, and she launched back into her sermon, howling of thumbscrews and broken bones, eager demons and weak flesh, evil liquor and the healing power of God's infinite grace. And she told about the coming resurrection, when our dead would rise from their graves and walk the Westside streets, when all the wounds we bandaged with liquor would finally be healed. She punctuated every paragraph by sweeping another heap of the mess she'd made over the edge of the vanished wall, where it crashed onto the street to startle the fleeing slummers. I reached behind the bar for an unbroken bottle, dropped a dime in the bucket, and poured myself a fresh one.

Before I could settle in, a hand brushed my elbow. Behind me was a sallow white man in a perfectly tailored suit that would have been the height of fashion thirty years before. His hands were bare, despite the cold, and he held a tidy wad of pamphlets that offered scriptural backing for Judy's unpredictable testimony. He was her brother, Enoch Byrd.

"A tract, Miss Carr?"

"I'm afraid I've read them all."

Enoch was at least a decade older than me, but there was something boyish about him. While his sister spoke in a rambling torrent, he chose his words with care, pausing for seconds at a time as he searched for one that fit. He reminded me of the sort of boy I met too few of as a young girl, who were too tongue-tied and pathetic to ever seem a threat.

I often saw him on cold mornings, pushing a soup cart down snowy streets, waking those who had passed out on the sidewalk, helping them get warm and get home. He ordered them about with the precision of a drill sergeant, an attitude that would have been irritating if it hadn't saved lives. A few years prior, my father had often been one of those woken on Enoch's morning rounds, and I had been deeply fond of this dull, middle-aged man and his rowdy sister ever since.

The business with the blue ink had started in late November, on what must have been our last tolerably warm day, when Enoch found me on my stoop pelting rocks at pigeons and watching night sweep over Washington Square. He was silent until I asked him to sit down, and then he pointed past the bare trees that filled the park to the clean, pale eastern sky.

"That blue," he said. "You only get it at this hour, when the sun is sinking and the shadows are long and day is just clinging on. It's my favorite color in the world."

"It's good enough."

"I have dreams in that color. Dreams of hell. Not nightmares. I've had them my whole life. My father used to preach about the blue flames of hell, and I've decided I'd like to do a tract in his honor, with three-color printing, that shows damnation as only he could paint it."

He slid a pile of meticulously printed religious blather, each eight pages long and printed in black, white, and a different shade of blue.

"And no matter how many different blues you try, none of them hits the mark?" I said.

"How did you know?"

"I know the look, that special brand of misery that comes from trying to make the real world line up with something perfect in your head."

"And these are the cases, the tiny mysteries, that are your specialty?"

I was wary. This was the type of thing I would usually turn down. It was tiny, sure, but it was also impossible. Enoch had standards—you could tell just by looking at his perfect little tracts—and that was hell in a client. But that fall I needed work, in every way a woman can.

"I'll turn the city upside down until you have the blue you want," I said. "As long as you can tell me what's so special about this shade."

I chucked another rock, missing the bird badly, and he told me a story about a little boy who grew up in the heart of Lower Manhattan, long before a fence divided Eastside from West, the son of a gifted preacher who loved his children, but loved his ministry more.

"Even when we did get Papa to ourselves, we never got to be alone with him," he said. "Except for one afternoon, when he took me to see the carriage parade in Central Park. Afterward, we walked the length of it. I was watching the sun set over the lake, when he told me to turn around and look east instead. He died soon after. My whole life, that blue has stayed in my heart."

Over the next months, whenever I had the pep to get out of bed, I stalked Manhattan up and down, sifting through shops for printers, authors, artists, stamp collectors, pen collectors, calligraphers, weavers, forgers, pornographers, and anyone else with an eye for beautiful things. To the Lower West I brought bits of paper stained with every blue I found, and to all of them Enoch apologized and shook his head.

At last I found an old woman in an underground shop on the Upper West, who promised she could make ink to match any shade in creation, so long as I could provide her with a sample. But of course that was impossible. In all of New York, there was no paint shard, no fabric scrap, no broken pot or torn dust jacket or dead bug that quite matched the flames burning inside Enoch Byrd's head. I didn't mind. The longer he was unsatisfied, the more I would eventually bill him, and the longer I put off finding something else to do with my days.

That night at the saloon, I smoothed Bex's array of blues out on the table and watched him run his finger down the rows of color, wondering how long it would take him to shake his head.

"Your instincts are good," he said. "Blue 72 is close to what I'm after."

"But close is . . ."

"Still a bit wrong. I'm sorry, truly."

"All part of the job."

With a final cackle, Judy cast the last of the broken glass over the lip of the building. She tucked her broom under her shoulder and sidled up to her brother, eyeing his purse.

"Any sales?" she said.

"Three dollars' worth," he answered.

"Berk says we owe two twenty-five for the glassware."

"You might avoid the ashtrays, sister. They are expensive."

"You know better than anyone that Christ demands a clean sweep."

Enoch sighed, counted the money, and dropped it in the bucket on the bar. Berk nodded, and Judy saluted with her broom.

"Have you nearly finished that drink, Miss Carr?" asked Enoch.

"Yes," I said, "but I haven't even started on the next one."

"I wonder if you would consider postponing it. You've done

such marvelous work looking for my blue ink and I wondered if, well . . . my mother wants a word."

I pulled the dregs of the gin through my teeth and remembered how Enoch would hold my father's hand as he trembled up our town house steps. My glass thudded, empty, onto the bar.

"Anything for the Byrds," I said.

Down on the street, on the frozen, broken pavement of that road some still call Broadway, the heat from Berk's felt far away, and the lights from the Eastside glowed only faintly over the top of the fence. Judy lit a cigarette and took a slow, sacred drag.

"I thought you were without vice," I said.

"I am opposed to the devil's intoxicants," she said, her Haitian lilt discarded in favor of a bracing Westside brogue. "That does not mean I am without sin."

"Mam is waiting," said Enoch.

Mam was a woman in a soiled white cloak leaning on the fence beside the barred Waverly Place gate. She had thin peach lips and, beneath her hood, hair translucent white. She wore a heavy ivory glove on her left hand. Her right she offered to me.

"Helen Byrd," she said.

"Matriarch of the Electric Church," said Enoch. "Widow of its founder, the prophet and martyr Bulrush Byrd. Mam. And this is my sister Ruth."

Ruth had a pointed chin and flat hair. A heavy scarf covered most of her face. She stared through me blankly, looking so much like her mother that it made me a bit dizzy. With only the flickering light of Berk's faraway fire to guide me, it was hard to tell if Helen looked young for her age, or if Ruth was old for hers.

"I'm not impressed," said Helen after she finished sizing me up.

"I'd be worried if you were. What is it you want?"

"Something has gone missing from our church. My children insist you are the woman to find it. I don't agree, but they don't care."

"If you're waiting for me to defend myself, don't bother. I'm too cold to beg."

She scowled more, somehow, and went on.

"It is the finger of Róisín of Lismore, a saint. Our saint. It is a fixture of our ministry, the centerpiece of our faith, and it was stolen from our church earlier this week. I am told you specialize in finding tiny things."

"It's the little finger," said Judy. I couldn't tell if she was trying to be funny, but I did my best not to laugh. "Left hand. Pickled."

"When was it stolen?" I said.

"After dark on Thursday night," said Helen. "Ruth noticed it missing at dawn."

"No one saw anything?"

"If we had, we would not have come to you."

"Who has access to the church after dark? Just the four of you?"

"The whole city has access to the electric faith."

"What?"

"We leave our doors open to the neighborhood," said Enoch. "That any passing vagrant might take shelter. We have nothing to steal."

"Not anymore, anyway," I said, ignoring Helen's and Ruth's irritation. "You're certain it was stolen? I find that the smaller the finger, the more likely it is to be misplaced."

"Saint Róisín's finger resides in a small glass case," said Helen. "It is never disturbed, even during services. The only key is kept in my office, and that door is always locked, no matter the needs of the city's vagrants."

"The case was smashed?" I said.

"To dust," said Ruth, so low I could hardly hear.

"Nothing else was taken?"

"As my brother said, there really is nothing to steal."

"And why do you need the finger back?"

"What kind of question is that?" said Enoch.

"It's, what, an inch and a half long? Shriveled? Pink? I can find you one to match in any snowbank on this avenue. I assure you, the donor will not mind."

"It wouldn't be Róisín."

"And you really believe that little scrap of flesh you keep in a box is?"

I thought they would be angry. If they were, it didn't show. Enoch blanched; Judy cackled, and Helen became, if this was possible, even more blank. Ruth's stern eyes softened, and she looked on me with pity as she took my hands in hers.

"You have lost quite a lot," she said, stroking my hands, searching my face.

"So has everyone. That's an easy thing to guess."

"You've lost a parent. Both parents?"

"What does that have to do with your stolen digit?"

"You have no family, few friends. You have seen too much bloodshed, too much pain. This winter has been hard for all of us, but harder for you. You try to carry the city on your back, and it has bent you double."

I tried to keep her from seeing that she wasn't wrong. I don't think I succeeded.

"Róisín is the patron saint of suffering. Her death was more horrible than you could imagine, and she bore it with a smile. Our family has lost much, too, and our parishioners have lost even more. Decades of suffering, and she has always been there. Without her to point the way, our family, our church, will be lost."

"Our city, too," said Enoch. "Without our church, the whole city is in jeopardy."

I had never been inside the building they called a church, but I had seen it. A onetime Italian banquet hall on Carmine Street, its old sign shone through the poorly painted marquee that invited the world to "Join the Electric Church." I had always wondered why they chose it. In a district overrun with abandoned churches, some in serviceable condition, they preferred a dump.

I looked at the four of them, their clothes and bearing as ridiculous as their faith. They were pathetic, but they were kind. In a city and a winter that fought so hard to crush those who believed in anything but greed and death, they pressed on. Delusional, certainly—Enoch couldn't really believe the whole city was counting on them—but their intentions were pure. If they thought the finger would help them continue with that mission . . .

"I'd be honored," I said.

"I still don't like her," said Helen.

"And I don't like you, but that doesn't mean we can't have a bit of fun."

Helen gave me the kind of look you normally expect from a Gorgon. Judy pulled her mother back and whispered, "She's the only one."

"Fine," said Helen. "Fine."

"A ringing endorsement," I said. "I can't wait to get started."

"Thank you, Miss Carr," said Enoch. "And while you're working for Mam, of course, you can let the blue ink go."

I appreciated that. I'm sure Bex would feel it was far more healthy to chase just one impossibility at a time.

I could have gone back upstairs for another drink, but instead I let them walk me home, as they had done so often for my father, to the town house that stood alone on an empty block on the western edge of Washington Square.

I stepped from the frozen street into my frozen parlor, lit a fire, and tried to drive the frost from my chest. I drew a fat album from a high shelf and laid it on the floor before the dancing flame. Inside were dozens of Bex's drawings of the old man and the young woman, drawings of them walking and eating and bathing and living lives too ordinary to be believed. He was the Glen-Richard Van Alen who lived in another New York, far gentler than our own. She was Juliette Copeland. Him I'd shot in the chest. Her I'd drowned. These drawings, which I'd started commissioning from Bex when I realized my guilt would not fade with autumn, were glimpses into the sorts of quiet days my victims would never enjoy.

I pasted the new pair onto blank pages. There was one more drawing inside Bex's envelope that I could not bear to see. I left it inside and fell asleep by the fire, hoping that if the finger of Saint Róisín couldn't save the city, it could at least save me.

The next morning I breakfasted in the Upper West, on a sliver-thin side street nestled between Fifth Avenue and the fence, where the smell of old money still hung in the air. In a double-wide town house painted a chipped, fading blue, I was greeted by a woman with tight white curls whose skin was as wrinkled and clear as cellophane. This was my grandmother: the distinguished Anacostia Fall.

"Did you bring it?" she said, as she welcomed me in from the cold.

"Is there sausage?"

"The way you can gorge without doing the decent thing and becoming monstrously fat—it simply baffles."

"I assure you—when out of your sight, I eat as delicately as a bird."

She honked out a laugh. I followed her across the polished parquet, beneath a dripping, wax-encrusted chandelier, past a heavenly staircase that twisted to the floors above. Candles flickered over photos of relatives long dead, posed as stiff as corpses but smiling, as the Falls usually did, like hoodlums. The final picture showed Ana, severely corseted, flanked by her children: a boy with hair as matted as beaver fur and a smirking young woman named Mary Fall.

In a dining room decorated with haunting landscapes of upstate New York, we sat at the corner of a table that could seat twenty-four paunchy men. Ana rang a bell, and a segment of wall shot open to reveal two steaming dishes of fatty sausage, buttered toast, and egg pudding. She carried the plates herself, hands shaking just enough to keep it interesting. The first bite warmed me down to my calluses, and I did not stop until I was numb with grease. I dried my fingers on the tablecloth.

Now it was time to pay the check.

I slid Bex Red's envelope across the table. Ana flipped it open and eased out the picture. She stared at it for a long time, then slumped back and sighed.

"Can I see it?" I said.

"You don't usually like to look."

"The dreams have gotten worse."

She handed it to me. Bex's effortless lines showed a middle-aged woman sitting at her kitchen table, a tomato sandwich in one hand and a neatly folded newspaper in the other. The table was my table. The woman was my mother.

Mary Fall died of pneumonia the summer of my tenth year. I'd thought that pain forgotten until last year, when I killed for the first time and she began to appear in my sleep. The dreams were violent enough to wake me, strange enough that I couldn't shake them, and when they became unbearable I began visiting the only woman in New York who might understand.

I'd hardly known Ana when my parents were alive, but she welcomed me without question and fed me well. When I told her how I was torturing myself with drawings of my victims living the lives I'd cut short, she asked if Bex could do the same for the daughter she'd lost decades before. We rarely spoke of Mary—we rarely spoke at all—but when we did, it was like opening a steam valve that eased the pressure and let me breathe again.

"She looks happy," I said.

"She doesn't. She looks normal. That's enough."

I gave it back to her.

"You didn't approve when she married my father, did you?" I said.

"Why would you ask me such an inane question?"

"I've always wondered how they met."

"Your father was a brute, and after she met him, Mary was never my daughter again. I never bothered to ask how it began."

I followed her down the long hallway, keeping my eyes on the photo of Mary for as long as I could. At the end of the immaculate passage, one of the doors was open an inch. Behind it I saw a heap of broken furniture, rotted books, ruined artwork, tarnished silver, cracked glass, and other refuse far past the point of identification. Ana shut the door, and I pretended I hadn't seen.

She insisted on helping me put on my coat. As I slid my left arm home, I asked, "Was she as good as I remember?"

"Better," said Ana. "There never walked a purer soul."

She called her carriage, an electric green behemoth drawn by a black horse speckled white with snow, and I glided home. As we crossed the Borderline, the tranquility of the Upper West fell away, and I steeled myself for work.

TWO

That winter had been all red gin and frozen corpses. Six months prior, my beloved Westside—a vast, desolate territory overrun with relentless vegetation but by unknown magic spared the tedium of modern technology like electricity, automobiles, and guns—convulsed into a civil war between the Upper West's hulking dictator, Glen-Richard Van Alen, and the Lower West's bootlegging bandit queen, Andrea Barbarossa. When their armies were slaughtered by the New York Police Department's savage Fourth Precinct, in a massacre that it disgusts me to say was already being romanticized as the Battle of Eighth Avenue, the lawless Lower West passed into Van Alen's hands.

He promised order and the pathetic trappings of civilization that are the hallmarks of the bourgeois Upper West. He gave us nothing but a tattered force of guardsmen who feared our streets and loathed our people, and whose only contribution to civic life below Fourteenth Street was to light candles nightly at each intersection and walk on, abandoning the corners to those who thrive in the dark.

Without Barbie's army of eager children to patrol the sidewalks and alleys, the few thousand who remained below the Borderline became the targets of robbery, battery, murder, and rape, a wave of street crime not felt in the city since the close of the last century. When his new territory threatened revolt, the feverishly teetotal Van Alen relented by opening a distillery on Morton Creek, churning out industrial-grade gin stained red with beets. The stuff was toxic, but he sold it cheap, along with a warning that if even a drop of the red stuff appeared on the far side of the fence, where it might arouse the attention of the Volstead agents, he would burn the distillery to the ground.

We had liquor. We had peace. But no dawn passed without one or two fresh bodies half buried under a snow that fell fat and yellow, like lard from heaven. When convenient, I reported the dead to the guardsmen or, on the rare occasion that I spotted one, a policeman. Mostly, I stared straight ahead as I walked past their stiffened forms, trying to forget the gray of their skin, the dusty red of their lips. These bodies were no mystery, and so they were not my concern. They were killed by anonymous thugs; they were killed by the city itself.

I saw plenty of them after the Byrds engaged me in the quest for the purloined pinkie, when I burned three days combing the gutters, alleys, and ruined houses of Carmine Street, and finding no fingers save those on corpses' hands.

On the fourth day, thick, wet flakes swept across the city, and the Westside hardened like wax. Once, each block would have been scraped clean by one of Barbarossa's little gangs of children—the One-Eyed Cats, the Gutter Girls, the Other Gophers, the Cut-Eyes, the Mercer Street Mercifuls, the Barkleys, the Toes—but they were all dead now, and Van Alen's guardsmen lacked the numbers to do anything but hack a narrow path along the major sidewalks. The rest of the Lower West was left to freeze.

When it was too cold to walk the streets, I brought a pound of brisket to Judson Memorial Church as an offering to Father Lamb. The defrocked priest's speakeasy was closed until spring, and he was happy to trade a lesson in Catholic history for a side of Jewish beef. I set the table, and he pulled down a volume on the lives of the saints.

"She was born on the south coast of Ireland in 632," he said between bites. "A noblewoman who renounced her inheritance to minister to the poor. Good girl. While working among the wretched, she picked up a pox that twisted her spine, causing un-told suffering until she perished in a poorhouse fire. The end."

"What was special about her finger?"

"Doesn't say. It might have been just a finger."

"Are there any other bits of her floating around?"

"This has no mention of any relics, fingers or otherwise."

"And the Byrds . . ."

"What about them?"

"Are they as kind as they seem?"

Lamb spent some time coughing down an oversized mouthful. I waited.

"What the hell do you care?" he rasped.

"They're a client. Before I can find what they've lost, I have to know them, inside and out."

He wiped a greasy hand across his mouth and beard, cleaning some parts of his face and leaving others grimier than before.

"Do you know why I got out of the business of God?" he said.

"I thought you were tossed out for blasphemy."

He scowled. People hate it when you answer rhetorical questions.

"I got tired of people needing something to believe in, needing what I couldn't give 'em. The Byrds never quit. Even people you'd think are beyond the reach of human kindness, they try to help."

"Like who?"

"Are you forgetting the many mornings Enoch saved your dad-dy's life?"

"All right, that's one. But have they helped anybody who de-served it?"

He stuffed the last wad of brisket into his cheek, wiped his hands on his pants, and said, "There's a woman at St. Vincent's you ought to meet."

Her name was Stacey Tarbell, one of an Irish colony that the guardsmen had herded into the quarantine ward at St. Vincent's, where the thick-walled rooms were small and easy to heat. Sitting in that little cell was like cozying up inside a tubercular lung. Even after too long in the cold, it was hotter than I could stand. I'd have liked to strip naked and lie on the stone, but the walls were plastered with images of the saints, and I didn't think they—or the defrocked priest sitting next to me—would appreciate the spectacle.

Stacey had two chairs, and insisted Lamb and I take them both. She sat on her bed and told me, in a voice too cheerful for me to trust, that Helen Byrd had saved her life.

"How?" I said, laying the skepticism on as thick as the syllable could bear.

"My Tom worked the high steel, hammering rivets one hundred, two hundred feet in the air. One day it was wet. He slipped. That was all."

"After the funeral, she asked me to pray with her," said Lamb. "I told her I quit that a long time ago."

"But he said he knew a woman who's devoted to widows."

"So what did she give you?" I said. "Money? Advice? A list of eligible widowers?"

"Lord, Gilda," Lamb grumbled. "Can't you have the smallest bit of faith in people?"

"I'm just trying to understand the nature of the services they provide," I said in my calmest, most open-minded voice. Quite a lot of sweat was dripping from my forehead, my neck, my upper lip. I dragged the sleeve of my dress across my face, sopping up as much as I could. Stacey was waiting for me, I realized, her smile undimmed. I asked her again: "What did Helen do?"

"It's funny," she said, "really, she did almost nothing at all."

"Very impressive."

Now Stacey laughed, a sound as clear and untroubled as church bells on Sunday morning, and it occurred to me that maybe I was the fool in the room.

"She prayed with me, sang hymns, but mostly we talked. After that, I could sleep."

"Did she show you the finger of Saint Róisín?"

"She knew I needed help, not mystery. She lost her husband so long ago, but she believes that someday he will come back to her. She helped me believe it, too."

"But that's ridiculous."

"Is it now?"

"Even children know it, Miss Tarbell, so I'll say it simple, like I'm speaking to a child. People don't come back from the dead."

"One man did, once."

"Maybe. But that was some time ago."

"In a city where water springs up from concrete and trees grow taller than the spire of Trinity Church, why couldn't it happen again?"

This woman's skin was thin enough that I could see her skull. Her smile was as fragile as bone china. I felt an urge to shatter her. Instead I excused myself and stepped into the long hallway, dabbing my forehead with my wrist, wondering how anyone could be taken in by such idiocy. A Westsider should know better. The dead do not return; grief does not subside. Our memories fade, until those we loved are no more real than paper saints on a wall.

"How are you finding the winter?" I heard Lamb ask her.

"It's hard without Tom. But Van Alen's guards bring food and coal, and the life insurance money should come through soon. When I get that check, I'll be going back to Ireland and sailing in style."

When he emerged from her room, I was already halfway down the hallway, making for the short flight of icy steps that led back to the tundra of Seventh Avenue. When Lamb caught up with me, he grabbed me by the elbow hard enough that I had to work not to slip.

"You should have some goddamned sympathy," he said. "That woman's hurting and you made fun."

"We all hurt. That's no excuse for her wasting my time."

"Since when does the detective of tiny mysteries care about wasting time?"

We walked down to Sixth Avenue, him grumbling about the transformative nature of faith, of prayer, of understanding, and me trying to understand why an impoverished widow's simple story had driven me so quickly to rage. In the shadow of Jefferson Market Court, whose multicolored shingles rose like a rainbow over the rank snow, I tried to atone.

"I'm sorry," I said, finally. "It was rude to point out that what she believes is stupid."

"That's a pathetic apology."

"Right now, pathetic is the best I can muster. This case has worn me thin."

"The next time you run out of ideas, bother someone else."

"Any suggestions?"

He pointed south. Past the snow, past the refuse, past the broken buildings and a half mile of buckled sidewalk, towering white trees bent against the wind.

"You want to understand the Byrds?" he said. "Get 'em to take you in there. Take a look at their first church. Make 'em tell you about the day their baby brother died."

The year the fence went up, pines sprouted on the south side of Houston. They hurled themselves through warehouses and shops, obliterating some buildings and swallowing others, absorbing bricks, concrete, and steel into a tapestry of pale wood. Today, this blank spot on city maps runs from Houston to Canal, from Sixth Avenue all the way to the fence. Nowhere on the Westside are the trees as thick, the shadows as dark, the roads as twisted. It is an insane place, and Judy and Enoch Byrd would serve as my guides. They hadn't wanted to come back here, but when I threatened to quit their case unless they gave me the tour I required, their mother ordered them to do as I asked. What a useful ally mothers can be.

The trees of the Thicket were evergreen, their branches thick enough to crowd out the sky. I walked slowly, watching every step, but Judy and Enoch strolled through the rough landscape like it was a fresh paved road. The path that had been West Broadway wound through monstrous vegetation and crumbled masonry. One building had been entirely overwhelmed by trees and vines, leaving a vegetative facsimile of the original structure in its place. Another had vanished completely, save for a network of copper pipes that stretched from the earth to the heights of the ramrod-straight trees.

"How long has it been since you lived here?" I said.

"We moved to Carmine Street after the fire," said Judy. "But I like the Thicket. It's a strange place to know your way around."

Our road dipped into a hollow and rose straight through a building, which had a gap in it as clear as a machine-bored hole. Branches rattled, small feet scuttled, and I felt the presence of tiny heartbeats and animal eyes. I had already lost track of how long we'd been walking, but the Byrds marched on. For the first time, I simply had to trust them. I was surprised by how natural it felt.

Finally, we came to a slouching archway and a pair of cross-shaped windows: the remains of Bulrush Byrd's original Electric Church. Beyond was a flat, snowy plain with an altar at the far end.

"You've seen it," said Enoch. "Let's go."

"I didn't come to gawk from the sidewalk. I need the whole tour, and the history, too."

"Mam didn't say anything about letting you inside. That's holy ground."

"I'll take her," said Judy.

"But she isn't family."

"I know, brother. But sometimes it's easier to just not care."

That's a fine credo, I thought as I followed her across the threshold. The walk had warmed me up, but I felt a renewed chill when I passed beneath the stone. Judy led me the length of the nave, hands stretched out to brush the backs of long-gone pews.

"Was it a grand church?" I said.

"Hardly more than a storefront. But Bully had the spirit, and that'll make any building feel like a cathedral."

"What did he preach?"

"The electric resurrection," she said with a sad flourish. "The miracle of miracles—that the gates of heaven would open, and our dead would come back to meet us. But really, he preached love."

The electric resurrection. For a few years in the late '80s, it was a sensation. I'd dug through old newspapers and found reports that Bully was a blessed speaker, able to make every sinner in the room feel he was bringing them the word of God fresh from the well. He preached to a packed house three times a day and was on the verge of launching what one Christian newsletter called "a major national movement" when his church was destroyed.

"Your brother won't talk about the fire," I said.

"No."

"Will you?"

She crouched, plunged her hands through the snow, and felt that holy ground. I didn't expect her to give me much, but I'd pieced together most of the story already. In March 1888, Bully Byrd promised the city a miracle. He had devised a ritual, he told his flock, that would call home the dead. The electric resurrection was at hand, and it would remake the world.

Hundreds crowded into his little storefront to watch their prophet work. Standing in a spotless white suit, he stoked a roaring fire inside a bronze brazier, mumbled some Latin, and hurled in a fistful of powder.

A jet of flame shot up.

The tapestries on the ceiling caught fire.

The blaze spread fast, but Bully kept his flock from panic. He led them out, single file, no one pushing, and nearly everyone was safe on the street when the children downstairs began to scream.

"What were you doing in the basement?" I said.

"Papa didn't believe in forcing children to sit through services. There was a playroom downstairs where Ruth and I watched the young ones. That day the back entrance was locked, but Ruth had a key and we went in anyway, with a few of the kids from the neighborhood. By the time we smelled smoke, the stairs were mostly flame."

As his church burned, Bully went back inside. He got the children out—as many as he could.

"The littlest were eating lunch," said Judy, "in high chairs. He took us, and he was going to come back for the youngest, but the fire was too high and the crowd held him back. Some of those babes knew how to walk. They could have gotten out. But they were strapped in tight, and they burned."

There were four who died, all under age three. One was Bully's youngest son, Barnabas. He loved sailboats, the *Sentinel* archives had the cruelty to inform me, and drawing angels. Bully was hailed as a hero. Two days later, he disappeared.

Out on the sidewalk, Enoch stared at the ground, twisting his foot in the snow like a boy who didn't understand why his brother and father will never come home.

"The finger saved us," said Judy, flicking her cigarette at the trees. "That was the year of the blizzard—it was like the whole city had slipped into some white hell. Me, fresh from Haiti, I'd never seen anything like it. Mam didn't know what to do without Papa, without the church. When spring came and the snow melted, we came here and found Róisín's finger on the altar."

"Who put it there?"

"God."

I made a face. She ignored it, which is usually the best thing to do with my face, and went on.

"We rebuilt the ministry around it," she said. "We survived."

"I'd like to see where it appeared."

"Go. I'll check on Enoch. Tenderhearted boy. Mam shouldn't have made him come."

She left me behind and I walked on to inspect the rough pile of half-buried stone. There I found the strange drift of snow and the body of the redheaded man. It was only a vagrant, I told myself. No one could get killed over a missing finger. His mystery was not mine.

As we walked out of the Thicket, I hung a few feet behind. Part of me still doubted the Byrds could be as innocent as they appeared. Part of me always doubts. That is the part that thrills at the sight of a murdered man, that relishes questions whose answers can be fatal. That is the part I wish I could silence forever.

"When was the last time you came by the church?" I said, seeing the blood, the red hair, the skin frozen and cracked.

"Years ago," said Enoch.

"Does anyone ever come here?"

"No one in the family," said Judy. "But there are people who live in the Thicket, and people who pass through. Why?"

We stepped onto Houston Street, where the trees stopped as sharply as a sentence. The wind blew in icy from the Hudson. Clouds hid the stars.

"I've spent a week and a half on this case," I said. "I've heard nothing but good things about you and your family. I've turned up no trace of the finger, no sign that anyone would do you harm."

"So?" said Judy.

"This is the Westside. No one is so pure. *Everyone* has enemies."

Judy looked at her brother, asking permission to say something she had been trying to keep to herself.

"It's not right," said Enoch. "He's family."

"He's a scoundrel."

"Still."

"Who?" I said.

And she told me about her other brother.

The Basement Club went on forever. The bar ran the length of the room; the earth floor was studded with melted snow, vomit, and blood. Built in a pit where a Bleecker Street apartment house used to be, it was below street level and had a low ceiling of irregular boards that kept out snow but let in damp. Rubber hoses snaked out of the bar at one-foot intervals. Drop a nickel in the slot and out slid a trickle of gin to be caught with a cup, if the patron brought one, or a mouth. A tangle of machinery ran the length of the place, whirring and clanging as the poison poured. There was no music, no talk, no chairs—just the cheapest drunk on the Westside. It was fiendishly popular.

Judy and Enoch left me at the door, proving that there were places of sin too filthy even for them. I entered through a turnstile that shot a ticket into my palm, which told me I was the seventy-third patron of the night.

I paid my nickel and cupped my palms under the hose, slurping up whatever didn't run through my fingers. I wiped my hands on the patron to my left, who was glassy with drink, his mouth stained bloody by the beet red liquor. The bartender surveyed his automated gin mill from a high chair, a lifeguard ignoring an ocean of drowning men. After several minutes' concentrated effort, and another few mouthfuls of gin, I caught his eye.

He was short and broad, with bushy hair and a nose like a ball of cookie dough squashed flat. His candy-striped uniform was a dizzying mess of black and green. On his chest was a wrinkled slip of paper, held with safety pins, that read "64." He smoothed it with his wrist as he climbed down from his perch and walked my way. His name was Abner Byrd.

"He's a scourge," Judy had said. "I'm sorry, brother, but it's true. Walked out on us when he was sixteen, and he's spent the last thirty years sinking deeper and deeper into sin. Doesn't speak to us except once or twice a year, when he crashes into the church, blind drunk, to scream that there is no god but death."

"He is a difficult case," admitted Enoch. "But God would ask us to forgive."

"I'll forgive when he gives us the finger back. He's the only rat on the Westside low enough to steal it. He'd do it just to watch us cry."

As I looked Abner in the face now, I wondered if that was true. The prodigal Byrd leaned on the bar and spoke, sleepy and slow.

"Trouble with the tube?" he said. "Sometimes a roach'll die in there and it'll get plugged. Let me get the pipe cleaner."

"The gin flows free."

"Then why the eye?"

"I'm looking for the finger of Saint Róisín."

I flicked out a card that read G. CARR: TINY MYSTERIES SOLVED. It landed in a puddle of gin on the bar and soaked up the liquor thirstily. Abner glanced at the panel of smoked glass mounted above the bar. A bell rang.

"I'm on the clock," he said.

"Your siblings think you took it."

He stalked mechanically down the bar, clearing each tube with a swift jerk, smacking awake any sleeping drunk and telling him to buy another round or get out. I followed him, calling questions from across the trench.

27

"But why?" I said. "A pickled finger's worth nothing. All it does is hurt your family, and why would you wound such fine people?"

"If you're not drinking, you need to leave."

I dropped another nickel and refilled my mouth. I swallowed without gagging and kept my eyes locked with his. He did not look like the vicious bastard Judy had painted. He was just another flop scrambling to hang on.

"Where were you on the night of the twenty-third?" I said.

"I don't know."

The bell rang, then rang again.

"What's that bell?" I said.

"My timekeeper. Behind the glass. Adjusting my rating. I'm only a 64. If I fall any further . . ."

"Did you take it?"

"No!"

"Can you prove it?"

He marched down the bar on that windup-toy gait, past glass so dark it was impossible to see what the timekeeper was doing or if he was even there. He came back with a fat ledger, which he dropped on the bar, taking care to keep it away from the gin.

"The twenty-third?" he said, opening to the most detailed time sheet I had ever seen. "What time?"

"Between dark and dawn."

"I was here. I'm always here. More specific? From 6 to 6:07, I'm in the chair. 6:08 to 6:22, I'm greasing the mechanism. 6:23 to 6:34, I'm fighting with that fat bastard at the end of the bar about how he can't bring food in here. 6:35 to—"

"I understand."

"I've had a lot of bad jobs," he said. "Sweeping floors. Hauling trash. This is the only place ever left me feeling less than human."

The bell rang three times, then a fourth, then a fifth.

"Oh, hell," said Abner, his puffy face suddenly oozing sweat. "Hell, hell, goddamn it to hell."

Abner slammed the ledger and rumbled off in an imitation of running. The bell rang faster and sharper until it was one long tone.

The patrons responded with a dull, animal roar. I launched myself across the deep wood. One of the gin swillers tried to drag me back, but I loosened his grip with a kick to the jaw. I ran after Abner. He threw open a panel on the far wall, gripped a smooth wooden crank, and whipped it around with all the speed he could muster. The drunks cheered him on.

"Why does Judy hate you?" I said.

"Why do you care?" he panted, his arms churning.

"Because their movement is dead, but they open that church every morning, they preach, they fight sin on every corner of a district that gets more evil every year. I care because I need to know—why do they bother? Why do they still believe?"

He bent himself double and, with a final thrust, drove the crank home. All the machinery came alive, groaning and screaming toward some impossible task. Abner wiped his brow and checked his watch. Only when he saw the time did he permit himself to breathe.

"If they're so sure I took that goddamned digit," he said, "why aren't they here to say so?"

"It's not their kind of place."

"That's a lie, and probably not the first they told you. Only reason Judy and Enoch don't do their act here is 'cause the Gray Boys pay them twenty bucks a month to stay away."

"Who are the Gray Boys?"

"The Eastside crowd that runs this place. That's just what I call them—I don't know their right name, or if they even have one. I just know they're gray, and as interchangeable as all the parts in this damn machine."

"Van Alen wouldn't stand for an Eastside gang in the Lower West."

"Van Alen might not have a choice."

That stopped me short. I hadn't heard of anyone tough or stupid enough to challenge Van Alen's grip on the Westside. I chewed on that as the bell continued to keen. When the noise was nearly unbearable, the machinery stopped, the ringing quieted, and the crowd fell into a seething hush. Abner put his hand against the wall. A metal chip fell out of the slot.

"Seventy-three!" he cried. "Who's got seventy-three?"

"Goddamn it!" cried a man from deep in the bar.

"This game is rigged," called a woman at my elbow.

I reached into my coat pocket, the clammy touch of coincidence sliding up my neck. I handed Abner my ticket.

"I'm seventy-three," I said.

"You would be."

"What's my prize?"

"The specialty of the house. A free drunk and a place to sleep it off."

From a narrow shelf above the mirrored glass, Abner took a chipped porcelain dog bowl. He set it under the nearest hose and filled it with a torrent of the awful gin.

"I've had my fill," I said.

"You drink it, or I gotta dump it out, and this room tears us both to pieces."

I nodded, and a path opened to the far end of the bar. Abner walked down it, carrying the dog bowl like he was escorting me to my coronation, and I followed at his heels. The crowd clapped, slow and mean, hating me for stealing their prize. At the end of our march, he handed me the bowl, unlocked a metal door, and bowed until I stepped inside. By the light of a greasy lantern I saw a glorified crawl space filled with a pile of stained mattresses, occupied by a single dozing drunk.

The door slammed shut. The lock rammed home. Cradling the bowl in one arm, I twisted the knob. It did not give.

"Abner, goddamn it, let me out!"

The drunk in the corner stirred and shushed. I continued shouting and he pushed himself onto his elbow. He was small, and his eyes were wet with gin, and when he grumbled, "Shut your mouth and for god's sake let us get a touch of sleep," I realized how bad I'd missed him. For here was a ghost, a myth from the past, the once-and-future chieftain of the One-Eyed Cats, a survivor of Eighth

Avenue, a hero of the docks, a Westside legend, my former lover, and a welcome sight for bloodshot eyes.

"Cherub Stevens," I breathed.

"Lord. Is that a brace of Gildas Carr I see swimming before me?"

"Tell me there's a way out."

"Not till Abner lets us out at dawn. Now are you sharing, or what?"

He patted his mattress, which was no more filthy than any of the others, and I took a seat. I lifted the bowl of increasingly icy gin, and we drank deep.

I looked him over, this beautiful black man, and saw the light had gone out of him. His coat was shredded; his hat was flat, and his hip, I was shocked to see, was bare.

"Where's your saber?" I said.

"Hocked it. I'm done fighting. After last year, I couldn't look at it without smelling blood."

"And you're not working?"

"Where would I go? Van Alen won't take Barbie's old soldiers, my papers don't allow me over the fence, and it's hard to find respectable work when all your references are dead."

I couldn't argue. We passed the bowl. We did not talk about last autumn, when war brought us together and fear of being happy drove us apart. We talked of our childhood—those days when death had only just taken hold of the Westside but had not yet begun to squeeze. We worked to remember the names of people lost, of places gone. We emptied our bowl and banged the door and did not complain when no one answered. But no matter how I tried to lead it elsewhere, my mind wandered back to the Byrds.

"Abner is wrong," I said, several times too many. "He's missed the point. It doesn't matter if his family's a touch crooked. What matters is, they show up. They're on a crusade for nothing, fighting against no one, all for something that no sane person could understand."

"That's what the Westside is all about," said Cherub, whose eyes would not stay open.

"That's what it used to be. It used to be fun. It used to be beautiful."

"It used to be that a few hundred people got killed every year for no good reason."

"But there was something . . . there was purity. Grace. Love. The Byrds have that, or they think they do. That's worth showing up for."

Cherub ran his hand through my hair. It caught on one of my knots, sending a wave of dull pain crashing over my scalp. I fell down on the mattress, and he fell beside me, and we laughed ourselves to sleep.

I dreamed of being burned alive. It was a theater dream—for someone too cowardly or foolish to have ever wanted to act, I have more than my share—in which a trio of stagehands lashed me to a pile of firewood and set me alight. An inferno of blue crepe flickered up around me, blown by unseen fans. When it touched me, it burned.

I screamed, and the audience was silent.

I screamed, and they booed.

A cry came from the wings in a nearly impenetrable Irish accent: "Pull her!"

The stagehands returned, and the crowd roared approval as they dragged me off, my skin starting to char.

The stage manager appeared, leading a hunchbacked woman who had four fingers on her right hand. I choked on the stench of burning hair.

"I told you," said the Irish woman, "the girl does not have the range."

"A mistake on our part," said the stage manager. She flipped open her notebook and crossed out my name. As the paper flames swallowed me, I recognized my mother's face, as serene as the day she died.

I woke with bile in my mouth, warm for the first time in months. Ash burned my eyes and smoke oozed in from under the door. A spike of fear pierced the fog of gin and dreaming. I got to my feet and found I was still deeply drunk.

The knob was red hot. The door remained locked.

"Abner, you bastard, let us out of here!" I screamed. No answer came save the gentle crunch of a happily growing fire.

My screams had not disturbed sweet Cherub, so I kicked him in the side.

"We have to break the lock," I said. Even drunk, he had the sense to feel his pockets, looking for an implement, and found nothing. In that moment, I was certain we were going to die.

I lifted my empty, beet-stained dog bowl and crashed it down on the doorknob. The bowl shattered. The knob held firm, and I almost gave in to despair.

But Cherub grabbed the heaviest chunk of split ceramic and swung it until the knob clattered across the floor. I kicked the door with optimism. It did not budge.

Flame spurted through the hole where the doorknob had been.

Flame soft and delicate, and turquoise blue.

It began a slow climb along the wood, moving like no fire I'd ever seen. It danced, languid and twisted, spreading like hairline fractures on cracking ice.

"I've gone mad," said Cherub.

"So have I."

I knelt on the floor, hoping to get a look inside the mechanism of the lock, certain that if I could see it I could pick it. Through the hole in the door I caught a view of the rest of the bar—a sight that made me lose hope.

The Basement Club's roof was a sheet of blue fire.

It fell to the ground in clumps, like wet snow melting from a tree. It reached down like swinging vines, then snapped back up, as though it were feeling for something. It was a living thing, a hungry thing that had swallowed the bar and the walls and anything else in the room unfortunate enough to be made of wood or gin—or flesh.

At the center of it, enrobed in fire, Abner Byrd lurched across the floor. Flames swept down from the ceiling, wrapped around his neck, and pulled. He clawed at them, screaming pitifully as his flesh burned away, and banged his bloody stumps on the front door. He pawed at the knob. It did not open. He gave in at last and fell to the floor.

"We're not getting out that way," I said.

"Then we're not getting out."

"I have no interest in dying in this awful bar."

I took a breath, trying to think, and quickly wished I had not. I doubled over coughing, landing on a mattress that went squish. As my hands sank into it, I saw a final chance.

Trying not to retch, I grabbed one end of the mattress. Cherub took the other. We thrust it against the door. It sagged, but did not fall, and its filthy damp stopped, for a moment, the flow of smoke.

"The mattresses," I said. "Stack them. Now."

There were eleven of them, as thick as bricks and just as comfortable. We dragged them into the center of the room, building a pile halfway to the ceiling.

"You go first," he said. "I'll hold it steady."

There was no time to argue. I clawed my way to the top of the stack, which sagged and swayed under my weight. Cherub handed me the shard of broken dog bowl, and I started to hack at the ceiling.

The wood was useless for keeping out the elements, but it held its own against the unremarkable strength of Gilda Carr. With the neck of my dress covering my mouth, I tore at the wood, which was soft and rotten but in no hurry to give. I had barely dented it when the mattress at the door betrayed us and erupted into turquoise fire.

"Help me," I gasped.

"But the mattresses—" said Cherub, no longer bothering to hide his fear.

"Will hold, or we'll die."

I helped him to the top of our little island. He took a few strong whacks at the wood, opening my dent a bit wider. Fire seeped across the floor, then the walls, and began to tickle the roof. Finally, the mattresses started to burn.

I pushed Cherub to his knees and placed my foot in his hands. I put my arms over my head. He stood, shoving me up, using my gin-numbed body as a battering ram to bash through the cracking wood. The night air was cold and sweet, perfumed with bonfire.

I dragged myself onto what remained of the roof, sat up, and reached back for him. He took my wrist and slipped, pulling me down as the flaming mattresses collapsed under him. I braced my feet against the hole.

"Climb!" I shouted.

"There's nothing to climb on!"

His grip slipped again. I grabbed his collar with my other hand. He thrashed, kicking his legs against empty air, and I pulled with everything I had left. I was too drunk and too tired to let a good friend die. I dragged him an inch onto the roof, just enough that he could get purchase and scramble the rest of the way on his own. I didn't loosen my grip until he tumbled into my arms.

He looked like he wanted to kiss me. I didn't feel like wasting time. We ran alongside the burning roof to the edge of the lot. I jumped down the steps to the club's front door. It was red hot and locked from the outside. I kicked at it, but what was the point? It wasn't going to open, and the only man inside was too far gone to save.

"What the hell just happened?" said Cherub. We scrambled across the ice into a night lit up blue, that useless question reverberating across my gin-softened brain.

What the hell just happened?

What the hell?

THREE

It was a short walk back to my house. It didn't take much to persuade Cherub to come inside.

I showed him to the bedroom that had once been my parents', where the bed was soft and the dust was thick.

"It's a crypt in here," he said.

"I found you passed out on a gin-soaked mattress in a basement's back room."

"Touché. I don't suppose you want to join me?"

"That's my parents' bed."

"In yours, then?"

"Go to sleep. Don't keep your hangover waiting."

He took my hand, not forcefully, not pleading, just gently enough that I could feel he was there.

"What was that fire?" he said. "Why was it blue? Why did it move like, like . . ."

"Like a nest of snakes? Those are the sorts of questions I do not ask."

"But somebody set it. Somebody made it like that."

"And that same person locked the front door, and that same person wanted to kill Abner or me."

"They could have been trying to kill me."

"It's sweet that you think that."

"What are we going to do about it?"

"You'll do what you do best: nothing. As for myself, I'll let the morning decide."

"I'm glad you're alive," he called as I walked down the hall.

"So am I," I said, and probably meant it.

Sleep grabbed me with both fists. As I drifted off, trying not to think of Enoch's blue hell, I wondered at the odds that the raffle machine chose me to be locked in that back room.

Breakfast came, a stack of Hellida's crepes as tall and unsteady as the pile of mattresses that saved our lives the night before. Cherub grabbed three in his fists and began to gorge.

"You look worse every day," said Hellida.

"That's not true," I said, taking a bite no more ladylike than Cherub's. "I had that cold last week. Looked much worse then."

She crashed around the kitchen for a moment or two, then sat down with a plate of her own.

"It doesn't matter to me," she said. "I told you that three times, now four. I'm not your nanny, not your maid, not your housekeeper, not your mother, not your cook."

"You did just cook her breakfast," said Cherub.

"I cooked myself breakfast. You're eating runoff."

"Hellida and I have agreed we are friends," I said, "nothing more."

"And friends don't care if their friends run headfirst into a wall, over and over and over again," said Hellida. "Friends don't say nothing."

I wanted to find something to quiet her anxiety, but my head felt like it had been flattened by a cinder block and my stomach was tipping back and forth like an hourglass. It was more important that I eat.

As Cherub finished his mound of food and started on the tureen of steaming Swedish coffee, Hellida fixed her gaze on him like a wolf stalking easy prey. She saw his patchy stubble, matted hair, and tattered clothes, and got a fiendish idea.

"We two," she said, pointing at Cherub. "We isn't friends. So him I can worry about. Him I can make take a bath."

"Do I get more of these pancakes?" said Cherub, and a bargain was made. She started boiling water, and I pulled on my coat. I was halfway out the front door when I heard a voice calling from up the stairwell. It was my father's—the voice I tried so hard not to hear.

"They're dirty," he said. "Everybody's dirty. So are they."

"I'm not sure," I said, soft enough that Cherub and Hellida could not hear that I was conversing with a ghost.

"So check! I've got files on every crook that ever walked Manhattan island. See if you can find their names."

"There won't be anything there."

"Jesus. Those pious bastards just about got you burned alive. If naught else, doesn't that piss you off?"

"You dead old man—why are you always right?"

I slammed the front door and stalked up the stairs. Sweating under my scarf, I threw open Virgil's office, hurled myself into his wobbly leather chair, and tore into his browning, dusty files, scanning forty years of criminal activity on the Westside. When I had taken their case, to look for the Byrds among this catalog of vandals, rapists, killers, arsonists, kidnappers, and thieves seemed pointless. But today my hair stank of smoke, and I was through being kind.

Trying to ignore my headache, I slid back through the years, finding nothing upon nothing until I reached my father's earliest days with the nascent NYPD. At the time of the fire at the Electric Church, Virgil was little more than a jumped-up thug, and his files were just a set of battered notebooks, roughly one per year, documenting in vaguely chronological fashion the violent escapades of a brutal cop.

I paged through his 1888, finding suspects beaten, innocents terrorized, and case after case cracked through sheer ugly force. March was a total blank, save mentions of a few nights lost at Lasko's Twenty-Seven, a Tenderloin dance hall where I happened to know his paramour, a young Andrea Barbarossa, once dazzled the crowd with dances most vile. There was no talk of the fire. On a page stained with either coffee or blood, I found a note from the first week of April: "Told widow Bully's dead. She smiled." I flipped through the entire book, finding no mention of Bully or widows, and so I stepped back to 1887. On the last page, I found two curt lines that sent a fresh wave of nausea through my coffee-addled stomach: "Met Anacostia Fall, 7 E. 20th, in matter re: Bully Byr—"

The note ended there. Virgil was too sloppy to ever write more. It wasn't dirt, exactly, but if the Byrds couldn't answer for it, I'd use the excuse to quit the case. Gods and devils didn't frighten me, but my family history was a book I did not want to open again.

In the entryway to the abandoned Italian banquet hall now occupied by the reborn Electric Church, Enoch Byrd welcomed the faithful. He stood in the doorway, coatless, distributing prayer sheets to all who came. He offered one to me, and I shoved it back into his hand.

"I want to know about the fire," I said.

"My sister told you everything we remember," he said, his church smile gone.

"Not that fire. The one at the Basement Club, early this morning, that looked so much like your particular hell."

He clasped his hands, shaking his head, looking ever so much like he wished he could help.

"If there was a fire, I can't tell you a thing. Judy and I have nothing to do with that establishment."

"Why not?"

"I'd like to give a high-minded reason, but the fact is . . . that place frightens me. It is so dark, so cold. Those who drink there are past our feeble help."

"So it's not that the owners have been paying you twenty dollars a month to preach your sobering gospel someplace else?"

He did not break eye contact. He did not flinch.

"Who told you such an awful lie?"

"Your brother."

"Then rest assured, I will have words with him."

"You really didn't hear about the fire?"

"Since we left you last night, Judy and I have been here, preparing for today's services."

I felt bad. I couldn't help it. I wanted to hate this softhearted hypocrite, from the cuffs of his fraying suit to the ink-stained tips of his fingernails, but god help me, I have a soft spot for chumps.

"He's dead," I said, as gently as I could manage. "Trapped in the fire."

For a long moment, Enoch closed his eyes. He tried to rub them, but his glasses were in the way, and his hand fluttered helplessly, unsure how to take them off. Finally he drew a breath and stood as tall as he could. He set the prayer sheets on the table.

"I'll need to tell my sisters," he said, and walked into the church. He didn't tell me not to, so I followed him inside. Candles filled the main hall. Pale blue sheets covered the many gaps in the roof, casting turquoise light across the stage and giving a sensation of being underwater. A stack of decrepit folding tables leaned against one wall, betraying the room's former function. In the center, five of the faithful joined in electric prayer.

Stripped to the waist, sweating despite the cold, they shook like undercooked cakes, moaning in protest of death. Two were under fifty. The rest were much, much older, and their wobbling skin showed every one of their years. There were men and women, black and white—a minute congregation held together by their refusal to admit that their loved ones were gone. Their prayer was silent, but intense. The service had not yet begun.

Enoch strode across the room to Judy, who was arranging a tragic spread of pastries. I walked in the other direction. I could not stand to see another person hear the news. A door to the right of the stage opened, and Helen Byrd surveyed the room with a look that could have meant satisfaction or disappointment or anything else humans can feel. I started toward her, needing to get there before she learned her son was dead and became incapable of answering foolish questions about a half-hearted police report written more than thirty years prior. If I were going to quit, this was the time. The knowledge of the blow Enoch was about to give her, and my guilt at bringing that pain into their house, slowed my step. Before I could interrogate her, the assembled faithful erupted in moaning. Ruth took the stage.

Besides the heavy scarf that still covered the bottom half of her face, it was hard to believe this was the bland woman I had met two weeks before. Even through the wool wrap, her voice filled the room. It was an instrument of gold.

"We are a district in mourning," she said, her fluid white gown swaying as she threw her arm high. "We have been hounded by hunger, disease, murder, crime. Our mayor cast us out of the golden city, calling us unclean. We were left to die, and die we did. Our families have been shattered, our friends struck down. Thousands and thousands have been lost to us, but I am here, friends, to tell you—our dead are coming back."

It went on like that for quite some time. Where Judy's sermons were a beautiful, improvised mess, Ruth's had the feel of carefully memorized scripture, performed so adeptly that it sounded fresh. It should have made me laugh, but the clarity of her voice, the love she poured into every word, was like a flawless icicle, and it pierced me deep. I was leaning toward the exit when Ruth caught my eye.

"Think of someone you have lost," she said. "Someone dear enough that instead of mourning, you fight to forget. Today, instead, remember. The curve of their jaw, the way their hair fell across their brow, their laugh, their hands, their smell. Close your eyes and invite them into the room. Don't say a word. Just watch. Take them in your arms and let the hurt go. Now open your eyes and tell me—don't you want that to be real?"

All around me, hearts were open. It would have been easy to fall on my knees and admit that yes, of course, I wanted what she had for sale. I could beg Ruth and her god to slice away the pain that coated my body like lead, keeping me so rooted to the earth that it was often hard to move. I could believe. I told myself that my father had raised me to keep my eyes open and my back straight, but the more she spoke, the more I wanted to kneel.

Helen and Judy dragged a brazier the size of a rich man's tub onto the stage and piled it past the brim with dry yellow wood. Enoch, pale and trembling, thrust in a torch, and the whole works exploded into flame.

Ruth sat beside it, her legs dangling off the lip of the stage, her toes scraping the floor. She spoke in an exhausted whisper. I got as close as it took to hear.

"Half a lifetime ago," she said, "my father attempted to change history. That man, that darling man some of you called a prophet, tried to pry open the doors to heaven with his own blessed hands, to call back the dead, to make broken families whole. It went wrong. Two days later he left this earth behind. I know his desertion wounded you. I wear that pain upon my face."

She loosed the scarf from her shoulders and let it flutter to the floor, revealing a face and neck whose flesh was buckled and torn, a mouth that was little more than a scar. The closest congregant was one of the oldest: a black woman with smooth skin and hair as soft as the snow outside. At the sight of Ruth's face, two fat tears rolled down her cheeks.

"This city has been mutilated," said Ruth, her voice thrumming even clearer now that the scarf was gone. "More than ever, we need the resurrection we call electric—electric because it is elemental, electric because it will shock a dead city's heart into beating again, electric because it burns hot enough to cauterize our wounds and make us whole. Today that resurrection is at hand."

Later I asked myself why I didn't stop her. At best, her ceremony would disappoint her flock. At worst, it would mean fiery death for every person in this fragile old tinderbox—and I was getting tired of fire. I could have dragged her off the stage, punched her in her ruined mouth, ended this now, but I'd spent all week asking if the Byrds were on the level and this seemed my last, best chance to find out.

Or maybe I really did want to believe.

Ruth stoked the fire until it leapt above the brazier's lip. She murmured something in a tongue I did not know. She took a roll of paper from her dress and fed it to the flame. Then, from deep in her chest came a roar unlike anything she had put forth during her sermon: thirty years of hurt packed into a single shout.

"Come back to me!" she cried, and launched a fistful of powder into the fire. It exploded as blue as the sky, as twisting and awful as the inferno that nearly killed me the night before. The light was so bright that I had to look away. Before my hands could cover my eyes, though, I saw a figure erupt from it, vaulting out of the fire as casually as a commuter taking the IRT steps two at a time.

When my eyes stopped burning, when the smoke cleared, Ruth was no longer alone. Beside her, in a white suit some forty years out of style, stood a man with blue eyes and a foolish, happy smile. His hair was singed, his skin sooty. He sagged against Ruth. She did not let him drop.

"You called me," he said. "You called me and I heard you and I came home."

With a mad whoop of pleasure, she embraced him, digging her fingers and face into his hair and clawing him to her breast, hard enough to drag him to the floor. She kissed him and sobbed, and only then did the rest of her family shake off their stupor. Enoch sprinted across the floor and leapt onto the stage with the grace of a much younger man. He threw himself atop the stranger, and he shouted, "Father!"

No. It simply couldn't be.

Beside me, tears poured down the old woman's face, running into her slack, smiling mouth.

"I remember," she said. "I remember those eyes."

The youngest congregant, a scraggly white man whose skin stretched tight across brittle bone, charged the stage. Judy and Helen dragged him back.

"Is it him?" cried the man. "Is it real?"

The stranger, his eyes fluttering and his breath staccato, slumped heavy enough that Ruth had to lower him to the floor. The Byrds crowded round. Enoch gave the man his coat. I climbed the stage, hoping to get a closer look, but Enoch looked at me, his face as tender as an open wound, and I stopped.

Ruth held up her hand, and the moaning congregants hushed.

"For thirty years and more, I have seen this face in my dreams," she said. "This is our miracle. Our wait is through. Bulrush Byrd has come home!"

Perhaps I expected applause. Perhaps bells from on high. Instead, the news was greeted with an expansive silence, like that which must follow battle—the sound of a roomful of weary believers releasing decades of doubt and pain.

"What should we do?" said one of the flock, a woman with long braids who held hands with a man who may have been her father. "What is your message for us?"

The answer was so obvious, Ruth could only smile.

"Tell the world," she said. "Tell everyone the electric resurrection is at hand."

They needed no more encouragement. The congregants pulled on their clothes and flooded out, ready to tell anyone who would listen about the miracle of Carmine Street. Ruth and Enoch helped the man to his feet. He mumbled incoherent thanks, and they eased him off the stage. I did what I do best—got in the way. I took the man's clammy hand and attempted to catch his eye.

"Our father needs rest," said Enoch. "Please."

"How do you know he's your father?"

"Surely, you cannot doubt him," said Ruth. "Not after what you have seen."

I gripped the man's hand tight.

"Who are you?" I said. "Where have you come from?"

"Far," he said. "I traveled far."

Ruth glared at me, as if those four words should have been enough to make me bow down and weep.

"He traveled far," said Enoch, softly, committing the words to memory, that they might someday be writ in stone.

A cough racked the man's body. He doubled over, and Enoch and Ruth guided him to the back room. I let them shut the door in my face.

Behind me, Helen collapsed the folding chairs. Judy watched

her for a moment, then erupted in a wild laugh. She bounded across the room, wrapped her mother in her arms, and spun her around, giggling and crying all at once. Helen was a statue. Judy pulled one of the chairs aside and forced her to sit in it. Helen draped a gloved hand across her forehead and closed her eyes.

"That's him," she said. "After all this time."

I sat beside her, and they did not make me leave.

"If you're here to talk about Róisín's finger," said Helen, "I'm afraid we've moved on."

"You're not serious," I said.

"Who needs scraps of dead saints," said Judy, "when you've got a live one in the flesh?"

"So you really believe that's Bully Byrd?" I said. She nodded at me, staring like I was the madwoman. "Did you know he was coming back?"

"Ruth has Papa's dramatic flair. She told us she had a surprise in store, she asked us to prepare the fire. I hoped, I've always hoped, but I didn't go further than that."

"What do you think, Miss Carr?" said Helen. "You saw what we saw. Your eyes are not clouded by sentiment. Do you believe?"

"I don't know."

It was the truth, and that lack of certainty felt very, very strange.

"If you can't believe a miracle when it occurs right before your eyes," said Helen, "well, I pity you, girl."

"I want it to be true, but I can't accept it until you let me see him up close."

"My husband needs his rest."

"Of course. He's traveled far."

I didn't mean it to sound as nasty as it did. A lifetime of cynicism is hard to shake in an hour. Helen's face hardened, and Judy walked away, disappointed, to finish picking up the chairs.

"Before the ceremony," said Helen, "you were eyeing me. Something else you wanted to say?"

It took me a moment to remember the doubt I carried in here— the line in Virgil's notebook about Bully and Anacostia Fall.

"It's nothing," I said. "You have a miracle to clean up after. Did Enoch tell you . . ."

"About Abner? Yes."

"I'm sorry."

"And here I thought I was finished losing children to fire." She ground out a smile. "But if Bully can come back, none of my boys are really gone."

I was too exhausted by what I'd just seen to argue. When I left, she was leaning on a table, her eyes closed. She looked like she was doing what Ruth had asked: picturing her dead returning to her arms. As I stepped down the frozen stoop of the Electric Church, I found myself doing the same thing. When I blinked, Mary Fall and Virgil Carr and every other loved one I had buried seemed closer than ever before.

Down the block in both directions, Ruth's acolytes fanned out to find people to tell the good news. I walked home, that crisp, cold morning, teetering between doubt and belief, wanting to fall toward faith and knowing I would tilt the other way.

FOUR

Houseguests are a pestilence. They eat your food. They disrupt your routine. They rob you of the feeling of solitude that is, I have always felt, a home's sole purpose. Worst of all, they make it nearly impossible to brood.

I was sitting by the parlor window, watching the sky turn black, rereading the baseball news from June 16, 1915—the Giants won and Brooklyn lost, a happy day—when Cherub entered, cradling a teacup between his hands. His face was scrubbed and shaved. His rags were gone, replaced with an ancient suit of my father's that could have swallowed him. He looked ridiculous and wonderful.

"Have you tasted this?" he said. "It's called grog or glok or something. It's got me warm right down to my toenails."

"A specialty of the house."

He snatched the newspaper so roughly that an entire column of racing news crumbled.

"They do make new newspapers," he said. "Every day, in fact. No need to keep them around."

I took back the paper, handling the newsprint as gently as it deserved. "These are my archives."

"It makes your house smell like food caught between an old man's molars."

"You know, you're staying here for free. Which means you're free to go."

"Have I complained? The bed is soft, the food bountiful. This is a palace, and you live like you're in a hovel. Why?"

There was no easy answer, so I said nothing. I shifted the papers and he sat down. Outside the light was nearly gone. Washington Square was gray, washed out, its branches bare, its overgrown paths drowning in snow. Past the mothball stench of Virgil's suit, Cherub smelled cleaner than he ever had.

"What are you waiting for?" he said.

"Dark."

He took my hand. It was strange to feel his calloused fingers so soft, to see his nails so tidy. I didn't mind it.

"We've known each other," he said. "We've seen impossible things. We've lost friends. You've been honest before. Don't stop now."

It would have been easy to deflect him with a joke or a kiss. It would have been safer. But he was right—there were few in the city whom I knew so well, and none I had loved the same way.

Cherub Stevens was the indulgence of a young woman who was trying to learn how to misbehave. The spring after the fence went up, I was a twenty-two-year-old with no interest in university or work, whose city was fractured, whose mother was dead, whose father was sinking into the case that would kill him after it drove him mad. I was not expecting to fall in love.

One day, the One-Eyes were making a vain attempt to hack a new path into the jungle of Washington Square. They were shirtless, sweaty, rippling, and obscene—a parade of vigorous flesh that even Walt Whitman might find excessive—all save the squat, bearded boy who slouched in a stolen wing-back chair on the sidewalk, sipping a pitcher of cognac and offering occasional words of encouragement. He had a cavalry saber across his legs and, beneath the patchy fur on his face, a smile he seemed unwilling to control.

I went up to him. "Are you the man in charge?" I said.

"What gave you that idea?"

"You're not working."

"That just shows I'm clever. The man in charge is Gilly, the redheaded girl swinging that ax like the tree did her harm. She leads by example, which is terribly inspiring if you've the intellect and initiative of a garden snail. Rather than exhaust myself trimming greenery that will regrow in the night, I've chosen to occupy myself in—oh heavens, I didn't offer you a drink."

He stood and bowed and compelled me to sit in his mildewy chair. He lowered himself to a knee and presented his tub of liquor like a knight offering the Holy Grail. In a neighborhood overrun with boys pretending to be brutes, here was a thug who styled himself a gentleman. It was absurd.

I was charmed.

That spring was the first dawn of a new sun. Having finally succeeded in evicting humanity, the Westside took its true form. Trees tripled in size. Vines erupted from brownstone. Earth buckled and split, swallowing some buildings and upending others, and in a matter of weeks, the map was redrawn. Each morning, I found Cherub on my stoop, and we explored our changing Westside arm in arm.

He was not the kind of boy I imagined myself being courted by, but then, I'd never really imagined being courted by any boys at all. I had no intention of treating him as anything other than a diversion, an amusing way to pass the weeks before it grew too hot to go outside, but in those years death was at our elbows, and that made it impossible to throw away something good.

Then one day, a year later, we were walking the banks of Morton Creek, which had recently overtaken a few sleepy blocks of the far Village. He asked me to marry him and I laughed in his face.

I still saw him after that—he was, after all, lord of my block—but only from afar. As the Westside settled into its own awful pattern, Cherub found his place. The older One-Eyes died or grew up, and the recruits got younger and younger, until Cherub was a man in his mid-twenties babysitting a gang of child soldiers. He discarded his beard, along with whatever savagery had lurked beneath his cheerful front, and settled into life as an old softie who liked to lie about how tough he'd once been.

Not long after my father disappeared, Cherub washed up on my stoop once more. He never said he'd come to help me forget, but that's what it had to be. To distract me, he gave me a case—a silly thing, a trifle—and I remembered how fine a friend he had been. But then his boys were killed at the Battle of Eighth Avenue, and I feared the light went out inside Cherub Stevens for good.

So now, in my parlor, as Washington Square faded away, I told him everything: the dreams of Mary, the missing finger, the prophet who had come back from the dead. I must have told it well, because when Bully exploded out of the fire, Cherub cackled and smacked his knee.

"Amazing! Beautiful!" he said.

"But it's a lie. Whatever magic there is on the Westside is indifferent, like those impossible trees outside, or relentlessly cruel. There are no miracles here."

"Why not? It's not hurting anybody. Why not let this be simple? Why not assume it's real?"

Through my grimy window, I saw the shadows were impenetrable. The time for nuance had passed. I felt right at home.

"Because I'm a pain in the ass," I said, slapping my gloves on his leg as I stood to leave.

"I wouldn't have it any other way. Where to?"

"The Electric Church."

"Breaking and entering! What fun!"

"You're not invited. I asked you into my house, not my case."

He stood. His eyes were wet. His cheeks were flushed. It was infuriating how handsome he got when he chose to be sincere.

"It's been four months since I had anything to think about but the faces of those boys I led to their death," he said.

"I know."

"So give me something to do. I won't cause trouble. I won't complain."

"Those are both lies."

"Maybe." His forefinger stroked the back of my wrist. "But it's dangerous out there, even for you, and if you don't take me along I'll tell Hellida and she'll insist on coming, too."

"Fine. But if there's a fight . . ."

"Don't worry. I can still run away, fast as ever."

He smiled, and curse that beautiful idiot, I smiled, too.

On a summer day, it was five minutes to the banquet hall. On the ice, in the dark, it took longer. There was enough moon that we didn't need the lantern, but the mediocre path Van Alen's guardsmen had cut along Sixth Avenue was too slick for us to move fast.

Cherub kept me entertained. There wasn't a brick in the neighborhood that didn't remind him of some story—gory, bawdy, or simply profane—from his days with the One-Eyed Cats, and I was happy to hear them all for the fifth or sixth time. I laughed at the right moments, gasped at others, and in between let my mind drift across the main hall of the Electric Church, wondering if there was anything I could find to prove whether or not Bully Byrd had really come back to life.

"I'd bring back Roach," said Cherub as we approached Carmine Street.

"Pardon?"

"If the miracle is true. If the doors to death are opened, if we all get to call a few people home—I guess the responsible choice would be someone really marvelous, Frederick Douglass or someone, but what would he and I even have to talk about? Roach always made me laugh, and the way he died was . . . I'd want him back."

I had never told Cherub that I had seen Roach after Eighth Avenue, trapped in a half death from which no miracle could save him. There were some truths it was braver to keep to yourself.

"What about you?" he said. "What lost soul would Gilda Carr call back from the grave?"

"Frederick Douglass seems a noble enough choice," I said, and pushed ahead before he could ask me again.

The windows of the Electric Church were dark. Despite Enoch's promises of openness, the door was locked. Less than a minute with my burglar's tools corrected that. How nice it felt to be doing something wrong.

Inside, we were greeted by stale, silent air perfumed by the memory of char. Cherub lit the lantern and swept the light across the room.

"Is this a quiet thing, or a talking thing?" he said.

"Perhaps a whisper."

"What, precisely, are we searching for?"

"Proof, one way or the other."

"I bet we find nothing at all."

The brazier had been dragged off to the side. Faint heat hissed from the smoldering wood. The stage was bare. A blue imitation velvet curtain hung behind it, hiding a brick wall. In the corner of the room was the chipped door to Helen's office. It was padlocked. It could wait.

I dragged a pair of folding chairs across the room and set one next to the brazier. I stood on it and prodded the ash with the other, kicking sparks into the air.

"Careful," said Cherub.

"Of what?"

"I don't know. Just seemed the thing to say."

I began to regret allowing him to come.

I dug and dug, not certain what I was looking for, until the chair swept across something other than ash. I tried to drag it out but couldn't snag it.

"Hold a minute," said Cherub. "I saw just the thing."

He loped across the room and returned with a long iron candle snuffer.

"Step aside," he said. "This is no job for such stubby arms."

"You're just as stubby as I am."

"Probably, but I'm the man with the whatsit."

I could have kept arguing with him, but at a certain point it is easier to let a man feel useful than remind him he is anything but. I hopped down and let myself enjoy the unique spectacle of Cherub

Stevens, warlord of the Lower West, stabbing the snuffer into a pot-ful of ash like he was spearfishing for his dinner. I'd nearly stopped laughing when he let out a Neanderthal roar, jerked the snuffer out of the brazier, and hurled his catch to the ground.

It was a shapeless bag—large, gray, empty—made of weighty canvas. It looked like the discarded skin of a mammoth snake. Cherub kicked it, scattering sparks across the floor, and I knelt to give it a feel.

"Asbestos bag," I said.

"So?"

"It's fireproof. Bully—or the man they're calling Bully—was in the brazier before they lit the fire. He was waiting in this bag. The ceremony was a fake."

Cherub chucked me on the shoulder in an altogether too brotherly manner.

"Don't look so gloomy, old girl," he said. "We're hard-bitten, cynical Westsiders. We didn't believe for an instant."

"Of course not," I said, unable to add any more to his lie.

"I only wish I'd been here to see those rubes fall for it. Must have been a sight. Only question is—"

Before he could ask it, the church was split by a scream. It was high and strangled, like a cat being sawed in half. It came from the back room.

Cherub, true to his promise, broke for the exit. I ran toward the sound. I yanked on the padlock, but it held firm. I kicked at the old, warped wood. The door buckled but did not break.

The scream grew worse.

"Help me, you idiot," I called to Cherub, who had frozen in the doorway, waiting for me to see sense. Remembering I never would, he hurtled toward me and threw every ounce of his slight frame into a flying kick. It was enough. The wood splintered. The screaming stopped. Cherub fell to the ground, dazed, and I shoved the door open.

Inside, I saw no one. I heard nothing. I swept the lantern across the room. A pair of swayback couches stared at each other across a lopsided coffee table. A desk held a mess of papers and candle stubs. Then, in the corner of the room, beneath a threadbare blanket, I saw the shape of the man who had stepped out of the fire. It was hard to believe that noise had come from him, but there was nobody else here.

I lowered the lantern and eased my way across the floor. I had to get quite close before I was sure he still drew breath. There was a bottle in his hand and a red stain around his mouth.

"That's our man?" hissed Cherub from the doorway. I nodded. "Alive?" I nodded again, and he stole into the room to pick over the desk while I inspected the would-be prophet.

His skin was puffy; his teeth atrocious. Up close, the clumsy stitching on his white suit shone plainly. I brushed my hand across his hair, knocking loose the powder that had made it look burned. I dragged my thumbnail over his cheek, scraping up some of the greasepaint that had passed for soot.

"Hmm," said Cherub. I turned to see what he had found. A hand grabbed my ankle. The man on the floor howled as loud as a person can. His eyes were open, but he did not see. I sucked in a breath and held back a scream, trying to pull away. He held on with a dead man's grip. I could not get free.

Cherub bounded toward me. I believe he had a notion of staging some kind of rescue. I held up a hand for him to be still. I shut my eyes, tasting ash in my mouth, trying to pretend I was somewhere far away. It was not easy standing still.

The man screamed for a minute or more before his eyes shut, his shoulders sagged, and his fingers released my ankle. I stepped out of his grip, walking backward, waiting for the monster to come alive. No matter how I willed them, my eyes could not break from his slack, sleeping face and my feet would not move faster than a crawl. Only when I passed the threshold of that filthy little room did I allow myself to run.

We got all the way to Sixth Avenue before I risked a look back and saw that we had not been pursued. Still, I didn't stop moving until we were across the avenue, when I threw myself onto a snowbank. My neck was so hot, I'm certain I heard it hissing.

"What the hell just happened?" said Cherub, a question that, this time, I could answer.

"He wasn't dead, just dead drunk and screaming in his sleep. A common affliction around these parts. Probably he's onstage and can't recall his lines. Or maybe he's just being roasted alive."

"Since when can you peer inside the minds of drunks?"

"He's an actor. What else would they dream about?"

"How can you tell?"

"The makeup looked professional. The asbestos bag is a stage trick. I don't think any of the Byrds have a theatrical background, so the man they hired must have provided it himself."

"You're sure he's playing a part?"

"If that was really their dear, departed father, would he be drinking himself to sleep, locked in a frozen room, or would he be at home, in bed, surrounded by the family that's waited so long for his return?"

Cherub hauled me out of the snow. We walked. He pulled his borrowed scarf tighter around his neck. In the moonlight his eyes shone yellow. His lips were chapped nearly to bleeding.

"What was it you found," I said, "before he started screaming?"

"The reason for the hoax."

He handed me a thin slip of paper, a spotlessly printed hand-bill advertising "A Grand Ceremony of Electric Resurrection" two nights hence on the Flat. It promised sermons from Ruth Byrd and her lately revived father, plus fifty sinners brought back from the dead. Two dollars bought admission, a view of the miracle, and a ticket to enter the drawing for the lucky fifty whose loved ones would be returned to life.

"Fake one resurrection," he said, "and sell tickets for fifty more. Hell of a racket."

I tore the handbill into careful shreds and dropped it where, if it weren't for the snow, the gutter would be. I had spent so long trying to understand how I felt. The answer was familiar.

Rage.

"They cannot *do* this," I said, surprised I could speak. "They cannot dress themselves up as saints, inflame the passions of the hopeless, and bilk them out of what little they have in exchange for a lie."

"They're going to make a fortune."

"No. I'm going to stop them if I have to tear their church apart, board by board."

I walked east. He followed, stumbling a bit as he tried to keep up.

"Are you really that embarrassed?" he said.

"What do you mean?"

"You saw that fire and you saw that smoke, and when Bully stepped out of it, you thought for just one second, if they can get their daddy back maybe you can have yours, too."

"I've met my father. I had a chance to have him back, and I said no. Death is final. Grief is permanent. Those rules aren't meant to be broken."

"You can lie to yourself, Gilda, but I hate when you lie to me."

I didn't answer. What was the point in telling a man the truth when he'd already read it on your face?

We reached Washington Square, where I'd paid a gang of Barbarossa's old men, unemployed and desperate, to cut a path along the sidewalk from the street to my front door. We stepped gratefully onto the pavement, our calves burning from the effort of keeping steady on the ice.

"My feelings don't matter," I said. "That ceremony has to be stopped."

"How?"

"I'll leave that for morning. Right now, I'm tired and cold and—"

"Look at that," he said. I turned my head and saw ice-packed trees glittering in the moonlight. When I turned back, he was two steps closer, leaning in for a kiss.

I'd loved him once for being an idiot, and it was nice to see he hadn't changed. His lips were frozen, but so were mine. It was like finding an old pair of slippers buried in the back of a closet and being surprised they fit as easily as ever.

I pulled away and found my breath. On the Eastside, I'd have been obligated to smack his face and stamp my feet and scream to the world that my honor had been insulted. But there was no one watching, and so I kissed him again. When I finished with him, I took him by the hand, opened my gate, and started up the steps. He looked up at me like a sunflower admiring the sun.

"You should let the Byrds alone," he said.

"Why?"

"Because what we're doing here, it isn't working for us anymore, is it? I haven't slept right since Eighth Avenue. I wake up six or seven times a night, even when I'm drunk. I'm grinding my teeth—by morning my gums are bloody and my jaw feels like I've been chewing rocks. And my dreams . . . you saw everything I saw, and more. You did everything I did and more."

Shot a man through the heart. Knocked a woman senseless and watched the river swallow her. It's all right, though. I only see them dying whenever I shut my eyes.

"Honestly," I said, "I'm doing fine. What's your point?"

"That's honesty?"

"The closest I can give."

He sighed. "Fine. If you can't talk straight, I will. Why not get out? You and me together, and Hellida to make those pancakes she does. To the Upper West or the Eastside or maybe even another city altogether, where things are passably normal?"

"And what would we do with normal?"

"Anything we want."

"This is the only neighborhood in the country where your skin and my skin can touch without fear."

"There are places we could go. It would be hard, but no less a hell than here. We're too young to give up. I'm through being an overgrown boy. Whatever kind of man you want, that's the kind I'll be. It's the same as I was saying earlier—why not take the thing that's simple? Why not assume this is real?"

If it had been summer, I might have let him down easy. If it had been summer, I might have said yes. But the wind was sharp and my hands were numb, and I lacked the patience to explain my fear that if I unpacked the iron around my heart, I would find it had died in its cell.

"Maybe not. But I still can't," I said, and he nodded like he'd been expecting nothing else. "Come inside and I'll find something to drink and we can talk about it, okay?"

But he was already opening the gate.

"It wasn't easy to say a thing like that," he said. "You're a tough audience when it comes to speaking the truth. I don't think I've got it in me to do any more tonight."

"At least come in and sleep."

"I've survived worse nights on the Westside, and colder, too," he said, and he closed my gate and he was gone.

I covered my eyes and breathed as best I could. In a minute or so I was nearly fine. I turned my knob and found that while I was away, someone had locked the door.

"Damn it, Hellida," I said. Deep in my bag I found my seldom-used keys. I stepped inside and closed the door, shutting out the wind and leaving me in silence so deep that I could hear nothing but my heartbeat and, worse, my own thoughts. Light was needed, and a few hours with the Giants' box scores, and I would feel human again. I reached for a match. Something hard pressed against my back.

"Mr. Burglar," said a woman's voice. "If you keep moving, I shall be forced to fire this revolver. It will put a hole in your back the size of a Granny Smith apple. Be good, stand still, and live."

"That's not a gun," I said.

"It most certainly is."

"There are no guns in my district. No guns west of the stem. And every New Yorker knows it. So who in hell are you?"

I spun around. It wasn't a gun, but it was still a weapon—something heavy enough that when she cracked me on the head with it, I fell down hard.

"I may be in hell," she said, "but I don't let anyone, even a demon, speak so disrespectfully."

"Who are you?" I said.

She swiped at me with the weapon.

"What are you doing in my parlor?"

She swiped at me again. I scrambled backward and found the match.

I scraped it against my thumbnail. It flashed into light and I saw my mother's face.

FIVE

She looked healthier than I remembered. Her teeth were white and her brow was free from worry. Beneath her coat she wore a thin, old dress—corseted, like always—and her hair, as knotted and uncooperative as my own, was piled on her head in a style thought becoming around the time she died. Today it looked ridiculous. Maybe it always had.

It didn't matter. I saw that face and did what I'd waited nearly twenty years for. I threw my arms around her, ready to cry.

My mother dropped me on the floor.

She raised the silver spoon she had cracked me on the head with and prepared to deliver another blow. I offered my hands in surrender, and she smiled—almost sneered—when she knew that she had won.

"You don't remember . . . ," I said.

"Quite correct. I don't remember a thing."

"I can explain."

That was almost certainly a lie, but I would take my best shot.

I scrambled across the floor and pulled a picture from the mantel: mother and daughter, posing against a set of Grecian ruins in a Seventh Avenue photographer's studio, circa 1901. Even at eight, I was unmistakably myself, and Mary could never be anyone else. The photograph would set things right, would clear the fog of death from her mind and bring her back to me. I pressed it to my chest and was about to turn around when she spoke.

"Your name wouldn't happen to be Gilda Carr?" she said.

Her voice echoed what I had seen in her eyes. It wasn't just that she didn't know me. She had looked at me, she had spoken to me, without an ounce of love.

"I'm Gilda Carr," I said. "This is my house."

"I wouldn't boast about that. What's that you're holding?"

In the photo, young Gilda stared straight ahead—dour, annoyed at being forced to stand still. Mary ignored the camera and gazed at her daughter with a look of infinite affection. I set the picture aside.

"It isn't anything," I said.

"It had better not be." She twirled the spoon. "I'm still armed. This is horribly tarnished, by the way. You really must polish your silver."

"I'll be sure to do that before the next time someone breaks in and brains me with it."

I yearned for a belt of gin. There was a bottle in the kitchen, but I did not want to risk turning my back on her, lest she disappear. It was strange to see her in the living room with her coat on, stranded in the middle of the floor, unsure where to sit. Of course, it was strange to see her at all.

I removed a few stacks of newspaper from the long sofa by the fireplace and gestured for her to sit. She placed as little of herself on the dusty cushion as she could without crashing to the floor. I sat, too. She lay the spoon across her knees.

"You entered like a burglar," she said. "When I heard the door I was quite terrified and reached for the nearest thing—that silly spoon. I thought my ruse about the pistol was rather clever, but you saw through it at once, didn't you?"

As casually as I could manage, I said, "Perhaps you could tell me what brings you here."

"I was rather hoping you could tell me. I appear to be suffering from a nasty case of amnesia. It's amazing. The sort of thing you read about in the papers and think, 'That will never happen to me.' And yet, here I am, mind as blank as a clear blue sky."

"Do you remember—"

"My name? Yes, and that's the extent of it. Mary Fall. A pleasure to meet you, Miss Carr. I do hope you can help."

She smiled with the serenity of a wealthy woman who is certain that wherever she goes, people will fall down at her feet, then sat there, perfectly still, waiting for me to work my magic. She was acting like a client, and if I had any hope of getting through this chat without breaking down, I would have to treat her like one.

"What brought you to me?" I said.

"Ah, of course." She slid the card across the couch, plowing up a trail of dust like an icebreaker on the North Sea. "G. CARR: TINY MYSTERIES SOLVED. Quite an amusing card. I do hope I'm tiny enough for you."

"Who gave this to you?"

"The man in the gatehouse. I suppose I should start at the beginning?"

"Please."

"The first thing I remember is the snow. I saw it piled on the streets, clinging to the trees, tumbling down in drifts from the tops of ruined buildings. It seemed infinite, and I was alone. I rather thought I'd died. I had never seen a city so broken—although it's so hard to be sure *what* I've seen before. The snow I didn't particularly mind, but the cold was terrible and my coat is thin. I went numb, and that was an irritant. After I don't know how long staggering about, looking for frankly anyone who might direct me someplace warm, I reached a road I recognized as Broadway and found that someone had put up a wall."

"We call it a fence."

"Well, it's a wall. Fences have posts."

I wanted to argue with her, but I had never bested my mother in a semantic debate, and I didn't think that would change tonight. I kept my mouth closed.

"When I see a wall, I want to go past it. The man asked for my papers, and of course I don't have any papers. He asked my name and I told him and whatever list he had, I wasn't on it. He wanted me to go away, to die in some snowdrift somewhere, but I wasn't having that and so I kind of elbowed my way inside."

"You forced your way into a gatehouse? People have landed in jail for less."

"I hardly had a choice. He had a little coal fire going in there, and you'll recall I was cold. He let me stay until I'd recovered feeling, but he began to lose patience when I ate his supper. Finally he said there was only one woman in the city who could handle someone as impossible as me, and he threw your card at my face and tossed me out and slammed his shutter and moaned until I left him alone. Quite a helpful man, in the end."

Her story had my head spinning. I was dizzy, and I was looking for a place to sit down when I remembered I was sprawled across a couch. I had not expected death would turn my mother into a chatterbox.

"And what is it you'd like me to do?" I said.

"Who am I?" she said. "Who is Mary Fall? What am I doing here, and how do I get back where I belong? I haven't a nickel, of course, but that shouldn't be a problem. I remind myself of the type of woman who has an easy time securing credit."

"Like the card says, tiny mysteries are more my line."

I don't know why I was refusing her. What other question was there to ask besides "Who is Mary Fall?" I wanted to keep her, of course, to hold her and love her and protect her from the world outside, but answering her question would mean pressing up against death itself, and tonight I was simply too tired.

"Tiny mysteries. Ridiculous. What does that even mean?"

"I find things for people. Small things, generally. Gloves. Ink. The odd finger. Or I answer questions—unimportant questions, but the sort you just can't let go."

"And that earns a living?"

"It's a niche service. 'Who am I?' is a bigger question than I have the strength to answer at the moment."

She stared at me, waiting for me to change my mind, and when I said nothing her smile crumpled like a deflating balloon. There was that look, that look I had spent my childhood trying to keep away. Mary Fall was disappointed.

But only for a moment. Before I could find something to comfort her, the light had swept back across her face.

"My glove!" she said.

"It's right there on your hand."

"Of course it is—that's where gloves go!—but look at it, won't you?"

She yanked off her left glove and showed me its third finger. Just where the knuckle would go, there was a tiny deformity: a wart in the supple black leather.

"Do you see that?" she said. "It's a dimple caused by a ring. But look at my hand."

Her ring finger was bare. I remembered the band my mother wore—plain silver with a single flawless sapphire. She'd inherited it from her grandmother. It was classic, simple, her. We'd buried her in it—Virgil had been adamant—and now it was gone.

"I must be engaged," she said, "or married even. And my ring has disappeared. Is that the sort of thing you help people find?"

I walked back to the mantel, where our picture lay facedown. I didn't pick it up, but lord I wanted to show it to her—not just for my sake, but to let her know that she was not alone.

I left the picture where it was. I didn't want to disappoint her again.

"I'll help you."

"Of course you will!" she said, and slapped her glove into her hand.

"But forget the ring. I'm far too busy chasing the blue of the evening sky."

"I suppose it's best if I just pretend that makes sense?"

"It means I don't need another tiny mystery—we'll recover your memory and go from there."

That's what I said, and she loved the sound of it, but I don't think that's what I intended at all. For now, she was beaming, and that's all I wanted in the world.

"We'll start tomorrow," she said. "For now, would it be a terrible imposition if I slept here?"

"There's a free room on the third floor." That morning, it had been Cherub's. He was long gone. "Before we head up, will you give me five minutes to tidy?"

She shrugged. I snatched the photo off the mantel and fled upstairs, sweeping up every photograph and memento I saw lying around my overdecorated house. I shoved a lifetime of memories under my bed, returned to the parlor, and invited her upstairs.

The moment her feet echoed on the wood, my tears came. Her shoes rapped against the steps, as clearly as they always had, and reverberated through me like a gong, until I was nothing more than a little girl excited to hear her mother had come home. I stared straight ahead and did not let her see me cry.

"There's one other thing," she said. "Now that I know you believe me, now that I know you won't laugh . . ."

"What?"

"It's just an image—or more likely, a dream—but I have a picture in my head of fire, blue fire, that danced up and down and side to side, zigzagging like it had a mind of its own. Have you ever heard of such a thing?"

I didn't answer. I could not stand for her to be tainted by the Byrds, by the Basement Club, by the blue flames or Abner's scorched corpse. Mary I wanted just for me.

I opened the door to the third-floor bedroom, wondering if the sight of her old quarters would provoke some memory of life in this house. If it did, she said nothing. She sat on the bed, and a cloud of dust burst into the air.

"Your five minutes didn't make a dent," she said. "But there's not much one could do in a room like this."

"I'm sorry."

"Don't be. It's not your fault you decorate like an old woman. This is a bed to die in, that rug is dizzying, and that dresser—lord, that's the worst of the lot. Perhaps in the morning, I'll give you a lesson in furnishing a home. For now, I sleep."

"I look forward to it. Good night."

I was leaving the room when she cried out: "The church!"

"What church?" I said.

"A church—a church. I remember it now! Before the snow I saw a church. Only it wasn't a church, it was just an empty lot. At one end was a pile of stone, at the other a doorway and windows shaped like the cross."

"Anything more?"

"Just that. Just the image. But it had to be a church."

And with my cancerous bad luck, there was no other church that it was ever going to be.

"Do you know any place like that?" she said.

I was too weak to lie. Mary Fall had come back from the dead, and there was only one outfit in town offering resurrection. My miracle was always going to lead back to the Electric Church.

"I do," I said. "I'll take you tomorrow." And I would keep her far, far from the body in the snow—and pray that the Westside lay no others at our feet.

"Miss Carr, you're a wonder. I think we're going to make a fabulous team."

I left a note on the kitchen table for Hellida, vague enough that if Mary found it, it wouldn't give the game away: "Don't act surprised." In my bedroom, I doused the candle, stripped my clothes, and climbed shivering beneath my many quilts. As I cinched them tight against my chin, it occurred to me that Mary was sleeping in the bed where she'd died.

When morning elbowed its way into my room, I kicked my bedding onto the floor and felt the guilt and confusion that had been suffocating me fall away as well. I leapt out of bed, not minding the chill. My mother had come home.

Hellida was no actor. The mood at breakfast was so strained that Mary got the impression Hellida hardly spoke English. It didn't bother her—she chattered happily to a woman too stunned to answer back, spending hundreds of words to somehow say nothing at all.

When Mary finished devouring a stack of crepes, sausage, and eggs, I sent her upstairs to find something warmer to wear. I cleared the plates and made a half-hearted show of washing them, waiting for Mount Hellida to erupt.

"You might have given a proper warning," she growled over my shoulder. "By your note, I thought you and Cherub were going to walk down those stairs engaged to be married. The thought made me sick, but I was prepared to fake a smile. You did not prepare me for this!"

I returned the dish I was washing to the pile in the sink and turned to face her. Her straw hair was pulled in a vise-tight bun, the lines in her face were smooth and narrow, and she wore a thin housedress that gave an idea of the terrifying thickness of her arms. As always, she looked half old and half young, but her weary expression showed she had been dealing with the Carrs for far too long.

"I couldn't have possibly prepared you," I said. "There's no way to brace oneself for this kind of Westside thing. I just wanted to make sure you didn't let your mouth dangle or rush across the floor to hug her or something ridiculous like that. Silent shock suited my cause perfectly—thank you."

"Happy to oblige," she said, sounding anything but. I shrugged. Her eyes narrowing, she continued. "Now, will you do me the honor of explaining what in the white Westside hell is going on?"

"She's come back from the dead."

"*How?*"

"She doesn't remember a thing, and I'm fighting the urge to speculate until I know a bit more. But I'm sure it's wrapped up in the Electric Church and Bully Byrd, who may have been resurrected as well, or may be a fraud. I'm waffling on that."

"And what is it that has you so giddy?"

"Am I giddy? I hadn't noticed."

She guided me away from the sink with her firm Swedish grip and sat me forcefully at the table, then pulled a chair around and sat alongside.

"You've wanted this for a long time," she said.

"Maybe."

"And you really think it's her? That she's come back to you, that she's yours?"

"I'm trying not to think along those lines. I just want to—I should like to show her a perfect Westside day. Remember the way she loved parks?"

"She practically lived in Washington Square."

"The Westside is the greatest park the world has ever seen. I want to show her how beautiful it can be."

"There's nothing out there but snow and ice."

"Ask any bride—there's nothing more beautiful than white."

Hellida squeezed her neck with her broad right hand, a practiced gesture used whenever she felt it would be counterproductive to smack me across the mouth.

"That isn't what she's hired you for, is it?" she said. "A bit of sightseeing?"

"She wants her memory back."

"So give it to her."

If I did, though, it would be over. Give Mary a piece of the truth and she would demand all of it. That would mean spilling the secret of June 7, 1903: a woman old before her time, lungs weighed down with fluid, drowning in her own bed on a sticky summer morning. A girl lying outside her door, praying the coughing wouldn't stop, because that would mean the end. A cloud of grief that filled the house, that claimed a father, that covered a city—a cloud that lifted last night when that spoon smashed into my skull. I needed time with her, just a little time, because if her memory came back there was nothing for her to remember but death.

But that wasn't a very tidy answer, and Hellida liked things tidy.

"Just telling her could be a shock," I said. "Better for her if things come back, bit by bit."

Hellida grunted a kind of approval. She inspected the few dishes I had washed, sighed, and began to wash them again. I knew I should stop her, but after nearly thirty years of her taking care of me, it had been hard for us to adjust to life as friends. One of these mornings, I swore, I would cook her breakfast. She was polite enough that I'm sure she wouldn't laugh.

"Say what you want. I know you're afraid. Don't argue," she said, just as I was about to start. "I also wouldn't want to tell that woman how she died. Put it off, like you always put off the dishes. This time, I don't blame you. So what's your plan for that perfect Westside day?"

"She wants to see the ruins of the Electric Church? Fine. I'll give her the briefest possible tour."

"After that?" said Hellida.

"The Upper West library, maybe a chat with Father Lamb. I want to dig up everything I can find about resurrection and amnesia, but mostly I want to keep her safe. If there are any dangerous questions that need asking, I'll attend to it while she's asleep."

Hellida set the last of the plates to dry. With the corner of her rag, she scrubbed clean a patch of window and squinted at the field behind my house. She wasn't looking at anything—she was just trying not to look at me.

"Will you let me handle her my way?" I said.

"You pretend you don't need your mother. Everyone does that. I don't know why. But I see you wanting to fall across her lap, to press your head to her bosom and cry twenty years of tears. She doesn't know you, though. And she doesn't love you. Don't give in."

"I won't." Of course I wouldn't. It would feel too good.

"And don't get excited. Whatever this is, you're not stupid enough to think it will end well."

I was worried I *was* that stupid. Because when the kitchen door opened, I fought the rush of sentiment that came from seeing my mother standing in the doorway, ready to go out for the day. She'd pinned her hair into some kind of shape and she wore a buttercup dress that I hadn't seen in years.

"Nothing of yours could have possibly fit," she said, "but I found this rather nice dress deep in my bedroom closet. Surely it doesn't belong to either of you."

"It was my mother's."

"She had good taste, and a fine figure. Now, quick quick. The world awaits."

Quick quick. She'd said that to me a thousand times—every morning I dawdled over my shoelaces or was slow buttoning my coat. It got me moving then, and it did still.

This time, my heart was racing as well.

SIX

Of the memories I tote around from childhood, few are more pleasant than mornings out with my mother. She loved the green spaces of the city and she patrolled them like an expert, recognizing each tree or wildflower as surely as she would an old school friend. Nothing made her happier than to find a bit of nature in a surprising place, whether a lovingly planted window box or an abandoned lot whose neighbors had converted it into a vegetable garden.

"No matter how much rubble they pile on this island," she told me once as we walked the narrow path of a pocket park, "green fights back."

Winter did not slow her. Even in thick snow, we went for our walks, tramping across empty avenues in homemade snowshoes and as many coats as we owned. We threw snowballs, snapped icicles, and stood beneath the awnings of the rich, watching New York drown. Of all the countless tragedies of 1914, one that stung was that Mary Fall did not live to see nature triumphant over the Westside. When the trees of Washington Square blotted out the sun, all I could think was how deeply she would have loved the shade.

That day's sky was a fragile blue. The breeze stung with the taste of snow. A long track of untouched powder ran down Thompson Street. We walked alongside it, single file, in a narrow, clumsily hacked path. Until that morning, I'd found the ice oppressive. Today, it was as beautiful as anything my embellished childhood memories could provide.

I stepped carefully down the icy pavement. When I looked up, Mary was half a block ahead.

"Quick quick, Miss Carr!" she called. "Don't make me tell you again."

My impulse was to snap that I was walking as fast as I pleased. I don't let people—even clients—talk to me like that, but she was not just anyone, and so I said nothing.

When I caught up, she was peering into an empty lot where the earth had swallowed a collapsed building. Broken walls lay in a heap, half underground, rising out of the snow like a mammoth's carcass.

"What's this wreckage?" she said.

"When the Westside grew into its own, the earth shifted. Some buildings came tumbling down."

"What was here before?"

"I don't know. A factory, I think. Men's hats, maybe, or trousers."

"Were there people inside when it fell?"

"Those are questions I try not to ask. Not exactly tiny, you know."

She pursed her lips at the ruined structure for a few long seconds, like she was trying to find a way to raise it back up through sheer force of will.

Finally, I said what I assumed we were both thinking: "It's beautiful, isn't it?"

"It is?"

"Not the building, not just that—the whole Westside. The fresh powder. The ice on the trees. Spring is my season, but a sight like this makes me admire the cold."

She shook her head, hoisted her skirt, and started across the street.

"A city should clean up its messes," she said. I hurried to keep up.

"But don't you find it beautiful?"

"Oh, perhaps. Beautiful like the bottom of the sea, beautiful as a frozen corpse. I see that untouched snow, and all I know is that no children have played there. It is a vision of hell."

My good mood crumbled like ash flicked from the end of a cigarette. We walked on, and I kept the guided tour to myself. A window blocked by dead vines hid an Italian restaurant where Virgil and I sometimes lunched before the fence went up. A slab of bare concrete, free of snow due to some invisible heat source, was once a florist's that my mother and I walked to on Sunday afternoons. And of course, a few blocks behind lay the ruined club-house of the One-Eyed Cats. All these memories were precious, but on this cold, still morning, I saw them as Mary did: wreathed in death.

We reached Houston Street, where the pines of the Thicket towered over the pavement. I waited for Mary to be impressed, but she didn't even notice. Instead, she simply marched right in, without any fear at all. I had to call her back and force her to follow my lead. As I picked my way over the sidewalk's winding remains, I sensed her straining behind me, an overeager filly pushing against her bridle, and I felt almost powerless to hold her back.

Above our heads, pines groaned in the gentle wind, dragging their branches across each other as steadily as a ship creaking on open water. Somewhere ahead of us, shrouded by the morning dark, a body waited in the snow.

"Being out in the city," I said, "does it bring anything back?"

"Such as?"

"Your fiancé, your family, your life?"

"If I remembered anything useful, don't you think I would have shared? Everything is a complete blank. It's embarrassing, honestly. Even basic facts escape me. For instance, what's the year?"

"1922."

"Who's the president?"

"A nonentity."

"The mayor?"

"Worse."

"What is the economic situation? Are we at war? What troubles face the city? Where are hemlines falling? How are we wearing our hair?"

She peppered me with those questions and more. I didn't bother answering. She didn't seem to care.

"This must be how a soldier feels," she said, "trying to clench a fist on an arm that's been hacked away. I reach for knowledge that I know is there and find nothing. I feel stupid, helpless. It makes me want to scream."

I was starting to feel the same.

The street split. To the right was sun, space, and a route that seemed to lead back to Houston. The left-hand path pointed straight into the close-packed trees. Judy and Enoch had gone right, I remembered, following some invisible markings until the path doubled back toward the Electric Church. I turned that way, but Mary did not budge.

"Don't be foolish, Miss Carr," she said, then smiled. "That's back the way we came."

"I know how it looks, but—"

"We're going left. Quick quick."

I didn't move. Neither did she.

"You're cross, aren't you?" she said. "Hurt that I wasn't more impressed with the awful specter of that sunken hat factory."

"It's not that," I lied. "You hired me. You should trust my expertise."

"I didn't engage you to get me lost in the woods."

"I came this way a few days ago. You don't even remember the president's name. Please, I beg you, listen to me."

She smiled gently, as one smiles at a harmless lunatic, and placed a hand on my shoulder.

"I will listen to you, Miss Carr, of course I will. As soon as you find something worthwhile to say."

Before I caught my breath, she turned left into the darkness, and once again it was all I could do to keep pace. The path was overgrown and rotten with switchbacks, and it took us an hour to cover ground we should have crossed in ten minutes. Nevertheless, I got us to the Electric Church, and refrained from strangling Mary as she boasted about her shortcut.

I leaned on the cold stone threshold of the church, trying to disguise how hard I was breathing. From here, thank god, we could not see the corpse behind the altar. I stood in front of her, ever so slightly, trying to discourage a jaunt across the snow.

"Does this bring anything back?" I said.

"I was here. It was night. I remember being surprised by the cold."

"What else?"

"My memory is empty. It's like the morning after drinking far, far too much champagne. I know I must have laughed, danced, sung, but I don't remember a thing. I lived a whole life before I came here, and none of it survives. That's a kind of death, isn't it?"

That was not a question I was prepared to answer at the moment.

"I do steady business helping people retrace steps taken while blacked out on bad liquor," I said instead. "Close your eyes. Forget I'm here. Tell me what you see."

"Oh, absolutely not," she said, her eyes wide open. "I'm not the type for spiritualist rubbish. Let's just have a look around."

She nudged me aside and leapt down into the snow, where she clapped her hands and laughed.

"What is it?" I said.

"Jump down and see for yourself, Miss Detective."

I loved her, but if she called me Miss Detective one more time, I wasn't sure I could keep from murdering her, just a bit.

She offered her hand. I hopped down and saw footsteps faintly preserved from two days before. Judy's tracks went halfway down the lot before doubling back. Mine went all the way to the corpse.

"I've heard rumors there are criminals, bootleggers, who move illicit goods through these woods," I said. "This could be their trail. That's a good reason, I think, for us to keep moving. Those are not men we want to surprise."

Instead, she knelt over the footsteps, running her gloved fingertip along the shallow imprint in the snow. She chuckled like a child enjoying a puzzle. I couldn't believe she was having so much fun.

"I don't think we've any men to worry about," she said. "These are women's boots. Two different pairs."

"Very astute," I said, understanding for the first time why people find detectives so annoying.

"I'm not going to have to worry about paying your bill if I keep doing your job for you," she said. "You'll be paying me!"

She stomped for the altar, and I remembered the blood frozen to the gash in the dead man's skull like congealed fat. I could not let her find him. I could not let his death stain her miraculous return, but she was nearly there.

"We have to stop!" I shouted.

"Why?"

"Because there's nothing here. This is a waste of time. This is—"

"Fun!"

"Stop walking now, or—"

"Calm down, Miss Carr. You're verging on a tantrum. You will find that sort of behavior has no effect on me."

I knew from bitter experience that she was right. I felt an unsettling desire to kick her in the back of the knee and send her face-first into the snow. I took a few long breaths, fixed a smile to my face, and pretended we weren't arguing at all.

"What's the matter?" she said, a sinister twinkle in her eye. "Have I hurt your feelings? Injured your professional pride? How would you rather we spend the morning?"

"There's a library in the Upper West. I want to—"

"No one ever solved anything lounging around a library. Try again when you think of something better. For now . . ."

She crossed the last few feet of open snow. She rested her hands on the altar and let out a shriek. I closed my eyes and saw every inch of that frozen corpse.

"What is it?" I said.

"There was a man."

"Was?"

"When I came to, there was a man here! A man, running across the snow."

She leaned on the altar, surveying the scene. Her eyes flicked back and forth, trying to see everything, almost like they were dancing. The cold had put strawberry red into her lips. She was so beautiful when she was getting an idea.

"What did he look like?" I said, afraid I already knew the answer.

"He had no hat, no winter coat. He was a big man—not fat, exactly, but large. And he wore—I can't believe I forgot this!—he wore a white suit. The moonlight shone off it like a pearl."

I walked away from the altar. The snow crunched beneath Mary's boots. Now it was her turn to keep up.

"Miss Carr!" she called, singing my name as joyfully as a Christmas carol. "Don't think you can fool me."

She grabbed my wrist. Her touch was gentle. Her smile was infectious.

"You know that man, don't you?" she said.

"I have an inkling."

"Then he must have something to do with what brought me here, what erased my mind."

"I'm believing that more and more."

"We'll have to speak to him."

She wrapped her arm in mine and led me away from the church, away from the snow, back the way we came. Holding on to her was like gripping a helium balloon.

"There's no chance of confining you to a library while I pay him a visit, is there?" I said.

"I'd tunnel out or burn it down."

"Then we'll go together."

"I knew having a detective would come in handy. What's his name?"

"You have to know—this may be dangerous."

"Spectacular."

"I have a plan, but it calls for subtlety."

"Subtlety is my trademark."

I let that slide. "And you must—you must!—promise to do everything I say."

She mumbled something that may have been yes and may have been no. It was the best assurance I was going to get. If nothing else, while we left the Thicket, she let me lead the way. I had failed to keep her away from the Byrds, but for the moment, I felt the sting of that failure faintly. Mary was happy, and there was nothing in the world as sweet as that.

We emerged onto Houston Street, where the sun was bright, if not warm. Behind us, the body stayed buried, its questions unanswered for now.

As we walked uptown, I told Mary what I knew of the Byrds, and we hacked together a sort of plan. By phrasing everything so that it seemed my ideas were coming from her, I was able to convince her to do things my way. We worked our way to Carmine Street, where a banner stretched from sidewalk to sidewalk, its four-foot-high red letters telling all who passed of "Bully Byrd's Spectacular Electric Resurrection: Tomorrow Night at the Flat." From afar, it looked impressive. Up close, I saw it had been painted on stitched-together bedsheets. Still, the lettering was tidy. Enoch was a professional.

"They're really promising to bring fifty people back from the dead?" Mary said.

"That's the pitch."

"That might be the stupidest thing I've ever heard. Or it might not be, of course. My memory is not to be trusted." When I didn't respond, she stopped to smirk. "Please don't tell me you believe they can do it."

"I didn't."

"What changed?"

"I woke up this morning and saw the sun shining bright on the Westside, and anything seemed possible."

"Hogwash."

"Or maybe I'm growing optimistic in my old age," I said. "Now remember—this calls for understatement. Recall Hamlet's advice to the players."

"And what was that, exactly?"

"Remember your lines and don't act like an idiot."

A trio of huffingly inefficient moving women was taking up space in the main room of the Byrds' banquet hall, dismantling the muddle of religious iconography that decorated the walls and dragging it, in bits and pieces, outside. Enoch tagged along after them, waving a scrap of notepaper like it was holy writ, begging them not to break anything. Judy, hammer in hand and nails clenched between her lips, repaired the smashed office door. On the stage, Ruth sat cross-legged, her scarf hiked up to permit the smoking of a cigarette, saying nothing and seeing everything. The brazier was gone, and I saw no sign of the fireproof bag.

"Everything must be in proper condition when it reaches the Flat," Enoch said, but no one heard him, because that was when Mary made her entrance.

She marched through the doorway and threw her infuriatingly slight form across a pile of orange Bibles heaped on the floor.

"Herbert!" she cried, loud enough that the movers stopped moving and Ruth uncrossed her legs. Mary rolled onto her back, looking like a petulant cockroach, and cried to the heavens: "Herbert—come back to me!"

Ruth hopped down from the stage and offered Mary a hand.

"That finger ever turn up?" I said.

"I thought my sister told you to quit looking for it," said Ruth.

"She did, but—do you really not care what happened to it?"

"Excuse me?"

"Someone broke into your church and stole your holiest relic, and you're all willing to just let that go?"

She ashed her cigarette at me. I shook my head.

"I simply cannot understand the pious," I said.

"No, you can't."

"Doesn't matter. That's not why I'm here." I gestured at Mary. "My cousin Mary."

"Why on earth do you look so proud?"

I tried to beam just a little bit brighter as I said, "She's visiting from the Upper West."

"And I'm utterly savaged by grief," said Mary.

"As I'm sure you can see. Her fiancé—"

"Herbert! Dearest Herbert!"

"Was killed by the Germans at Belleau Wood."

"And each night I see him in my dreams, begging me to bring him home. I am told you have this power. I will do anything—pay *anything*—for you to bring him back."

Mary pulled out her bulging pocketbook, which we'd fattened with a shredded copy of the *Sentinel*, and waved it over her head in a gesture, I am certain, that no human being had ever made. Ruth smiled, puzzled at the eccentricity.

"It is true that the electric resurrection is at hand," said Ruth. "But not this instant."

"Tomorrow night we raise fifty from the dead," said Enoch, with sickening pride.

"I cannot wait so long," said Mary.

"Miracles cannot be rushed," said Ruth.

"It's my fault, then," I said. "I told her you could help."

"I'm sure there's something we can do to tide her over," said Enoch.

"I've spoken to widows who received comfort from your mother. If you can't offer a miracle, a shoulder to cry on could suffice."

"My mother is at the Flat supervising construction of the stage," said Ruth, "and I am a preacher, not a healer. My shoulders carry the weight of the ministry. They are not built for crying on."

I took Mary's hand. Tears swept down her face. Enoch was so distressed, he looked ready to dissolve. Even Ruth seemed moved, in her way. Despite Mary's hysterics, it had gone the way I wanted. It was time for my only important line.

"If you can't help us," I said, "perhaps your father can."

Ruth and Enoch shared a look. What it meant, I could not say, but I did notice that across the room, the hammering stopped. The hammer dangled at Judy's hip as she waited to see what happened.

"Papa is resting," said Enoch. "The ordeal . . ."

"I know," I said. "Of course I know, but if he knew one of his faithful was carrying so much pain, perhaps he could—"

"No," said Ruth, like a steel shutter falling into place. "Tomorrow night, Papa will perform the greatest miracle since Christ walked out of his tomb. He cannot be bothered with matters so trivial."

"Tragic though they may be," said Enoch. He took a pair of bright blue tickets from his coat pocket and pressed them into my hands. "Perhaps this will salve the wound. Premium tickets to tomorrow night's ceremony, for a reserved section right at the foot of the stage."

"Thank you," said Mary.

"We'll see you there tomorrow night," I said. I turned to the exit. Mary did not. She was simply terrible at following cues.

"I'm not leaving until I see Bully Byrd," she said.

"He is in no state to speak," said Ruth.

"I don't care."

"Mary," I said, unsure how to rein her in, "I'm sure we'll get everything we need tomorrow at the Flat."

"I cannot wait!" she shouted. "They talk of helping widows? I envy widows. A widow has status. A widow may grieve. A girl who has lost her fiancé is nothing but alone."

It was far from what we had planned. Mary's improvisation made me want to take her by the neck and drag her out by force, but even through my rage I had to admit that it was the best acting she had done all day.

Enoch looked like he wished he could vanish into the floor. Ruth stood tall, considering the simplest way to expel this madwoman from her church. Judy joined her siblings to present a united front.

"Please," I said. "You must excuse my cousin. She's had such a hard time."

"You have no idea," said Mary. "None of you have *any* idea. If Bully Byrd can help me, I will not leave until he's been given the chance."

"We have so much work to do," said Ruth. "If you don't leave us to it, we'll have to compel you."

"Please don't make me compel you," said Judy, thwacking her hammer against her empty palm. Mary shoved her in the chest, broke through the Byrds' rank, and strode across the floor. I followed, walking backward, hands outstretched, ready to protect Mary if the Byrds charged. They advanced, first at a walk and then at a run as Mary pounded on the recently repaired door.

"Wake up, Bully!" she said. "You're not dead anymore. You've got work to do."

"Papa is sleeping," said Enoch. He charged at Mary, and I caught him by the waist and held him firm, glad it wasn't his sisters I had to fight. He shoved and clawed feebly, and I tightened my grip as Judy stepped closer, shaking her head and preparing to do what we had driven her to. She raised the hammer and Mary kept banging—kept banging until the door swung open, and Bully Byrd entered the room.

He was sober and awake, his cheeks shaved close and hair scrubbed clean. He was bigger than I'd realized—he filled the doorway—and the white suit clung to him like a second skin. He was handsome, if you were the sort of woman attracted to tree trunks, and it occurred to me for the first time that he was the youngest Byrd there—younger than his children by a decade or more.

Of course he was, I thought. Bully was thirty-five when he died, and death is a wonderful preservative. Stranger than that, I realized, was that I had begun to think of this man as Bully, and the three apologetic misfits who stared at him as his children, just as they said.

"I'm so sorry, Papa," said Enoch, eyes fixed on his father's shoes.

"It isn't his fault," said Mary, as sweet as you'd expect from a well-heeled young woman talking to a preacher. "I'm mad with grief."

"I heard," said Bully, his voice as smooth and deep as the Hudson. He stared down at me, and I wondered if he knew that he'd seen me in his dreams.

"You can go back to sleep," said Judy.

"They're leaving," said Ruth, glaring at me. "Aren't you?"

"No," I said. "We're not. My cousin is hurting. You are people of God, and if you'd rather sleep than help a woman in need, your god must be ashamed."

Laughter rumbled out of Bully's chest. He clapped me on the shoulder, and it was all I could do not to fall down. Mary stared at me with unmasked pride. It filled me with a warmth I hadn't known since summer died.

"I don't know that I can stop you hurting," said Bully, "but I'll do whatever God permits. Let's go somewhere we can talk."

I started for the office, but Bully did not step aside.

"That room's not fit for a dog," he said. "Helen's got a place for these little chats, hasn't she?"

"Across the street," said Enoch, unsure.

"Perfect."

"I'll help you over."

"I can cross a damn street by myself," said Bully. "But come if you want, old man. Can't see as you're doing anything worthwhile here."

Mary and I followed him out, with Enoch bringing up the rear. The moving women got back to work. Judy and Ruth stood in the middle of their church, lighting cigarettes and staring at us with hate or pity or a cold blend of both.

Across the street was a creamy stone tenement with boards over the first-floor windows and broken glass where the rest were meant to be. In place of the front door, strips of fabric hung across the threshold, twisting in the slow westerly wind. Enoch held the curtains aside and welcomed us into the entryway, which was lit by a pair of candle stumps burning low. Boards blocked off the apartment doors. A slightly questionable set of stairs led us to the second floor. At the second-floor landing, the building disappeared.

Westside real estate is so unpredictable.

The outer walls were still there, but the four floors above our heads were gone, leaving a space as vast and empty as Grand Central Terminal. Wind twisted through broken windows. Far away, a pair of gulls screeched beneath the pressed tin roof. At the end of the long, gray room, two chairs flanked a table that held a tea service, waiting for the widows of Helen Byrd.

"Well!" said Mary. "What an unusual room."

"I don't know why she uses it," said Bully. "Must be hell to heat. Come on, let's sit down."

We started walking, and he set his paw on my shoulder.

"Not you," he said. "It's a private talk she wants, and private it's gonna be."

"Anything you say to my cousin, you can say to me."

"Your choice," he said to Mary. "We talk alone or I go back to sleep."

"Miss Carr can wait with Enoch in the stairs. There are things I have to say that only a man of God should hear."

Mary gave me a nod that was supposed to be reassuring, but that just made me want to scream.

"Before I go, Bulrush, a question," I said.

"Yeah?"

"It's a warm summer evening in Central Park. The sun plummets to the horizon. What's your favorite place to watch it set?"

"That's a stupid question."

"My specialty."

"Miss Carr," said Enoch, sweating more than a healthy man should, "this is really not the time."

"He's right," said Mary. "Go downstairs."

"I'd love to, but I have an obligation to a client. So what is it? The Harlem Meer? The Kinderberg? The Green?"

"None of them. A sunset's overrated. I'd turn my back and watch the eastern sky. I'm no poet, but there's a color you get that time of day that you know came straight from God's own brush. That good enough?"

Before I could answer, Enoch grabbed me by the elbow and marched me down the stairs.

"That's a stupendous answer," I said. "Could you have planned that with him? If it was anyone else, I'd say no, but you do think of everything."

He just about shoved me off the bottom step. I was grinning when my feet hit the floor.

"My father is engaged in work that will rewrite history," he said, smoothing his hair. "You must not pester him with trivialities."

"That blue wasn't trivial when you had me running up and down the whole goddamned Eastside looking for it."

"I'm no longer concerned with three-color printing."

"So I'm fired from that case, too, am I?"

"These are questions of life and death. You are not qualified."

"Why am I the only person in this city who understands that life and death are nothing next to a missing finger or the right shade of ink? When someone like your father points at the heavens, it's just to distract everyone else from the fact that everything that matters is right here."

"So you admit he's my father."

He allowed himself the faintest smile. He'd taken the point. I tried to steady my breathing. I'd let my anger show, and that meant I was no longer in control.

"You want to get metaphysical," I said. "Fine. Have you raised anyone else from the dead this week, or was it just him?"

"You ask the strangest questions, Miss Carr. It's a delight."

"Your father just did a Lazarus act. I don't think it's my questions that are strange. So let's try another one: Why isn't Bully sleeping at home?"

"Excuse me?"

"I happen to know he passed last night drunk on bad gin, curled up in a shivering ball in your church's back room. Why?"

His cheeks turned red, and he shook a little bit. He looked as angry as I'd ever seen him, which still wasn't that angry.

"How do you know that?" he said.

"I'm a detective. I'm terribly clever. Why wasn't he nestled in the bosom of his family? Is it because he's an actor? Or is there something more sinister going on?"

"I will say this as plainly as I can. My father, whom I lost when I was a boy, is back from the dead. Why would I question a miracle?"

"Because you're smart enough to know better, which means you're either lying, or you're trying like hell not to see the truth."

He peeled a strip of gray off the wall. When he looked back at me, his cheeks were porcelain and all was cheer.

"I will state plainly that you are no longer engaged by my family on *any* business," he said, "metaphysical or otherwise. Forget the finger. Forget the ink."

"So if I happen to stumble on the truth of who set the fire that killed Abner, you wouldn't care to know?"

A sharp breath. "Abner's death was a tragedy, but it was one of his own making. He chose his life, and that meant he chose his death as well."

"Why not just bring him home? When you're dragging those fifty lost souls back from death, why not throw out a line for your poor misguided brother as well?"

Enoch opened his hands and raised his eyes, a sweet hopeful look on his face. I wasn't sure if his gaze was directed at his father or his god.

"I don't pretend to understand how this works," he said. "I'm just a printer and a servant of the Lord. It all depends on how tomorrow night goes. Bully believes he can prop open the gates to death. If he's right—and I know in my heart he can never be wrong—the fifty will only be the beginning. Thousands, millions will follow."

"And that's supposed to be progress?"

"What do you mean?"

"Ever consider that we're better off letting the dead stay buried?"

"As I said, Miss Carr, when it comes to cosmic questions, you're out of your depth. Are you all right waiting for your cousin here? I have quite a bit of work back at the church."

I let him go. I'd hate for him to know it, but two minutes of spiritual debate really was all I could stand. I had smaller matters to attend to.

SEVEN

When Enoch left, the breeze stirred the snow scattered on the floor, carrying it toward the back of the darkened hall. I followed the current. At the end of the hallway I found a door covered by just one board, held in place with loosely hammered nails. I popped them off and let myself in, looking for a pickled pinkie or a pot of ink and expecting to find anything but.

Here the windows were not boarded up. Gray airshaft light cast dim shadows across a two-room apartment crowded with far more furniture than it could hold. The walls were covered from baseboard to molding with photos of a family: a girl, a boy, a mother, a father, all with the same stooped shoulders, wiry hair, and eager smile. In the kitchen, a wobbly table was set for four. On the stove, a tall pot held the mummified remains of an unidentifiable stew. I had to wonder—even though I knew I would never find the answer—where had this family gone?

A square hole in the ceiling revealed a network of ducts and gears of uncertain purpose. I stared at them for some time, but they neither moved nor rattled, and at last they lost my attention.

There was a pen on the table and a stack of honey-colored sheets, thin as dragonfly wings and printed with blue ink as delicate as the evening sky. At the sight of that color, that unmistakable color, I felt dizzy and had to sit down. I almost called for Enoch before I remembered that I was trespassing and decided he did not deserve to witness any more of my brilliance today. But I would take one with me to rub in his face and force him to pay my bill.

Block letters in the top left corner identified the sheet as something called an R-913. Space was provided to write a subject's name, address, age, physical description, occupation or trade, and estimated monthly income. The rest of the form was given over to a large blank space marked "Particulars." I lifted one and felt something on the paper. Holding it to the limp light, I saw an italic lowercase *r*.

There was a pair of filing cabinets beneath the window. I wanted rather badly to know what was inside. They were locked, but that rarely stopped me. I picked them both and found them full to bursting with R-913s. I grabbed a file at random and found the story of Helen Byrd's meeting with Clark Howe, a widower whose wife had been murdered by street thugs, and who said he would pay anything for a good answer to his children's question: "Where is mommy now?"

He was a clerk in an Eastside shipping company who lived in the Lower West because a family apartment on the dignified side of the stem was more than he could afford. He felt his frugality got his wife killed, and he was more than willing to answer every question Helen had about his work, giving information about his company's payroll, shipping schedule, and accounting system, all of which were recorded in mind-numbing detail under "Particulars."

Here was the final response to the question I'd been asking everyone on the Westside: unquestionable proof that the Byrds were swindlers, set down in soft blue. I'd expected to feel satisfaction—at getting my answer, at proving that nobody in the city besides the woman upstairs was really worth a damn—but all I could taste was bile. I spit on the floor and pressed on.

Howe was an outlier. Most of Helen's interview subjects were widows. An Eastsider whose childhood sweetheart drank poison three months after their wedding; an ancient woman from the Upper West whose husband had been dead for decades; one of my few neighbors on Washington Square, whose man had been found dead in the park when the first cold snap hit this year. From them Helen teased details of their husbands' lives, recording everything that might be useful to a blackmailer and quite a bit that could not. I found a file for Stacey Tarbell, Father Lamb's friend, and deep in the oldest cabinet, where the papers were dry to crumbling, I found a file for Anacostia Fall.

Did my hands tremble as I lifted the cover? It should have felt strange to touch such a relic, but that week my family's past was closer than ever.

The notes on Ana were not recorded on an R-913, nor were they constrained by the tidiness of the newer files. They were written in a man's clumsy hand, every letter capitalized, words wandering across unlined paper like a drunk working his way home: "ANACOSTIA FALL, RECENT CONVERT. PIERREPONT FALL, DEC. $2,000 ASKED AND PAID. AF SATISFIED."

Another note followed: "AF TO POLICE. DET. CARR INTERR. BB. NO EVIDENCE. NO FURTHER TROUBLE EXPECTED."

That was all.

I climbed onto the decrepit table and took another look at the ducts. A thick canvas tube that ran straight down from the floor above hung just a little loose. I tugged on it. It stretched readily. I pressed my eye to it and saw nothing. As I turned away, I heard something whispering from inside it—my mother's voice. I pushed my ear against it and heard every word that was said upstairs, as clear as the sky outside.

"I see your fiancé in the leaves," said Bully, in a voice not quite his own.

"They just look like wet leaves to me," said Mary.

"I see a violent man."

"Herbert was as gentle as a lamb, but he was a soldier."

"A soldier he may have been, but he never wore an army uniform."

"What do you mean?"

The bravado she had shown across the street was gone. Mary sounded disarmed, even honest. It worried me. She was not that good an actor.

"He was a brawler," said Bully. "A soldier of the Westside. A skull-cracker. A thug."

"That is not my Herbert."

"And his name was not Herbert, either."

No. The brawler Bully described could only be one man—my dear departed brute of a father, Virgil Carr.

"He wants to speak to you," said Bully.

"It isn't possible."

"He wants to tell you to stop lying to me. He wants you to hear how he died."

The gears above my head spun to life. Wind rushed through the tubes, and from upstairs came an awful, inhuman scream. I wondered how Bully did it. Was there a pedal under the table? A switch hidden inside the arm of his chair? It was a classic medium's trick, and it stunned Mary into the kind of silence I did not think her capable of. "I don't believe that was his voice," said Mary, after some time.

"Why not?"

"Because you are a fraud."

"How could you say that, when you came here on the same road as me?"

"And what road was that?"

"Do you really not remember? When I saw you at the church . . ."

"Tell me what we were doing there."

"I'm not the fraud here. You came to ask my comfort, but you lied. There is no Herbert. You do not grieve. It's fine. I don't care about your motives. But if you won't be honest with me—"

In the hallway, the boards groaned. The apartment door opened. I let the tube drop from my ear. A polite man gasped in horror at the sight of me teetering on the kitchen table, gorging on his family's secrets.

"Miss Carr," whispered Enoch. "You mustn't be here."

"And yet, I am." I hopped down. "What the hell is an R-913?"

"Pardon?"

"What are they, Enoch? Who designed them? Who printed them? Who filled them out? Was it you?"

"I have no idea."

"But you knew about this room. A place to listen while Helen comforted her widows. A place to keep their secrets."

"I assure you, Miss Carr, I was only looking for you. I wanted to apologize. I followed your footprints down the hallway. I have never been here before."

"Keep your mouth shut if you're just going to lie." I threw a file at him. He caught it as the papers fell to the floor. While he picked them up, I stuffed my bag with as many files as would fit and pushed past him. I was halfway out the door when I heard him start to cry.

"What is it?" I said, wishing I didn't care.

"That blue. That blue."

"I thought that might be the one. So where did it come from?"

He didn't answer. He just pressed the paper to his face like he was trying to draw the color into his lungs, and I tried to take comfort that I'd at least made a convert to the church of tiny mysteries. They are powerful things indeed. I might have questioned him further—to see if he was lying about the room, the ink, the eavesdropping apparatus—but before I could think of any clever questions, my mother began to scream.

I rattled down the hall and up the stairs as fast as the sagging wood allowed. I burst into the long, mostly empty room. The gulls scattered out the missing windows. The scream echoed off the walls.

Forty feet away—too far for me to reach, too far for me to do anything but watch and howl—Bully Byrd had his hands around my mother's throat. He pressed her into the arm of the chair, his awful bulk crushing her lungs as his hands twisted her neck.

I took a step. Mary got her arm free.

I took another. She reached blindly for the table.

I took one more. She got two fingers through the handle of the teapot and smashed it into Bully's head.

As cold as it was in that room, the tea couldn't have been hot, but a faceful of china is enough to make any man pause. He clawed at his eyes, blood-infused tea streaming across his skull, and fell to his knees. Mary kicked until he was down. She reached for a shard of china and was about to bury it in his neck when I dragged her away.

"Let me!" she said.

I saw no point in letting my mother, who had never hurt anyone in her first life, become a killer so soon into her second one. I pointed at the doorway, where Enoch stood frozen, as white as the china clutched in Mary's hand. I didn't think he would let me breeze past him a second time.

"We've outstayed our welcome," I said.

Enoch ran our way. Behind us, there was a window. Outside the window, there was an oak. Mary didn't complain as we accepted the tree's invitation, leaping off the rotted windowsill and into its stiff embrace. Before Enoch reached the window, we were gone.

The sidewalk was slick. Mary's breath came in sharp bursts as she stalked across it. Beneath her loosening scarf, red streaked across her neck.

We turned onto Seventh Avenue, where a clump of people gathered around a long table, waiting for soup. On the other side, two of Van Alen's guardsmen dished out bowls of something thin and beige. As the people grumbled that the servings were getting lighter, I forced Mary onto a bench.

"Why are we stopping?" she said.

"Because you're wheezing."

"Not half as bad as you."

"What happened back there?"

"I don't want to talk about it."

"I don't care."

I sat beside her. I knew I should take her hand, put my arm around her shoulder, but her anger was infectious. I couldn't feel anything else.

"He attacked me," she said.

"Why?"

"Do men need a reason?"

"I heard your conversation. You had quite a rapport."

"You were eavesdropping?"

"Of course I was! What else is a detective for? He knew you. He said you'd traveled together. What did he mean?"

Her eyes were red. Her fists were clenched. I did not want to see my mother cry.

"Don't you wish I knew that?" she said. "He knew more about me than I do."

"And he knew your fiancé, too. Not Herbert. The real one."

She took off her glove and rubbed the spot where her ring should have been.

"I should have asked him the man's name," she said. "Where he comes from. Where he is. And the ring, too. A friendly psychic could be quite helpful—except, of course, that every word was an obvious lie. What else did you hear?"

"Nothing. My attention was elsewhere. What happened next?"

"He said, 'I won't have you ruining this for me,' and that's when he pounced. Lucky for me, I've always been handy with a teapot."

"Silver spoons, too."

She gave a small smile. "And what were you doing while I was wasting time getting strangled?"

That morning, it had seemed easier to let Mary wallow in her amnesia. But if Bully Byrd knew her, if they had returned from death together, it was worth seeing what we could drag up from the depths. That was what I told myself, anyway. In truth, I was too cold and too tired to stand another minute of her looking at me with eyes empty of love.

"Have you ever heard of a woman named Anacostia Fall?" I said, expecting the words to explode her amnesia like a cigarette popping a balloon.

"That's a perfectly ridiculous name. Where did you hear it?"

I tossed the oldest of the Byrds' files into her lap. She read what little it contained.

"Does that bring anything back?" I said.

"Should it?"

"Anacostia and Pierrepont could be related to you. They could be your parents."

"Maybe."

A squirrel, dizzy with hunger or some invisible illness, struggled to leap from the ice to the nearest tree. Mary stared at it. I stared at her.

"How hard are you trying to remember?" I said.

"Not hard enough to satisfy you, I suppose?"

"You gave me a case. Asked me to find your past. This is an intriguing lead, and you don't seem to care."

Her hands curled tight around the ancient file. A sneer bloomed.

"I've been trying," she said. "Every second since I came to in that blighted church, I've been scrambling for some detail of who I am. Every building we pass, every face I see, I ask myself, 'Have I been there? Have I known them?,' but it's like nothing in this city has any connection to me. I feel like my brain is rotting from the inside out, and I am *terrified* that it will never be whole again. If you haven't noticed that, either I'm a better actress than you seem to think, or you're not much of a detective."

"I'm sorry. I doubt. It's my job."

She prodded the file. The first line made her cackle.

"This is dated 1887," she said. "Just how old do you think I am?"

May 5, 1867, to June 7, 1903. Just a hair over thirty-six. A final birthday party, a picnic in Washington Square. Cold chicken and potato salad and a mother I thought I would have forever.

"Thirty-five," I said. "Thirty-six?"

She prodded her skin, scowling.

"It's possible. I'd have guessed a touch younger, but then I've always been generous with myself. Thirty-six? Then yes, it's conceivable old Pierrepont and Anacostia—those names!—are my parents, but the file doesn't mention them having a one-year-old."

"It doesn't mention much of anything."

"No." She squeezed my hand, and life felt easy again. "So what do you think the Byrds gave Anacostia for her two thousand dollars?"

"I know a woman who might have an idea."

She smoothed her skirt and tightened her scarf until the bruising skin did not show. She stood, clapped her hands, and smiled anew.

"Well! Which way do we walk?" she said, striding away before I could answer. It had never occurred to me how false her cheer could be. I wondered how often it had been so in my childhood, and what it had concealed. I wondered what else it was hiding now.

In the quarantine ward at St. Vincent's, the coal had run out. Beneath her paper saints, Stacey Tarbell was a mass of blankets, coats, and scarves. Her eyes peered out, bloodshot and aching. Her breath steamed through cracks in the cloth. I leaned close, trying to smile and hoping the result was friendly instead of terrifying.

"You lied to me before," I said. She nodded. "You lied to the father, too, but that doesn't matter now. I understand why."

"Mrs. Byrd told me that if I said anything, her prayers wouldn't work, and Tom would be turned away at the gates of heaven. I couldn't take the chance."

Mary, who was crouched in the corner perusing Stacey's R-913, scoffed. I gave her a nasty look that she didn't notice at all.

"How much did you pay Helen Byrd?" I said.

"Please don't ask me that."

"You told me she prayed with you, that she talked. Sang hymns. You made her out to be a saint."

"She helped me. What does it matter how?"

A cough rattled down the hallway, where it was joined by two or three more, a little orchestra of ill health.

"You told her quite a lot about your husband's work," said Mary. I winced at the venom in her voice. This woman had already been abused by me for reasons that had nothing to do with her. She did not deserve another interrogation.

"Did I?" said Stacey.

"How the foreman pushed the riveters to work higher than they wanted, in bad weather, sixty, seventy hours a week."

"She asked how he died. What else was I to say?"

Snow oozed from a crack in the thin, frosted window. The walls were bumpy with frozen condensation.

"Why are you still here?" I said.

"The guards told us it would be safe."

"And when was the last time you saw the guards?"

"Four days. Since then, no coal, no food. Two of us left, night before last, to go for help, to make them come back. We've heard nothing since."

On the wall, beside the saints, a 1920 calendar topped by a faded drawing of green, green hills and blue, blue water.

"You were going to go away," I said. "Back to Ireland."

"That's what everyone in this hallway is dreaming of."

"You were going soon." I took Tarbell's thrice-gloved hands. Her cheeks were chapped. The blue in her eyes was nearly gone. "You signed over your life insurance money, didn't you?"

"Yes."

"All of it?"

"It was the only way."

"And what did Helen give you in return?"

"Nothing."

"Pardon?"

"I mean—she took the money. That was the gift. When I met with her, she saw how sad I was, how lonely. She read the leaves and told me why. Tom's spirit was caught between heaven and earth. That money, cursed blood money, was weighing it down. I brought it to her, and she wrapped it in a little sack, and we burned it. The fire died and Tom was free and so was I."

"You believed that?" said Mary.

"Please," I said. "Be gentle."

"There's no sense being gentle with fools. You fell for that idiotic lie?"

"How could it be a lie?" said Stacey. She stood, defiant. Some of her layers fell away. Holding up the fabric, she raised her arms, as thin as curtain rods. "What other reason could there be for the sleepless nights, the nausea, the weight on my heart? Tom needed my help. I did what I had to."

"For being that stupid, you deserve to lose everything. You deserve to freeze."

I could not believe my mother would talk that way. I could not believe that *anyone* would talk that way, in fact, but Stacey took no offense. She fell onto her bed, exhausted from the effort of standing, and with infinite patience, she whispered, "You're young. You never lost anyone. You don't know."

Mary crossed the little room to continue the attack. I pushed her back.

"Get out of here," I said. "We've learned everything we came for."

Mary stomped out. I helped Stacey back upright and leaned her against the wall. I wanted to do more, but my bag held no money, no food, no fuel.

"I wish there was something I could give you," I said.

"What else do I desire? Those I love are safe in heaven. Someday, if you're lucky, you'll say the same."

I wrapped her blankets tight and left, not knowing how to say goodbye.

Mary was halfway down the hallway, waiting by the stairs, not looking my way. I didn't care. The true audience of our scene with Stacey Tarbell was leaning by her door. Max Schmittberger, rising star of the *Sentinel* city room, wore a soiled hat and an indefensibly plaid coat. His moustache was thinner than when we last met, his face fatter, but he still wore the ravenous expression of a man whose hunger for attention could never be sated.

"You heard it?" I said.

"I heard it."

"And Mary gave you the R-913s."

"Every one."

We walked away from Stacey's room, passing cell after cell that held men and women exactly as desperate as her. Teeth chattered like hail falling on pavement. The coughs grew worse. Max tucked the files under his arm.

"This is quite a haul," he said. "I got dirt in here on the biggest construction firm on the Eastside, a shipping outfit, the cops in the auto squad, and basically the whole BRT."

"That's all incidental. What matters is *how* it was collected."

"Hardly. A holy woman bilking widows out of their life insurance money? On the Westside? Could see a few inches on page four."

"A holy woman whose husband just came back from the dead, who plans to bring fifty lost Westsiders back to life tomorrow night at the Flat."

"And that's juicy stuff . . . *if* it pans out. But I tell Gish that, I can hear him saying, 'This is an honest paper, Max. Keep that Westside rot out of my office.' So until then, I'll focus on the goods," he said, holding up the files.

I stopped, and took a step toward him. He backed into the icy wall. It was good to know he was still afraid of me. I snatched the files out of his hands.

"Hey!"

"You'll print it," I said. "The Byrds are criminals, and you're going to make the bastards pay."

"Tell you what. I'll go to that resurrection shindig tomorrow night. Get a little Westside color, maybe get us closer to page one. And hell, if he does start bringing people back from the dead, that smells like a Pulitzer Prize."

With a quickness I didn't expect, he grabbed the files back and busted out of there. I watched Max bound up the stairs, feet light with dreams of all the awards he would never win. I thought of the people behind me staring down another frozen night. I took Mary by the hand.

"What now?" she said, and didn't wait for my answer. "You simply must get me over to the Eastside. I want to dig through the

Hall of Records—see what I can find about myself. Maybe that will shake my memory loose."

I didn't answer. I just pulled, and we walked up the stairs. I was fed up with being cold. I was taking us home.

I filled the fireplace past the point of safety, prodded in the match, and watched the paper burn. My hands were as cold as sepulchral marble. Even if I plunged them into the growing fire, it would take an hour before they felt warm.

Mary marched past the window, her coat off and her shoulders bare, showing an infuriating indifference to the cold. I remembered why I had been trying to keep her out of this room. While we were here, the urge to call her Mother was far too strong.

"You were hell on that old woman," I said.

"She lied to us. She lied to herself. Why be gentle?"

"Because she's hurting."

"That's exactly the kind of stupidity that lets hucksters like the Byrds flourish. It should be stamped out."

"I've never seen you looking so cruel."

"You haven't known me very long." She leaned on the window-sill. A sly smile danced onto her face. "Don't try fooling me, Miss Carr. You're not clever enough. You think I'm lying about—well about what?"

"I don't think you're lying. But to forget your age, your city, your family . . . I've never read of such an extreme case of amnesia."

"Then something fairly extreme must have happened to me." She smiled broader, shaking her head as sharply as the movement of the branches outside. I was probably the only person in the city who might recognize how angry she was. "At any moment, I'm torn between desires to sob, sleep, and scream. Instead, I've kept moving, trusting that if I don't let my smile drop, something will start to make sense. So far, it hasn't. Now I've just been throttled by a madman and the only friend I've made in the entire city tells me she thinks I'm lying. What else would you have me do?"

The streaks on her neck were turning purple, like night coming on fast. I had rarely felt like such a nitwit.

I wanted to trust her. But it was a wide room, and there was no way to close the gap. I was trying to find the strength to take the first step when the window exploded. Glass rained down on Mary. Her blood stained the floor.

EIGHT

As the glass crashed over her, Mary threw her arms above her head and twisted away from the window. I crossed the room in one, two, three long bounds, leapt over the couch, and smashed her to the floor. The glass cut, but I needed Mary down.

We landed at the base of the window seat. I pushed my back against it like a sensible soldier cowering in a trench. A stiff wooden rod poked out from the torn upholstery of my sofa. An arrow. I reached out to touch it, and another whipped through the broken glass and buried itself in my floor with a hideous *thunk*.

"Someone is shooting arrows at us," said Mary.

"What gave you that impression?"

"Arrows!"

"Two so far."

"It's ridiculous. Does this sort of thing often happen to you?"

I shrugged. "It could be worse. Last fall it was rifles. Are you hurt?"

"I'm fine." She said it and realized she had no idea if it was true. She patted herself down, confirming the arrow had missed her, and that the many cuts on her neck and arms were nothing that might threaten her life. She said again, rather more brightly: "I'm fine!"

The moment that the window broke, that the glass rained down, had been one of the longest of my life. I wanted to clutch her to my chest, to hold her until night fell and day returned. I could not bear to lose this woman again.

"Miss Carr," said Mary. "You're crying."

"It has been a difficult year."

"There's no time for weakness. There's an archer outside intent on spilling our blood across your hideous parlor rug. What are we going to do about it?"

Other children's mothers held them when they were sad, and I'm sure it was a comfort. But for a lifetime on the Westside, there was no better training than a parent who wasn't afraid to say shut up.

I crawled across the floor, keeping as close to the outside wall as my stiff joints would allow, and wriggled to the front hall. In the center of my great wood door was a brass mail slot that had not been used since the mail stopped, eight years before. I poked it open. An arrow thudded into the door and shook the whole house. I let the slot close.

"He's in the red oak, the big one, just inside the park," I said. Mary crawled across the floor and sat next to me, breathing hard against the door. She smelled of blood and sweat.

"No use screaming for the police, is it?" said Mary. She was whispering, and for reasons I didn't understand, I did the same.

"No."

She drummed her fingers against her cheek, a gesture I remembered from rainy days when she was stumped by a particularly vicious segment of jigsaw puzzle.

"If we open that door, we'll be impaled," she said.

"Like rotisserie pigs."

"So we don't leave through that door. We sneak out the back— there is a back, isn't there?"

"Through the kitchen."

"Then we go out that way and head west to Sixth Avenue, and on into the safety of the night."

"Six months ago, that would have been the plan. But the tall grass is dead, and there's nothing out the back door but snow. We'd be targets in a shooting gallery."

"Oh. Damn."

I looked over my front hall, examining it closer than I ever had before. Just as in the rest of my house, there was too much furniture: tables and an armoire and a thoroughly misplaced chair that half blocked the foot of the stairs.

"What do you think is the sturdiest piece of furniture here?" I said.

"Hard to say, it all looks cheap."

I rolled my eyes. "Just choose."

"That table, I suppose." She pointed to a long, low table, once used for storing hats and mail and now retained mainly so I would have something to bang my shins on in the dark.

"What a shame," I said. "I've always liked that table."

I strode across the floor, reasonably certain I was out of the archer's line of sight, bent low, and hefted the table with both hands. I walked up the stairs, turned, and hurled it back down. It exploded across the front hall, scattering splinters of wood and making Mary laugh like I didn't know she could.

"Delightful!" she said. "Do I get to break something, too?"

"Maybe later." I came back downstairs and handed her the largest fragment of wood—a piece of the table's top that was just a little longer and a little wider than Mary's slight torso. I took the second-largest piece. It wouldn't cover all of me, but it would have to do. "When I open the door, run."

"Which way?"

"Whichever looks safest. Toward Fourth, probably, and then west."

"Which way are you going?"

"That archer attacked my house. He broke my window. I'm going into the park, I'm going up that tree, and I am going to drag him back to earth."

She let out a kind of bellow and banged her shield against mine, hard enough to knock me back onto my heels.

"Miss Carr," she said, "your attitude is improving all the time."

Or I'm finally loony enough to keep up with you, I thought. It didn't matter now.

She took her position at the side of the door, and I gripped the knob. Even through my glove, it was cold with the chill from outside. I yanked the door open, expecting an arrow to fly across the threshold. None did.

"Perhaps he's gone," said Mary.

"No," I said.

"No."

She shook her head, took a long breath, and charged out just as I was realizing that I was a fool to let her go first. She screamed, and my heart stopped for the awful, endless moment it took me to realize that she wasn't hurt but was simply having a good time.

I leapt around the door, held the wood in front of my face, and started down the front steps. I'd planned to take them two at a time, but I'd forgotten about the ice, which forced me to inch pathetically down my stoop. I was nearly at the bottom when the first arrow hit.

It ripped into the wood, its silver point coming half an inch from my right eye, and opened a long crack along the already abused timber. The shield withstood one hit. I did not think it would absorb a second.

"This isn't a pleasure walk, Miss Carr!" shouted Mary, who waited at the bottom of the steps, crouched low, mostly hidden behind her fragment of table. "Are we running or aren't we? Quick quick!"

"Run," I said, and run we did—across the sidewalk, onto the snow, our boots slipping and our bones aching as we fought to keep our footing on the frost.

An arrow took a bite out of the snow between us, plowing up a furrow as long as my leg.

"Not so close!" I shouted. "And not in a straight line."

Perhaps Mary listened. If she did, it was the first time that week. I zigged a bit and zagged a bit more, and was almost at the edge of the park when the next arrow came.

It bit into the side of the wood, almost severing the fingers of my left hand and tearing the shield apart as neatly as a cracker snapped in half. I felt the wood disintegrate. As it tore, I saw the park before me, and I saw the marksman in the oak.

He wore a long black coat and a neatly blocked felt hat, and he looked as at home in the tree as a toucan in a boardroom. He clutched the bow like an expert, though, and without taking his eyes off me, he reached over his shoulder for another arrow.

I leapt over the low, snow-swamped fence that separated park from sidewalk. I slid on the ice, grabbed the trunk of the archer's oak, and did not fall.

"Gilda?" cried Mary, worry in her voice for the first time. I did not see where she was. I looked up and did not see the archer, either. I covered my head and waited for the blow. It came from the side, as Mary flung herself over the fence and tackled me to the ground. I was looking for the correct words to curse her when an arrow slammed into the snow where I'd been standing.

"Oh," I said.

"Yes."

The ground shook as the archer leapt down, landing a few feet in front of us. His quiver was empty. He tossed his bow aside and ran deeper into the park. I sloughed off Mary and ran after.

In the summertime, I know the twists and turns of Washington Square better than any sane person in the city. In the winter, when the light fades early and snow clogs the paths, it is not clear.

The archer ran beneath the trees, where the snow was sparse and his tracks were harder to see. When I emerged at the ruined fountain at the square's center, he was gone.

I looked up at the arch, badly cracked but still standing, the grime on its marble stark against the purity of the snow. The sun was gone and the moon not up. The darkness smelled cold.

Mary bolted out of the trees.

"Where is he?" she said.

"I don't know."

"Well show some goddamned imagination!"

"Shut up and follow me."

I ran south. We emerged onto West Fourth just in time to see the archer step out of the trees, halfway down the block.

Once, we would not have been alone. Once, the One-Eyed Cats ceaselessly patrolled the southern edge of the park, terrorizing outsiders and welcoming locals with a smile. Once, a killer would have had no hope of crossing their territory without being struck down by a hail of brickbats and stones. Once, they'd have beaten him bloody, or lashed him to a tree and left him there howling and embarrassed as a warning to others. But those children were dead now, and the One-Eyed Cats were not coming to our rescue.

At least, not all of them.

The archer was nearly past the park when Cherub Stevens intervened. The onetime lord of Washington Square leapt out from behind a skinny old cherry tree and blocked the archer's escape.

"Stop right—" Cherub managed to say, before the archer, hardly breaking stride, punched him in the jaw. I hate to admit it, but I'd seen it coming. Cherub fell hard but was able to grab the man as tight as he could—and failed utterly to drag him down. The archer shook him off and kept running. We reached Cherub, and I had to choose between helping this poor, daft man and continuing the chase. My legs ached and my lungs were doing little better. I decided to be generous.

"Running on snow is simply impossible," said Mary, as I helped Cherub up. The archer rounded Mercer. I let him go.

"That was awfully brave," I said.

"You don't have to place so much stress on the word 'awful,'" he answered. He looked cold, hungry, and cruelly sober. Mary inspected him, smiling charitably, as one might greet a particularly bedraggled alley cat.

"And what is the name of our would-be savior?" she said.

"This, Mary, is a Westsider born and bred, a soldier of the gutter, a legend of Eighth Avenue. I give you Cherub Stevens."

She offered her hand. He bowed low, unable to resist, and gave it a smacking kiss. Mary blushed. I did not know she could blush. I did not like that she blushed because of Cherub.

I didn't really like a lot of what was happening.

"Come back to my house," I said finally, really just to say anything.

"I told you I'm not going back there," he said.

"Then what are we going to do with you?"

"Food wouldn't hurt."

We walked north, and I found myself standing between two people whom I felt utterly unable to hold as tightly as I should.

"You were mad to try to stop him," said Mary. It was the first time all week I'd heard her properly impressed. "That man was a terror with a bow and arrow."

"Well," said Cherub, not even bothering to feign modesty, "he had no arrows left."

"It was stupid," I said, "and a waste of effort if you weren't going to at least knock him down."

Cherub was too proud of himself to be bothered by my jab. He flicked up his fingers. There was a slip of paper clutched in his hand—a creased square torn where he had ripped it off the archer's coat. Aside from the fact that the number on it read "83," it was identical to the bit of paper Abner Byrd wore when he died.

I took it from Cherub and felt it with my bare fingers. The paper wasn't flat. In the light of the rising moon, I saw an italic lowercase *r*.

I didn't bother to tell Cherub good work. But his smug smile showed he knew he had gotten to me anyway.

A block west of the fence, flames flickered in the side of a hill that had once been a line of town houses. A year or two before, an enterprising cook dug a hollow in the earth and installed a long firepit, creating a makeshift restaurant. Between the dirt wall and the heavy canvas that cut out the cold, it was smoky, crowded, and mercifully warm. A metal grill rested atop a long trough of burning coals. Hunks of pork and bread sizzled and burned on the iron.

I slapped down our money and took three dented plates piled high with pork, bread, beans, and root vegetables unidentifiable but delicious. Mary waited at the counter, her eyes watering from the smoke. Cherub leaned beside her, telling one of his interminable stories of Westside heroism. I'd heard it a dozen times. It had never seemed so funny as Mary seemed to think.

Cherub gave me an icy look as I approached them, then returned to charming Mary. She was taller than me, more slender, her skin clearer, her hair an artful mess rather than an intractable quagmire. As he looked at her, an old gleam crept into his eye. It was childishly obvious that he was trying to make me jealous.

It worked.

I dropped the plates before them, and Mary tore fearlessly into the heap of crisped meat, looking with every passing hour less and less like the mother I thought I knew.

She finished in minutes and took a sip of water, leaving greasy fingerprints on the glass. She pushed her plate away and leaned an elbow on the splintered wood. Most of her cuts had stopped bleeding. I wanted more than anything to take her hand, but did not have the strength, and knew she wanted none of my comfort, anyway.

"So what now?" she said. "We've passed the evidence to your newspaperman and been chased about the park by a cut-rate Robin Hood. Shall we take the fight to them?"

"Not until we know who they are," I said. "The Byrds' blackmailing operation, the torched saloon, and your Robin Hood are all linked by this lowercase *r.*"

"*R* for rancid?" said Cherub, not quite helpfully.

"*R* for reindeer?" said Mary.

"*R* for ragamuffin?"

"*R* for really rude repairmen repair really rudely?"

For some reason, they considered all this hilarious. When they had stopped chuckling, I continued, feeling something like a sour kindergarten teacher who couldn't understand why her charges didn't find her fun.

"I know a woman who may know what the *r* stands for," I said, "but it will have to wait till morning."

"Why?" said Mary, serious again.

"She's busy."

"With what?"

"Everything."

"That won't give us much time before the resurrection ceremony."

"We'll have to make it count."

"Then we've a night off?" she said, sharing a smile with Cherub that made the pork tap-dance in my stomach. "How shall we spend it?"

"When it comes to wasting an evening on the Westside," said Cherub, "you could have no better guide."

He offered Mary his hand, knelt low, and swept her off to see a miracle. As ever, he didn't let my grumbling sour his mood.

At the Borderline, the bonfire burned hot and the snow was clear. We tipped our caps to Van Alen's guards, crossing Fourteenth Street with an ease I had still not gotten used to. Technically it wasn't a border anymore, but it still marked the line between Lower West and Upper, between desperation and simple poverty, between nightmares and pleasant dreams.

It was snowing softly as we walked up Fifth Avenue, the wind whispering the fresh powder back and forth on the spotless sidewalk. After months tramping across the imperfectly cleared pathways of the Lower West, it was like walking on a cloud.

We turned right on Seventeenth Street, just a few blocks south of Anacostia's manse, and made for the fence. From over the iron came the blinding light and howling noise of the stem.

"Is that . . . ," said Mary, gawking at the glare.

"The Eastside," said Cherub.

"It's pointless," I said, "but it makes an awful lot of noise."

Mary stepped to the fence, gliding like a sleepwalker, and I wondered if somewhere some memory was rising out of the muck. What might Mary Fall remember of the Eastside lights?

We would not learn that evening. Cherub guided her back into the dark. He had quieter entertainment in mind.

He led us to a limestone-fronted town house, holding out his hand to help Mary across the packed snow between the sidewalk and the servants' entrance. On a street of broken windows and smashed doors, this house was protected by a stout silver padlock. Cherub had the key.

"After Eighth Avenue, I started a campaign of exploration around the Upper West," he said. "Wanted to see if it was as charming as I'd been told. Mostly I was disappointed, but here . . . here I found something worthwhile."

"Whose house is this?" said Mary.

"No idea."

"Does it look familiar?" I asked her.

"I feel like . . . I feel like I've seen it in a dream."

Cherub, never one to waste time on metaphysical questions, lit the lantern that hung inside the servants' door. He led us through the butler's pantry and larder to a flight of stone steps that wound down to the wine cellar. He pocketed two bottles and handed me two more.

"We came all this way for wine?" I said. "We have liquor downtown, and it hits a lot harder."

"But it doesn't taste half as good. That's a Château Something or Other, straight out of the 1890s. But the wine isn't why we're here."

Cherub took Mary by the hand and led us down more twisting steps into the earth. We walked for some time, until the air grew hot, with a hint of the funk of the riverfront in summer. I ran my finger along the stone walls. It was damp.

"Where are you taking us, Mr. Stevens?" said Mary.

"Don't bother," I said. "He considers himself a showman. He'll never waste a surprise."

We turned into a cavernous black room. Our feet echoed on tile. Mary took a step and Cherub wrapped his arm around her waist, pulling her back. I felt a temptation to rip them apart.

"If this basement is your miracle," said Mary, "I'm not impressed."

"Just wait," he said, and started lighting candles. As each flame caught, the darkness of the great, lost room seeped back, inch by inch, and Cherub's wonder was revealed.

"A swimming pool," said Mary. "Here."

"And all for us."

In the candlelight, the tiles were a deep ocean blue. The water, opaque black, lapped at the edge, throwing up little wisps of steam and stretching farther into the darkness than our light could reach.

I splashed water on my face. It was hot and tasted of spoiled eggs.

"It isn't possible," I said.

"It isn't half bad," said Mary.

"This pool should have emptied years ago. Who's maintaining it? Who is *heating* it?"

"I haven't the faintest," said Cherub.

"It could be fed naturally," said Mary. "Some lost hot spring bubbling up out of the earth."

"In *Manhattan*?"

"Or it could be just one of those beautiful Westside things," said Cherub, standing closer to Mary than I could bear. He tossed a pair of bathing costumes at our feet.

"Don't be a fool," said Mary. She shrugged her shoulders and her dress fell to the floor. Either through gentility or shock, Cherub did not goggle but simply followed her lead. She dove into the pool, an arc as perfect as a rainbow, and Cherub splashed in after.

"Gilda," said Mary, "even you can't be sullen enough to turn this down."

"You'd be surprised."

"Wear a suit," said Cherub. "The water's astonishing."

"That's all right. You have fun. Someone has to work on the wine."

I popped a cork, yanked off my boots, and dangled my feet in the water. It was warm enough to blot out the entire awful winter. I'd have liked to dive in, but that black water called to mind the hungry shadows at the bottom of the Hudson, and the woman I sent to her death. A foot bath and a bottle of vinegared wine were all the fun I could stand.

They splashed about, farther and farther into the dark, their laughter bouncing off distant tile. I fought the urge to shout for them to stay where I could see.

Finally Mary climbed out, her hair slick against her head, her skin reflecting the flickering orange. I had not imagined my mother could ever be so naked. She pulled her yellow dress back on and reached for the wine.

"That Cherub is an amusing fellow," she said.

"Do you think so?"

"Don't look so threatened. I don't recall much about my taste in men, but I'm sure my preferences don't run so short, filthy, or crass. I believe I lean more toward the powerful, the brooding." She lost herself for a moment in contemplation of men imaginary, then brought us back to the earth. "Besides. He's in love with you."

Somewhere in the darkness, Cherub splashed and cackled like a happy seal. It was a pleasant sound.

"I have broken his heart too many times," I said.

"It's mended."

"Why do you say that?"

"As soon as you were out of sight, he lost all interest in me. He only wants to make you green. I can see it's working."

She sat down, close enough that I could smell the sulfur in her hair. She breathed deep, eyes squeezed shut, and said, "The Lenstaadts."

"Bless you," I answered, unable to resist a bad joke.

"They lived in this house. I came for parties. I didn't know they had a pool."

I looked at her sharply. I'd never heard that story before, but there was so much about their youth my parents never bothered to tell. "What brought that back?"

"When we crossed Fourteenth Street, the city looked sane again. I began to remember. This district was my home."

She wasn't looking at the water; she wasn't looking at me. She was staring into the dark, plumbing a memory as infinite and obscure as Cherub's sulfurous pool. I didn't want to push her, but I had to know what else she had found.

"Anything more?" I said.

"Anacostia Fall. Pierrepont. You were right. They were my parents."

"You're certain?"

"How could I have forgotten such outlandish names?"

I didn't dare ask another question. After a while, she went on.

"I remember them, my parents. Not a lot. But Ana—everyone called her Ana—she was an eccentric. She painted our house pale blue, and everyone said she was insane. She taught us to think for ourselves. And Pierrepont—he was a painter, quite a serious one. Landscapes. Roamed all over the city, all over the state, painting scenes that I thought looked like heaven on earth. He was happiest when he was painting ruins. That burnt church? He would have made it a masterpiece."

She looked at me. I don't know if it was the candlelight or the damp, but she looked older than I had ever seen her—wrinkled and gray and ready to sleep forever. Worse than that, she looked afraid.

"What troubles you?" I said.

"That file of the Byrds, it was dated when?"

"1887."

"And it said Pierrepont was deceased. But I remember him. A man dead thirty-five years."

She wrapped my hand in hers. The warmth of the water was gone, and she was as cold as anyone out on the street.

"How old, Gilda?" she said. "How old does that make me?"

I hugged her, and she didn't pull back. I had no better answer.

"This afternoon," I said, "before the excitement, you asked me about doubt."

"I did."

"You should know—I do believe you."

"All the way?"

"All the way."

"And you'll help me find out who I am? What I'm doing here?"

"You hired me, didn't you?"

Cherub staggered out of the pool. He drained the rest of the bottle in one draught and hurled it into the dark. It splashed and was gone.

"In a minute I'm going to go back in," he said, curling up on a towel and falling fast asleep. Mary draped a second towel over him, and I opened a fresh bottle. She watched him as tenderly as a mother looking down on a sleeping child.

She took a long sip from the bottle and winced.

"This wine's past it," she said.

"By ten years or more."

She took another sip, but the bottle didn't quite meet her mouth, and most of it spilled across the dress, staining soft yellow with sour red.

"Hell!" she said. "Your dress. I've really ruined it now."

"My clothes have a way of being ruined. I'm used to it. When the sun comes up, we'll swing by my house and put you in the least offensive of my black frocks."

"You're a good friend, Gilda Carr. The best on the Westside." She thought for a minute. "And your family. Who are they?"

"My father was a cop. My mother died young. I hardly think of them."

She shook her head, drank deep, and slumped backward across Cherub. I pulled my feet from the pool, dried off, and heaped a few towels on top of them. I lit another dozen candles, trying to beat back the dark as far as I could, and leaned against the wall, falling asleep certain that there was no way but cowardice to keep us both alive.

Dawn broke into our underground oasis through a strip of frosted glass panels in the ceiling. We woke with crushing headaches and bodies aching from a night spent on unforgiving tile. In the silver light of morning, the room was smaller than it had seemed in the dark, the pool nothing more than a few hundred gallons of murky, stinking green.

NINE

The woman had been screaming for a minute or more. I hoped she was nearly done.

It wasn't a scream, really, but a rumble that started deep in her gut and vibrated out of every part of her. Her arm was wrapped around my neck, gripping it so tight that I worried my spine might crack, but I did not complain. Of the two of us, she was having the harder day.

The contraction ended, and the woman—a Portuguese mother of two come down from the Upper West to deliver her third—sagged against me to catch her breath.

"That was an easy one," she gasped. "Was it too easy? Are they slowing down?"

"You're fine," said the woman who knelt at her feet. She wore tortoiseshell glasses and a white dress so fashionable that I couldn't be sure if it were for medical use or simply style. She was Ida Greene, right hand to Glen-Richard Van Alen. Undoubtedly the most important person on the Lower West, she may have also been the most powerful black woman in the country. I could imagine no one else who might know who had sent that archer to kill me. As predicted, she was busy.

We were in the ballroom of a Fifth Avenue mansion abandoned before the fence went up. Blackout curtains covered the towering windows, and clusters of candles gave soft light for the ten laboring women who ranged up and down the polished parquet. There were beds provided, but the women preferred to crouch, lean on their partners, or brace themselves against the white paneled walls. Others occupied the hallways, dining hall, parlor, and library of the faded house, filling it with laughter, screams, and noises inhuman. The entire place smelled irresistibly of women. I had not predicted how happy it would make me feel.

The Portuguese woman began rumbling again. Another contraction was on its way. Mrs. Greene signaled for her midwife, just back from catching a baby, wearing a pink sweater flecked with blood. As the midwife stepped in, we stepped out, but the Portuguese woman would not let Mary leave.

"She's helping," she said, gripping Mary's wrist. "She stays."

"Of course," said Mary, with a warmth I had not seen since I was a child.

"Twenty hours," said Mrs. Greene as she led me across the room. "A third child will usually come quicker, but something is holding this one up."

"Will she live?"

"Yes!" She chuckled. "She'll be fine. An Eastside doctor would have sliced her open ten hours ago and she'd be bleeding out on his table. We let her go at her own pace. The baby will come."

When Van Alen took over the Lower West, he pledged to bring civilization with him. Candles were distributed. Food was given away. Libraries, schools, soup kitchens, shelters, concert halls, and food stalls were promised—all the amenities Van Alen provided in the Upper West, available below the Borderline for the first time. The birthing center was the first to open, to provide for women whom Eastside doctors refused to treat. None of the other promises had been fulfilled, but the center was thriving.

"We have women coming down from the Upper West," said Mrs. Greene, "we have women crossing over from the Eastside because they've tired of their doctors' rough, patronizing care. I have three times as many patients as I can handle, too few midwives, too few beds, too few supplies, and I'm wasting time talking to you. Why?"

I showed her the scrap of paper. I let her feel the lowercase *r*.

"Oh hell," she said. She nestled a cigarette into her ivory holder. She pressed on the wall, popping open an entrance to an old servants' passage. She closed the door, and the din of life faded. She lit a lantern, then the cigarette. "Where did you get this?"

"From a man who shot my town house full of arrows and tried to do the same to me. A late employee of the Basement Club wore one like it. And I found the same mark in forms used by the Byrds, who have been spying on those who seek comfort in prayer."

"Why did you bring it to me?"

This was less a question than a lamentation. I answered it anyway.

"I wanted to know what kind of syndicate is bold enough to adorn criminal evidence with an official seal. I know that when you're not delivering babies or butternut squash, this is the sort of thing that keeps you up at night."

"I advise you to change course."

"I'd like nothing better. Were my time my own, I would content myself searching for blue ink and missing fingers. But those things didn't try to kill me. The man who wore this paper did. That makes me mad."

"Don't play tough, Gilda. It doesn't suit you."

"Fine. I'm scared past the limits of my senses, for me and for that nice young woman out there, who matters more to me than I can reasonably explain. I need to find out who wants us dead. I need to change their minds."

Ida Greene did something that, in our brief acquaintance, I had never thought possible. She removed her glasses. Without them, her face was rounder, her gaze softer. She truly seemed worried for me.

"That's the mark of Storrs Roebling: a dull, dangerous man. His outfit is the Roebling Company. They've been a power on the Eastside since before you were born."

"I've never heard of them."

"They prefer it that way. You're accustomed to the Westside, where criminals are baroque. The Roeblings are different. They own tenements, tanneries, warehouses, mechanics' shops. Their money pads the pockets of the NYPD; their stock is traded on the Wall Street exchange. And all of it is supplemented by saloons like the Basement Club, where they profit off the city's worst vices, without any pretense of pleasure or class. They push liquor and heroin and kill anyone who wastes their time."

She finished her cigarette and lit another off the butt. The air in the narrow tunnel was close and getting closer all the time.

"And blackmail?" I said.

"I wouldn't be surprised. What you've described sounds like Roebling to a T. He's ravenous for information. Slurps it up like a baleen whale taking mouthfuls of ocean, then strains out whatever dirt he thinks might be of use."

"But the form—why the form? What kind of lunatic puts his brand on something like that?"

"A lunatic with nothing to fear. Roebling is rich, powerful, respectable—to the people he needs to appear respectable to—and ruthless. Every minute of his employees' time is tracked, every movement is watched, every action is recorded, checked, double-checked, and written down. They have forms for everything. Why should blackmail be any different?"

"And you let him open up in the Lower West?"

Mrs. Greene took an extra beat to answer that question, blowing smoke out of the side of her mouth in a long, narrow stream, amused that I could be so stupid.

"How much control do you imagine we have?" she said.

"Enough to stop parasites like the Gray Boys from infesting the Lower West. If a man like Roebling had tried to cross the stem when Barbarossa was in charge—"

"She'd have let a few hundred children die to protect her bottom line. We don't do that. We're not an army. We're not thugs. We provide social services and protection to people whose city has given up on them."

"Then you should have protected us from Roebling."

"With what? Half our guardsmen died at Eighth Avenue; most

of the rest deserted. We're trying to run twice as much territory with a tenth the men. When Roebling opened up the Basement Club, I had to allow it or start a war I couldn't win."

"But that didn't stop you from selling him your red gin."

"What can I say? I'm a businessman above all else."

A businessman. A humanitarian. I had seen her with a switchblade. She dressed better than Barbarossa, but she was no less ruthless.

"If you couldn't stop them building the Basement Club," I said, "could you be the one who burned it to the ground?"

"Miss Carr, you demonstrate admirable imagination."

"That's no answer."

"It's the best you'll get. Lord, I hate this intrigue. All I want is to help people—give them food, shelter, a midwife, a chance. But all that costs a hell of a lot of money, and crime is the only thing that pays."

A horrid roar came from the other side of the thin wood panel: a woman in the throes of something I could not imagine. Ida Greene shook her head.

"We tell them not to scream like that," she said. "It's a waste of energy."

"It seems like a reasonable response." I tried a new tack. "Did you know the Byrds are working for Roebling?"

"Until this week, I was blessedly unaware that the Byrds existed at all. Then I started seeing handbills for their electric resurrection. Idiotic." She rapped her knuckle on the door. "If people want to beat back death, they should work a shift here."

"What if the Byrds can really do it?"

"Don't be a fool. We seem to be the only two people in the Lower West who know that death is final. The district is buzzing about this ceremony. It's going to be a mess."

"Could you stop it?"

"Only if I want a riot. Unless I have cause, the best I can do is contain it."

A banging on the door. Mrs. Greene opened it. On the other side was a sweat-soaked midwife's assistant whose graying hair hung limp around her face.

"What?" said Mrs. Greene.

"Towels. We're running low, and the washing women are all backed up, and—"

"I keep a reserve store hidden in the cupboards beneath the stairs. Take all you need and send two of the attendants to help with the wash."

The door slammed shut. Mrs. Greene put her glasses back on and gave me a look that said our audience was coming to an end.

"Your time is precious," I said.

"And you've taken up more than your share. You obviously want a favor—what is it?"

"Arrange a meeting for me with Storrs Roebling."

"We don't have that kind of relationship."

"Then tell me where I can find him."

"Whatever you're planning, Miss Carr, it's a mistake."

"You have no idea."

She pressed the "83" tag against the wall, scratched out an Eastside address, and handed it to me. Then she popped open the door and returned to the ballroom. The flood of light, of pain, was almost blinding. Mrs. Greene sliced through the chaos like a butcher through bone, and I struggled to keep up.

"I'll need you to get me across," I said, following at her elbow.

"Did you misplace your papers?"

"I'm in order. My companion is not. Can we use one of your tunnels?"

"Fine. But if Storrs Roebling doesn't kill you, I'd like you to tell me everything you learn."

I nodded, and we took our places at the sides of the Portuguese woman, who was now laboring on her hands and knees. Mary bent over her, pressing hard onto her lower back, while the midwife wet a towel for her neck.

"There is one more thing," I said, as softly as I could. The

Portuguese woman glared at me, and I wished I had the power to sink into the floor.

"What?" hissed Mrs. Greene.

"There's a few dozen people freezing to death in the quarantine ward at St. Vincent's. You owe them food and coal."

"I'll see that they get it—now be quiet."

When the contraction ended, Mary stepped back, stretching out her muscles but not making a sound of complaint. Mrs. Greene took her place, one woman's hands replacing another's. When we left, the mother was screaming again.

Ida Greene's Twelfth Street passage was a narrow crawl space wedged between Broadway and the thundering BRT. It was cramped, badly lit, and wet with melted snow. I had brought a skinny package wrapped in newspaper, and keeping it out of the muck made the trip an ordeal. Mary chattered the entire time.

"It just seems a waste, crossing over to the Eastside if we're not going to visit the Hall of Records as well," she said. "What does any of this have to do with me?"

"These things always connect."

"That's a stupid thing to say."

I did not disagree. But I also wasn't wrong, and she didn't turn back. My hand splashed into a puddle of black slush. We crawled the rest of the way in silence.

It had been gray, dark, and threatening snow when we went into the tunnel. When we emerged from its terminus, a Van Alen–owned lamp shop, snow fell like powdered sugar on Broadway's glittering sidewalks. The lights were blinding and the noise, as always, was more than I could comfortably bear. Motionless, blaring automobiles filled the narrow strip of asphalt between the sidewalk and the fence, stuck in the kind of traffic jam we are never subjected to on the Westside. Pedestrians weaved around them freely, cursing, shouting, and shivering from the cold.

The spectacle hit Mary like a hammer to the forehead. I was

two doors down before I realized she hadn't followed me. She stood frozen before the lamp shop, speechless and pale, stunned by modernity's gaudy face.

"Tourists," I muttered, and took her by the hand.

Eastside crowds are notoriously sluggish, and the snow made them worse. Three months prior, they would have greeted the gentle dusting with holiday cheer, but we were in the pit of winter now, and the mood on the avenue was frantic and depressed as people fought to get home.

"I've never seen anything like this," said Mary.

"You don't know what you've seen."

"I don't. I don't, of course, but I know . . . nothing like this."

We were halfway across Tenth Street when Mary stopped and cackled at the gutter.

"What?" I said.

"They clear the sidewalks here. No snow. No trash."

"No corpses, either."

"It puts your Westside to shame."

A horn blared. I jerked her out of the crosswalk before she was squashed. The driver bellowed a few choice oaths, and I returned fire so forcefully that Mary almost looked impressed.

"What are those machines all over the street?" she said.

"Autos. Horseless carriages."

"Are they a recent invention?"

"Hardly. They're more common all the time."

We slogged south, block by block, passing stationery stores and dress shops, chophouses and oyster rooms, pawnshops, a billiard hall, three newsstands, a speakeasy disguised as a doctor's office, and a doctor's office that was filthier than any saloon. Mary stopped at every one, marveling at the cheap baubles that were the great achievement of our age, so impressed with it all that she couldn't see how deeply I did not care.

At Waverly, where the herd fought for admittance to the subway, a nickelodeon barker begged Mary to come inside.

"One minute to showtime, ma'am, which means you're in under

the wire! The season's finest motion picture, 'Sally Out West,' and I've got two seats left, fine seats, perfect for a pair of young women with ten cents to spare."

"Out of the way," I said, but Mary was transfixed.

"Motion picture?" she said.

"Not just a motion picture, *the* motion picture: seventeen minutes of giddy joy from Sally Feeney, comic sensation of our age, only a nickel, only a nickel, but hurry up, would ya, because picture's about to roll."

"We don't have seventeen minutes," I said, "and I don't have a nickel. Let's go—quick quick."

"Maybe next time," apologized Mary. I dragged her south, her eyes fixed on the blinding colors of the theater marquee. For all my admonishment, I failed to convince her to pick up speed.

"Is the Eastside always so startling?" she asked while gawking at a wigmaker's dummies.

"It hits me like a toothache: one I'd thought I'd shaken and forgotten how much I hate."

"You're a terrible grouch, and if you hate the Eastside I think that's the finest recommendation there is."

"That's because you literally don't know anything."

"Hmph."

The snow picked up. We were nearly at our destination. Mary stopped again—not to peer into a barbershop or cobbler's, but to look at me with a curiosity whose ferocity was almost frightening.

"Why does this all seem so new?" she said.

I knew what she was driving at, and I did not want to let her get there.

"Most of it is new, and it won't last a week," I said. I tried to press on, but she held my wrist tight.

"Before my memory was taken from me, I must have seen thousands of autos, watched hundreds of motion pictures. None of this should surprise. But it's struck me like a girl's first taste of liquor. Why do I feel I've never seen any of this before? Where have I been?"

On a quiet side street in the Upper West, under an elm, in the yard of a Methodist church. The Fall family vault, where some ancient endowment ensured that no weed may grow on New York's holiest ground.

"I don't know," I said. "Perhaps you don't get out much."

It stopped her questions, but it didn't make her happy. We walked the rest of the way at a nice clip, all the wonder that had animated Mary's face wiped clean.

In a whitewashed cast-iron palace at the corner of Third Street, the Roebling Company looked down on the stem. A small door marked "ROEBLING" opened onto a lobby with an elevator. An old man in a tidy uniform sat behind a gold desk. He informed us that the Roeblings occupied floors five through seven. We signed his book, and he waved us on to the elevator.

"What name did you use?" asked Mary.

"Sally Feeney."

"I'm Fairy Mall."

I couldn't help it. I giggled, and she looked at me like I'd sprouted polka dots.

"I didn't think you knew how to laugh," she said.

"I didn't know—really, I never had any idea—that you were funny."

"Keep watching. You'll learn a lot."

The elevator was old but spotless, every brass fitting shining bright. The operator, a middle-aged woman who looked like she was built out of railroad iron, guided it up with a touch so gentle that it made Mary say "Oh!" Another unexpected surprise.

We stepped off the elevator and were greeted by a massive gold-plated *r*. Beneath it, a frail young man with hair as wet and rounded as a scoop of ice cream eyed us like we were a stain. After our trip through the tunnel, we might as well have been. The plate on his desk read "Sullivan." Pinned to his breast was a little slip of paper that said "71." He set down his glass of water and said, "We don't get many women here."

"It's a matter of lost property," I said. "An employee of yours was—"

Mary ripped the long package from my hands and slapped it on Sullivan's desk.

"This is the property of Storrs Roebling," she said. "We shall return it to him personally, or we shall give it to you in the neck."

"Hand it over and I'll make out a receipt," he said, not looking at Mary.

Mary tore open the package, revealing a sparkling silver arrowhead. She pointed it at Sullivan's throat.

"Oh," he said. "Perhaps you should speak to the floor manager."

There was a little noise at his waist—a snap popping open, I realized a moment later—and the soft tap of something heavy brushing against polished wood. He'd drawn a pistol. I believe it was a semiautomatic, although I am happily no expert in these matters. It looked large enough to blow a hole through an elephant, however, and it was pointed at Mary's gut. With his other hand he lowered the arrow until it pointed at the floor.

"I thought you said there were no guns here," said Mary.

"Just west of the stem. Here, they are an essential accessory."

"You'll come with me," said Sullivan.

"You are absolutely right."

Sullivan shrugged toward the door behind him. I opened it, and Mary stepped inside. He followed us into a long room of clerks scribbling numbers at little desks with little lamps. There were windows along the western wall, but the shades were drawn tight. At the back of the room, a smoked glass bubble protruded from the wood.

Our feet were silent on the white carpet. I tilted my head toward Mary, feeling that even my softest whisper was louder than the room could bear.

"What happened to sweet-talking our way in?" I said.

"Sometimes it's better to do something loud."

Someday, I would give Mary a talk about the importance of patience. It would go brilliantly, I'm sure.

The clerks wore their ratings on their jackets: 77, 74, 79, and one terrified 62. Their suits were spotless and well-trimmed, cut to accommodate the blue steel pistols that dangled from every waist. I had not seen so many guns since the year before, when I emptied a boatload into the Hudson River, and the sight of all that gleaming death made me shiver.

"Mr. Sullivan," said Mary, in her calmest Sunday school voice. "It's quite difficult to follow you when you're behind us with that gun."

"Back wall," he hissed, "then we'll talk."

We stopped before the smoked glass bubble, where a hairline crack in the paneling marked a hidden door. I leaned close to the glass, trying to catch a glimpse of who might be inside, and was rewarded only with a twisted view of my own ridiculous face.

Sullivan tapped his pistol on the door, and it popped open. Mary stepped through. Sullivan went after, and before I could follow, the door slammed in my face. I reached for the knob, but there was none. I banged on the wood. No answer came.

"Mary," I said. "Mary?"

The clerk nearest, a grease-slick man with a 68 rating, sneered. Others snuck glances before returning, as quick as they could, to their work. Panic snaked through me like wildfire. My feet felt heavy, my mind sluggish. I was surprised by how scared I could feel.

I decided it was time they felt a little fear, too.

I grabbed the back of 68's chair and spun him around to face me.

"What the hell, woman?" he said, straining to return to his desk.

"How do you get in that room?"

"You don't."

He pushed me, hard enough that I stumbled, and got back to work. I leaned over him and caught a stultifying glimpse of the long ledger he was reviewing, line by line, whose every minute character was inscribed in Enoch's sunset blue ink. I snatched his inkpot and screwed the cap on tight.

"That's my ink," he said.

"Shut up," I told him, and I took his lamp, too.

I pulled it from the outlet and threw it across the room in one smooth motion. It may have been the most graceful thing I'd ever done.

The smoked glass wall fell slowly, like a sheet of ice cracking off a mountainside. The scratching of pens stopped. The only sound was the relentless ticking of the great clock at the end of the room.

Behind the destroyed glass, Mary stood between Sullivan and an ancient man in a slim-fitting black suit who leaned on a silver cane. His skin was like week-old oatmeal, scaly and soft, and an ashy moustache drooped across his mouth. Sullivan looked like he yearned for death, but the other two smiled cheerfully.

"Miss Carr," said Mary, "meet Jerome. I was just telling him we needed to speak to his boss."

"Welcome to the Roebling Company, Miss Carr," said Jerome.

He prodded the last remaining shard of window with his cane. It landed on the carpet with a soft thump that was as loud as a starter pistol. The clerks got back to work.

TEN

The elevator swept us silently to Roebling's seventh-floor citadel. There was no operator. Jerome handled the machine himself.

"I guess subtlety's gone out the window," said Mary, pleased with herself. "Or through it."

"I was simply following your lead."

She shrugged, a far-too-satisfied smile on her face.

Jerome dipped his fingers into his jacket and handed us each a paperclip.

"Thank you," said Mary, making it sound like a question.

"Our flagship product," he said. "The Roebling Paperclip, developed by Mr. Roebling's father some thirty years ago. It is virtually indestructible. Imagine that: an empire founded on a twisted bit of wire. Now please indulge my curiosity: Where did you get that silver arrow?"

"One of your men shot it at my head," I said.

"I'm terribly sorry to hear that. A misunderstanding, I'm sure."

Mary flicked Jerome's lapel. A shudder went through the old man, like a tree shaking off its last dying leaves. He smiled, and I fancied I could see his skull. He was one of the most polite criminals I had ever met, but something about him made me feel like ice water had just been poured down my back. As we passed the sixth floor, I realized I was standing as far from him as the little compartment allowed.

"You're missing your number," said Mary.

"Timekeepers don't wear their ratings on their chest."

"But you do have one?"

"Oh yes. Everyone has a rating. Ours are confidential."

"Even from you?"

"Even from us. The executives believe an air of mystery heightens the timekeeper's effect."

"And what is that supposed to be?"

"To remind the men that every second counts."

I gripped the brass rail to still my quivering hand. It seemed impossible that Mary was standing there, leaning against the wall of the elevator, tapping her foot on the crimson rug. Just a few minutes before, she had left my sight, and the terror of that moment had not ebbed. I had been a fool to let her come here, I realized, to involve her with any of this. I should have followed my first instinct and confined her to the library, to the town house, to bed. Some treasures were too precious to be let into the world.

"But you sell more than just paperclips," I found myself saying, as a way of forcing myself past the fear of losing her again.

"Ours is a diverse business, yes," he said.

"Bootleg liquor?"

"We see no reason to let a law as misguided as the Volstead Act stop working men from taking a drink."

"Heroin?" said Mary.

"A phenomenally popular recreational narcotic."

"A plague," I said.

"There are some who see it that way, yes, but I remember a time when it was available in every drugstore for twenty-five cents a bag, prescribed for everything from toothaches to children's coughs to women's ailments. Modern prudishness about drug use does not stop it from being a useful product."

"What about murder?" I said, nodding at the arrow that Mary clutched tight to her chest. Jerome shrugged, and the elevator glided to a stop. The trip had not put me at ease.

We walked down the hallway, which was as dim and silent as a crypt. He followed close behind. His stride was awkward, as though his legs were tortured by arthritis or some old injury, but he let no pain show on his face.

"Your conception of business is typical of a woman," he said, putting a healthy sneer into the word, "or a child."

"Is it?" I said, speaking quickly before Mary could say something rash. "Please enlighten me."

"The product is not important. What matters is that there is a need, and that we can make a profit by filling it. The Roebling Company offers many services that ignorant people consider illegal or immoral. What you might call murder, racketeering, bribery, fraud, or theft, we understand to be capitalism in its purest form."

"What about blackmail?"

"It's one of our fastest-growing departments."

He smiled broad enough for me to see every yellow tooth in his head. I couldn't tell if his pride stemmed from the company or from putting two women in their place, but I knew it made me want to run.

At the end of the hallway, Jerome stopped before a door whose smoked glass was inscribed "ROEBLING." I put my hand on the doorknob, but Jerome touched my wrist with a grip so clammy that I simply could not move.

"May I ask what you want of Mr. Roebling?" he said.

"He tried to kill us," I said.

"We want to know why," said Mary.

"Hmm. It is a fair question to ask," said Jerome, trying his best to look grandfatherly. "But I beg of you, for your own sake, please do not waste his time. People stronger than you have been killed for less."

"Death doesn't scare me," I said. "I live on Washington Square."

I unclamped his hand from my wrist and opened the door.

The office of this Eastside crime lord was hardly bigger than a coat closet. A tidy wood-paneled room, it had just enough space for a bare desk, a filing cabinet, and a clerk's chair. A window as narrow as my hand let in a sliver of light from the stem and gave a look at the white expanse of the Lower West, whose snowy streets were lit only by a swelling moon. On the far wall was the smoked glass window that was the organization's trademark. Not even the boss was trusted with his own time.

The man himself hunched over a leather book, scratching out something illegible in pale blue ink. He was younger than I'd expected—around thirty, probably, but graying fast. He was trim and might have been handsome if his skin had any color at all. He wrote fast, glancing every moment or two at the clock on the wall, whose second hand swept along as relentlessly as floodwater. When he saw the boss was occupied, Jerome stretched out his hands to block us from coming in farther. I wanted to hurl that book out the window, with the pen and its owner along for the ride, but I was mesmerized by the sight of the executive enslaved by his own clock. The label on his chest rated him a 96. Even in the executive suite, perfection was out of reach.

He lowered his pen, blotted the paper, gave the clock one more look, and glanced at his watch for good measure. Now he acknowledged Jerome.

"Westside business?" said Roebling, syllables clipped as tight as a military haircut.

Jerome nodded. Roebling snapped his fingers at the smoked glass. The door in the wall popped open, and a stooped old man who could have been Jerome's double slunk out from behind it. Jerome took his place, shutting the door behind him.

"They watch you, too?" said Mary.

"Time is precious, and no man can be trusted with it."

"And who tracks the timekeepers? How do you know they're not sleeping back there?"

"Jerome has been with the company for a long time. You have twelve minutes."

He pulled a folder from the cabinet and opened it on his desk.

It was a file, on Roebling stationery as tidy as the R-913s, and it was all about me.

"Gilda Carr," he said, his voice flat and his eyes dull. "The detective. What do you need?"

In the elevator, I hadn't been sure. Now I knew. The misery of that winter, the guilt, the awful unsatisfied yearning for my mother—all of it fell away in a flash of acid rage. In a single motion, I yanked the arrow out of Mary's hands, raised it above my head, and plunged it into Roebling's desk, impaling my file. It bit deep into the wood. I was proud to leave a scar.

"Twice you've tried to kill me," I said. "Twice you've missed the mark. You're not going to get a third chance."

"Your file makes no mention—"

"Shut up. I'm here to tell you to keep your goons, and your liquor, and your drugs on this side of the fence. The Westside is ugly, but it is pure. It is a sanctuary for the weak and broken and insane, and it will never be yours."

Maybe he was frightened. Maybe not. I didn't care. His hand slid to the side of his desk, where he pressed a small black button that summoned a man from the hall. This fellow was no clerk. He had a face as flat, soft, and red as sirloin, and he drew his gun as he stepped into the room. For a moment I was certain he was the archer from the park, but this man had none of the archer's leonine grace. After a while, all angry men start to look the same.

"Yeah?" he said.

"Miss Carr has wasted my time with a display of emotion intended to intimidate." Roebling looked at me, puzzled, like he was deciding between buying me or throwing me in the trash. "That was your goal, wasn't it? Intimidation?"

I was hot in my coat. My heart thudded in my ears. I didn't answer him. Mary gave me a look that was either terror or pride.

"It doesn't matter," said Roebling. "If she tries anything along those lines again, shoot her in the leg."

The man with the gun grunted and leaned on the doorframe,

his pistol trained lazily at my calf. Roebling tugged the arrow out of his desk. It took just a little more effort than he'd expected. I liked watching him struggle. He inspected the arrowhead and laid it down, perfectly parallel with the open file.

"You have ten minutes," he said.

"One of your men put that through my window," I said. "Tell me why."

"As I was explaining before your outburst, your file mentions nothing about an attempt on your life."

"You write that sort of thing down?" said Mary. Roebling did not look at her, but contempt swept across his face.

"We write everything down. You said I tried to kill you twice. What was the other time?"

"The fire at the Basement Club."

"You were there?"

"I won a raffle. A dog bowl full of gin. I nearly died."

"It's a shame you didn't. Anyone who would drink a dog bowl full of gin deserves to die. Why would I burn my own saloon?"

"To kill me, or to kill Abner Byrd."

"Ridiculous."

"Then what caused the fire?"

"Our investigators call it arson. They are divided as to whether the culprit was simply a lunatic, or in the employ of Ida Greene."

"Only the Byrds traffic in blue fire."

"And only sick drunks believe what they see from the bottom of a bowl of bootleg liquor."

He glanced at the clock and smiled at the second hand's steady progress. It was the first indication I'd seen that he felt anything at all.

"Women have no head for business," he said. "Supply and demand work as surely as water finding its level. The Westside is empty. The Eastside is full. The company's business must flow across the fence until both sides are level."

"And how many have to die before that balance is achieved?"

"I don't have the figures at hand, but our actuaries calculated it at somewhere around seven hundred forty per annum—drunks and addicts poisoned by their own vice, any guardsmen foolish enough to object, and whatever detectives get in our way."

It was all so stupid and monstrous and clinical, I could do nothing but laugh. Mary simply stared.

"You're surprised I had an answer, aren't you?" said Roebling. "You thought you were being clever. Again, it shows how little you understand."

"Those are people's lives!" said Mary. "Not just numbers in a ledger. You can't just—"

"We can't what?" said Roebling. "Give them what they're asking for? 'Numbers in a ledger'—that Sunday school morality won't shame me. This is a place of business, ladies. Life and death mean nothing here. Six minutes."

"But the Lower West isn't empty," I said. "There is Van Alen."

"Is there? He promised so much last fall, but what has he given you? Frostbite and starvation and darkness. He has no hold on the Lower West, and so it will be ours. Five minutes."

"What about the Byrds?" said Mary.

"What about them?"

"They're defrauding mourners on your behalf and passing their secrets along for you to use as blackmail."

"So what? We've contracted spiritualists and fortune-tellers all over the city—Eastside, Westside, Brooklyn, and the Bronx. We pay for secrets. Occasionally, we turn those secrets into profit. Our methods are generally far more subtle than blackmail. I have no material connection to the Byrds."

"Abner kept bar at the Basement Club," I said.

"I employ many such unremarkable men."

"You pay Judy not to preach her gospel at your clubs."

"She is a pest. Money is the easiest way to keep her away."

"And the resurrection ceremony tonight?" said Mary. "What do you hope to gain from it?"

"You're really not understanding this?" said Roebling. He stood and looked out the window to the blank expanse beyond the fence. "Perhaps it's my fault for speaking above your level. The Byrds do piecework for us—you know, like a woman taking in sewing. I do not give them orders. Perhaps they hired one of my men to kill you. I wouldn't blame them. But whatever silly performance they put on tonight has nothing to do with me. Two minutes. If you have anything important to ask, I would ask it now."

"Why does your window look out on the Westside?" I said.

"That's not important," said Mary.

"Even so. Why? Every boss on the stem wants a window that looks east, south, or north, so they can admire the healthy city and forget the lesion on its back. But you picked this office. Why?"

"It was the smallest on the floor. I didn't want an inch of space wasted on me."

"I think you have designs on the Lower West."

"Of course I do. It is a great untapped market. I should like to see a Roebling Club on every corner, but I have no interest in ruling it, as Barbarossa did, as Van Alen pretends he does. I wish only to sell my products to those unlucky enough to live there."

"You're disgusting," said Mary.

"That isn't a question. This was a very important meeting for the two of you, and you've approached it with all the weakness of women. Less than a minute left, and so far you haven't asked anything worthwhile."

"What about the finger?" He raised an eyebrow. It was the first thing I'd said that surprised him. "Two weeks ago the pickled finger of Saint Róisín was stolen from the Byrds' church. It still hasn't been found, and—"

"Let's save thirty seconds. You can leave now."

The gunman knew his cue. He stepped between me and the desk, his gun pointed at my chest now, instead of my leg.

"Why did you agree to meet with us?" said Mary. "If you knew we were going to be such a waste of time?"

"To let you know I have this," said Roebling. He dropped a stack of papers on his desk: the R-913s and other notes that we had stolen from the Byrds and passed on to Max.

"Where did you get those?" I said.

"Strike that look of concern off your face. Your little reporter is unharmed."

"Did you bribe him?"

"I didn't have to. Who do you think owns the *Sentinel*? Who do you think has an interest in half the papers in town? Your friend brought his editor a story so outrageous that Mr. Gischler had no choice but to pass it on to me. He was relieved when I told him he could put it on the spike. Miss Carr, I'm disappointed that you thought this would work."

"What's your point?" I said, utterly beaten, trying to salvage something from this meeting even if it was only a scrap of my much abused pride.

"You'll waste no more of my time, here or on the Westside. Interfere with my business in any way, and I'll kill you as casually as I tally numbers on a ledger."

"Braver men than you have tried," I said, feeling not one-tenth as tough as I was trying to sound.

"Of course I wouldn't start with you." He ran his finger down the paper on his desk. "You have a companion, a Swede named Hellida Krag? How would you like to wake up one morning and find her chopped up like steak tartare?"

I felt a sudden urge to see if he *could* fit through that little window. Mary held me back. The gunman gave us a shove toward the door, and we let him push. There was nothing left to do in this office but get ourselves killed, and I really didn't see the point.

Before I left I looked back at the slight, graying man shifting numbers and bodies on his ledger, killing with the stroke of a pen. He had already gone back to work.

"Do you spit on us?" I said.

"What?" he snapped.

"When you look out at the Westside, do you ever spit at the dark side of the fence? Because we spit on you."

I slammed the door as hard as I could—an adolescent gesture, satisfying all the same.

Night had solidified by the time we got back to the sidewalk. The snow had stopped. Eastsiders muscled their way along Broadway with their collars up and heads down. No one seemed to care that in a few hours, a miracle was to occur on the Flat. I didn't care myself.

Back on the Westside, the mood was different. There were fewer people, as always, but everyone we saw was walking south and west, for Bully Byrd, for relief from death. For the first time since summer, I saw people walk my streets with smiles.

When we reached Washington Square, Mary kept on toward Sixth Avenue, but I turned for home.

"I thought the Flat was that way," she said, "past the Thicket?"

"There's nothing there we need to see."

"And what are you going to do while the people of the Westside gather to witness the miracle of the age?"

"I'm going to go inside, light a fire, and get warm."

"Won't be easy—you've no front window."

"That's right. Damn it. Then I'm going to go inside, light a fire, and shiver. I'm going to get a little drunk and sleep for a year, and when I wake up, I'm going to meet with Ida Greene and form a plan to annihilate the Roebling Company, Westside and East."

I grabbed her wrist and dragged her down the overgrown lip of the park. Even through the anger and the cold, I felt ridiculous, but that didn't mean I stopped.

We were halfway to my door when she succeeded in wrestling away from my hand. She sneered, showing not just an absence of love but a wealth of contempt. For the first time, I didn't want to throw myself into her arms. I just wanted to bring her to heel.

"Roebling has nothing to do with this," she said. "It's the Byrds, and it always has been. Don't you want to see what they've got planned?"

"I'm too tired and too hungover to waste my evening admiring their theatrical fraud."

"So they're fraudsters again now? I thought you had come around to the idea of Bully Byrd's resurrection."

"I still think he may have come back from death. Anything is possible. Tonight, I just don't care."

"He tried to kill me. That doesn't matter to you?"

"Storrs Roebling tried to kill me *twice*."

"He said otherwise."

"And the fact that you believe him shows just how daft you are."

I regretted it as soon as I said it, but I didn't take it back. The effort of holding back with this woman, of guarding her feelings and guarding her life, had rubbed me raw. I was no closer to telling her I was her daughter—not because I didn't want her to know, but because in that moment, I didn't think she deserved me.

"I'm glad you finally admit it," she said. "You think I'm stupid. Since I hired you—"

"Hired me! You haven't paid me a cent!"

"And I'm getting what I paid for. Since I *engaged your services*, you've done nothing but lie, scold, and treat me like a spoiled, useless twit."

"If you act like a moron, people will treat you like one."

Tears welled up in her perfect blue eyes. I suddenly wanted quite badly to stop them, but I didn't know how.

"You have given no thought to how I feel," she said. "I am lost here. I am frightened. I don't know where I came from, much less how to get home. And the detective I trusted to answer those questions has done nothing but condescend and get in my way."

"Listen to me and I can help. Otherwise—"

"It's too late. This has been a mistake from the start, Miss Carr. You are incompetent, callous, and utterly unsuited to your work. I should never have hired you at all."

For the second time that week, someone I loved left me at my stoop, and I lacked the strength to make them stay. As she stepped toward Sixth Avenue, the same panic that had gripped me in the clerks' room at the Roebling Company flooded my nerves, but this time I was paralyzed.

"Come inside!" I shouted. "Get warm. We can compromise."

"Compromise is a waste of time."

"Please. Just stay. I can help you remember who you are. I can help you remember everything."

The swelling moon caught her curling brown hair, and she looked like every dream I'd ever had.

"Your services are no longer required, Miss Carr. If you ever need a recommendation, ask someone else. And if you find that ring of mine . . ."

"Yes?"

"Choke on it."

The moon slipped behind a cloud, and my dream turned away.

"Mary!" I called, putting everything I had into it, certain that when she heard her daughter's voice, the fog would lift, and she would see me with the love I needed so badly.

Love let me down. She kept walking, and by the time I had gathered myself to run after her, she was gone.

ELEVEN

In a city where unseen forces had toppled buildings and grown hills, thrown up forests and sunk roads into swamps, a block between Sixth and Seventh Avenues, a few blocks south of Houston, was curiously smooth. A long flat rectangle, it was shaded from the summer sun by the Thicket and shielded from the winter wind by the tenements of Seventh Avenue. Once used by Barbarossa's child army as a parade ground, the Flat's grass was as dead as its old master, and its earth was frozen hard.

Tonight it was lit by Chinese lanterns and ringed with thick rope. The view of the Thicket was blocked off by a mountain of cleared snow. The crowd entered from the west, where hand-lettered banners whose paint seeped through the bedsheets like blood asked "$2, silver ONLY" and warned that Westsiders alone would be let through.

The people who had fought across the ice congealed into a mass, like a chunk of fat ready to clog an artery, as they tried to get inside. I shoved to the front. I was through waiting for this city to get out of my way.

I slapped down my ticket. I wasn't sure how Mary would get in without hers, but I knew she'd find a way. One of the youngest members I had seen at the Electric Church—a chunky fortysomething who managed to sweat despite the cold—took the blue slip with a smile. Past him, more rope divided the crowd into halves, with an empty corridor down the middle that led to the stage. The place was nearly full, and there were hundreds more outside. He offered me a raffle ticket. I shoved it back into his hand.

"Have you seen a woman in a black dress that matches mine?" I said, knowing it was a hopeless question.

"Every widow in the city is here tonight, ma'am."

"Then can you point me to Enoch Byrd?"

"Please, ma'am. People are waiting."

I was about to step inside when a voice I had hoped to never hear again called my name. Max Schmittberger had found me. He elbowed past everyone else in line to speak to me across the rope, drawing a stream of curses that he didn't seem to notice at all.

"Gilda Carr, you gotta get me in there," he said, fumbling with a Turkish cigarette before he managed to jab it into his mouth. I'd never known smoking to be so annoying.

"It's Westside only."

"That's what they tell me, and I tell them I'm press, and they tell me they don't care, and I tell them—"

"I don't care either, Max. I gave you the best scoop you'll ever get, and you let Storrs Roebling take it away."

"I didn't let them take anything from me, Gilda, honest to god. They had to drag those papers out of my clenched fists. When Gish gave it the spike, I threw myself on his floor and screamed at him like nobody never screamed before. I cried so hard I near about drowned the ad boys downstairs. Nothing doing, but I swear I tried."

"For god's sake, stop shrieking."

"Sorry. I just love my work. Now can you get me in or what? I saw an extra ticket there peeking out of your coat."

The crowd pulsated with impatience. A tinge of fear crept into the ticket taker's smile. He put a light hand on my wrist.

"Please, ma'am, step inside or get out of the way."

I had spent too much time that winter being hard. What a relief it was to take pity on something so pathetic. I handed Max the ticket, and he clutched it to his chest.

"Gilda, Gilda, how can I thank you?"

"Just please don't mention my name."

He slapped his ticket onto the box and gave the acolyte a truly lewd tip of his cap, then took my elbow and led me inside. We stood between the two long banks of believers, like Moses dawdling in a parted sea of black fabric. It really was more widows than I'd ever seen.

"What do you think?" said Max. "Can this Byrd really bring fifty stiffs back to life?"

"You couldn't possibly believe that."

"I don't, no, not really. But it would be a dream if he could. Say—you all right? You look a little corpsey."

"My mother's come back from the dead."

"Don't you hate when they do that?" He saluted me and melted into the crowd. I hoped he'd stay disappeared. I jogged down the muddy, trampled earth, searching for a woman who would surely not be easy to find. The faces became a blur. They were frostbitten and hungry, their clothes torn, skin scarred and stained, hair matted with dirt, and mouths black with missing teeth. They were in the depth of another hard winter in a lifetime of hard winters, but tonight they held hope in their hands: a raffle ticket that promised a chance to ease the pain. It seemed foolish to me, and sad, but I was spoiled. My mother had already come back, and I'd let her slip away.

If she was here, I didn't see her. I found Enoch Byrd instead.

He was halfway to the stage, hunched and walking slowly, supporting an ancient woman in a coarse black dress on his left arm. I yanked him away from her. She managed not to fall.

"Miss Carr, I simply do not have the time," he said, paler than ever.

"Everyone's always in a hurry," I said.

In the pocket of my coat, I found something small, cold, and hard. I unscrewed the lid.

"You wanted blue ink?" I said. I snapped my arm out of my pocket and flung the whole bottle at him, drenching him from necktie to navel in the Roebling Company's own special blue. He froze—really froze, like he'd been dipped in cement—and the widow backed away.

"Why?" gasped Enoch.

"I'm tired of being lied to. I know you want to hurt me or throw me out, but there are hundreds watching, and if you want to keep them calm, you'd better lower your arms, straighten your tie, and escort me to the reserved section."

He looked left, then right, and found himself in the unfamiliar situation of being the center of attention. He tidied his tie, smoothed his ruined coat, and walked to the front of the crowd. I followed, firing questions nearly too quick for him to answer. I didn't want to give him time to come up with any more lies.

"Have you seen my cousin Mary tonight?"

"No."

"This is the shade of ink you've had me looking for?"

"Unquestionably."

"The same as on those papers I found yesterday?"

"Yes."

"Had you ever seen them before?"

"I swear to you, I hadn't."

"Then how the hell did they come to be printed in ink the color of the evening sky?"

"If I say it's a miracle, will you throw another pot of ink at me, or will it be acid this time?"

I don't think I'd ever heard Enoch make a joke before. It didn't suit him, but he looked like he was telling the truth. He looked tired, too, in a way I found familiar.

"Where is Bully keeping himself?" I said.

"Nowhere you're allowed to go. Please, Miss Carr, for once in your life, sit back and enjoy the show."

"I wish I were the type. Since he came back, has Bully seemed himself? Is he what you remember?"

"I remember my father as a very big man," said Enoch, speaking slowly, as though interrogating himself about this for the first time. "Warm and captivating. Full of life, always the loudest, happiest man in the room. Bursting with love for my sisters and me, for all mankind."

"And how does he seem now?"

"He's all of that," said Enoch, not quite selling it, "but smaller. It's to be expected, isn't it? He's younger than I am now. He's just a man."

Nearly at the front of the crowd, among a group of people who must have shown up at dawn to be so close to the stage, I saw a face I knew. Bex Red stamped her feet to keep warm, raffle ticket clutched in her hand. She looked away when she saw me. I would not let her off so easy.

I tapped her on the shoulder and she shook her head like she knew she'd been caught. I tried not to let her see how disappointed I was that she had fallen for Bully's lie.

"I didn't expect to see you here," she said. "And I bet you didn't expect me."

"We're too smart for this, Bex."

"In the summer, maybe, but this winter has been cold."

"You wasted good silver on that ticket?"

"What else should I spend my money on? It's just two dollars, and they're never gonna call my name, and even if they did I know it's all hooey, but still . . ."

"How early did you get here?"

"Dawn. I brought a sandwich. If you're going to be a fool, why not go all the way?"

Enoch took Bex's hands and looked deep into her eyes the way only a preacher's son can.

"I see you found your shade of blue," she said, nodding at his freshly dyed suit.

"There's no need for irony," he said. "You hurt. We all hurt. And we are so, so grateful to have you here tonight."

The unexpected sympathy hit her like hot water on frozen skin. She squeezed her eyes tight enough that not a single teardrop stained her cheek, and she put on her old, chipper smile.

"Thanks for having me," she said.

"And if your number is called," said Enoch, "who will you invite back?"

"Her name was Ellie. The best painter I ever knew, and a wizard with charcoal. We met at school, and we lived together for a long time, and . . ."

"She vanished?"

"In 1910. Went to walk the dog and I never saw her again. The dog, either."

Now the tears came: two plump ones that rolled down her cheeks, making tracks in her powder. I wanted to hold her—she was my friend, damn it, not Enoch's—but for the first time, I found him impossible to shoulder aside. Every ounce of her pain was mirrored in his face.

"You never told me about her," I said.

"You're not the only one who likes to hide."

"Good luck." There was nothing more to say. Enoch let her go and led me on to the front of the crowd, where a small area had been roped off for honored guests, including the withered electric faithful, who wrapped their white robes tight against the frigid wind.

Billowing torches ringed the whitewashed stage. At right, three rows of bleachers awaited the winners of the resurrection lottery. At left, seats were provided for the Byrds. Dead center sat a massive brazier, and looming over the entire scene was a towering black cross framed perfectly by the snow piled behind. From afar it looked like steel, but up close I saw it was flat, painted cardboard.

"You'd better shut the gates soon or you'll have a crowd too big to control," I said.

"There's no crowd my father can't handle."

"Don't look so proud, Brother Byrd. That's a sin, isn't it?"

"I can't help it. I've waited for him for so long."

"Where did he come from?"

"From the flames. You saw him leap out, remember."

"I saw the asbestos bag, Enoch. Quit fooling."

"Miss Carr . . ."

Ruth and Judy walked onto the stage. The crowd roared, but the show was not starting yet. Behind the brazier, an ax leaned on a pile of freshly chopped wood. The sisters started stacking lumber for the fire.

"How can I hurt you now?" I said. "The electric resurrection is at hand. You must have brought in two thousand in silver, and I couldn't shout loud enough to stop this ceremony even if I wanted to. The Byrds have won. Why not tell me how?"

A little smirk, and he was ready to spill. I think he'd been waiting to share for some time.

"The ceremony you saw was staged, yes, for the benefit of the faithful. They'd been praying for it their whole lives. They earned it. Bully put it together—the bag, the blue fire, everything. He is a professional."

"You mean an actor?"

"Of course not! He *is* my father, Miss Carr, and there's nothing else I can do to prove that to you. He appeared at the church the night before—just walked through the door, dazed and frozen but undeniably ours."

"Did he recognize you?"

"Not at first. But then, we have all changed quite a bit since he saw us last."

"Where did he come from?"

Enoch started twitching, kicking the ground like a bull about to take off, scanning the crowd, looking for a soul to save—or for someone to save him. He found neither. I put my hands on his shoulders. He shrank back, unused to the touch of even an unremarkable woman.

"Where?" I said.

"He killed himself, Miss Carr. We'd always suspected it and he said it was true. He couldn't bear the loss of Barney, the church . . . he swallowed a bullet and woke in fire."

"With snakes pricking his pecker?"

"He did not stoop to my sister's colorful language. He described a forest of blue fire, boiling like pitch, swinging like vines.

An eternity of agony—not just physical torment, but watching his own son, strapped in a high chair, burning to death endlessly, and always calling for Papa, Papa, Papa."

"You believed him?"

"I am a believer. That's what I do. He killed himself, and hell was his reward, until, after uncountable seasons of torment, he heard another voice calling his name. He walked toward it and awoke in the Westside. Home at last."

"Whose voice?"

"He didn't recognize it."

The fire was laid. Ruth, alone now, stepped before the brazier, raised her hands, and bellowed, "Who is ready to defeat death?"

It was like flipping a switch. A cataract of noise erupted, louder than the Polo Grounds during a pennant race. Enoch's eyes went wide.

"I have to join my family," he said. "We're starting."

"A last question—what is your relationship to Storrs Roebling?"

"I've never heard the name."

Before I could press him, he slipped under the rope, scooted along the stage to a short flight of steps, and bounded up behind the curtain. In the moment the drapery was open, I saw Bully flanked by Judy and Helen, his white suit shining in the candlelight, his hands massaging his temples.

"Brother!" cried Ruth, and Enoch emerged onstage carrying a wooden barrel. Behind him came the four stoutest of the faithful, hauling a chest painted gold. Its impact shook the boards.

"You paid your money, friends, a gesture of faith more moving than this old sinner has ever seen," said Ruth. "You paid it because you have God's light in your heart and sorrow on your breast, and you are praying for the Almighty to pass His power through my father and ease your grief. Well, I assure you, your faith will be rewarded, just as mine has been.

"I was a girl when I lost my father, and for years I dreamed of him—the funniest sort of dreams, because there was nothing strange about them. I dreamed of watching him drink a glass of milk or choose an apple at the market. I dreamed of saying hello in the morning and 'night night, Papa' in the evening. I dreamed of normal, and I never got it until this week, when my daddy came home.

"I know you didn't come to hear me talk. I'm just filled to the brim with joy, and you'll forgive me for bubbling over. I'll still my tongue now, because the electric resurrection really is at hand, and it's time to choose our lucky fifty."

She dug into the barrel, pulled a ticket, and called a number. The crowd disgorged a grinning young man in a patched black overcoat who sprinted down the center aisle like he was beating out a play at first base. Ruth called number after number, and though the crowd responded gratefully at first, the novelty wore off fast. By the time the thirtieth person had scaled the steps, the audience was bored and so was I.

I was shifting on my feet, trying to decide which one was more numb, when I saw Mary in the crowd. It was the first time I'd seen her when she didn't know I was looking. She looked older than ever, and as cold as a switchblade.

I ducked under the rope and pushed into the horde on the far side of the aisle. Impatient for the miracle, the people were in no mood to step aside. I stomped on toes and dug my heel into ankles, throwing elbows and squirming as forcefully as I could until I found myself where I'd seen Mary—right at the steps that led backstage.

I could see Bully's wingtips beneath the bedsheet curtain— where were the Byrds getting all these bedsheets? I wondered—and between Ruth's shouts, I heard Bully clear his throat, beat his chest, and run his golden voice up and down the scales. Ruth called the fortieth name, and the crowd's interest revived. Every face was on her. Even the acolytes tasked with guarding the stairs were looking the wrong way. It was better than a formal invitation.

I darted up the steps and through the curtain, into an indifferently heated tent where Bully Byrd massaged his throat. Beneath five pounds of stage makeup, he looked savage.

"I don't want another thing to do with you or that crazy bitch of a cousin," he said. I took great pleasure in ignoring him as I squatted down and forced him to meet my eye.

"Why did you attack her?" I said. An utterly disgusting look of satisfaction spread across his face.

"I didn't. She came after me."

"That doesn't make sense."

"If a lifetime at the pulpit's taught me anything, it's that women usually don't."

There were a hundred or so different ways I might have answered that stupid comment, but I was startled by the fact that beneath his makeup and bluster and misogyny, Bully seemed to be telling the truth. Mary had disappointed me again and again that week. It was shockingly easy to believe that she had lied.

He swept me aside and walked to the edge of the stage. A corner of the crowd spotted him and screamed his name. He did not look their way.

"How did it happen?" I said.

"Our little talk was a waste of time. I could have helped her, but she didn't want it. When I got sick of banging my head against her nonsense, I told her to leave. She leapt across the chair and tried to smash a cup of hot tea against my face. I dodged it, and she went after my throat. I got hers instead."

"Why?"

"The hell do I know? All I could tell was I had to fight her off. When she caught me with that teapot, I thought I was finished. You dragging her out the window just about saved my life."

He said this without gratitude. It was a statement of fact—everyone on earth was here to protect Bully Byrd.

"Where had you seen her before?" I said.

"If she didn't tell you, there's no way you'll believe me."

"Did she follow you back from the other side?"

"The other side of what?"

"Of death."

"You want the gospel, darling? There is no other side. Every person in this world is dead already."

I smacked him across the face. It probably wasn't a good idea, but I'd had enough of being lied to and pretending I didn't care. My hand came away slimy with blush.

"I don't know what gave you and that cousin of yours the idea that you were strong enough to hurt me," he said. Lord, but I wanted to hit him again. "Got any other stupid questions while I wait for my cue?"

"Tell me," I said. "Why did the ceremony work this time? How did you and Mary wind up at the Electric Church? Whose voice called you back from death?"

"Wanna hear something that'll make you chuckle? I got no goddamned idea. That gate opened and I walked through, and since then, things have been dreamy for Bully Byrd."

The man had timing. As soon as he finished oozing out the syllables of his own name, Ruth called the final number, and disappointment spasmed through the crowd.

"Don't weep, my friends," she called, gesturing for them to settle. "This is only the beginning. Today we bring back fifty—next week it will be a hundred, then five hundred, then a thousand. My father will make your families whole."

At that promise, the crowd erupted, and Bully Byrd strolled onstage carried by a wave of applause. I followed like flotsam.

Two dozen torches cast two dozen shadows, flanking him with an army of flickering doubles. In the orange light his makeup did not show. He looked healthy, strong. I hung a few feet back as he walked to the brazier, watching for Mary, certain that if she hurt even a thread of his white suit, the crowd would tear every person on the stage in two. For being where I was not welcome, I drew glares from the Byrd women and jeers from the audience, which stopped only when Bully raised his hands, coughed for effect, and spoke his piece.

"What is there left to say?" he began. "What prelude would be more appropriate than three decades dead? What words could prepare you for what is about to happen better than the years you have suffered, the tears you have cried? What would you say if this old preacher just got on with the show?"

The answer was a fresh burst of applause. Ruth lit the fire and stoked it high, as Bully mumbled words that might have been Latin and might have been gibberish. As the flames licked higher up the brazier, I looked for Mary in the crowd. The torchlight was blinding, and I couldn't make out their faces.

When the fire burned hot enough to make us sweat, Bully took the first of the chosen worshippers, the skinny boy in the dying coat, by the hand.

"What's your name, son?" said Bully. The boy coughed a little, trying to answer but producing hardly a sound. "It's the crowd, isn't it? I know the feeling. The first time I spoke the gospel, it was just a few dozen faithful, and I about sweated through my suit."

This earned a laugh that put the boy at ease.

"My name's Mitchell Pepper," he said.

"And who is it you lost?"

"My brother, sir."

"What was his name?"

"Raymond. He died in the war."

"In a few minutes, Raymond will shake your hand."

He went down the row, asking every lottery winner who they had come to recover from death, and their brief stories—simple and heartfelt and true—might have made my eyes water if I weren't so horribly scared. God, I hoped Bex had left when they hadn't called her onstage.

"Why do we die?" Bully called to the audience. "Why do we suffer? Why do the people we love walk out the door? They are questions that had no right response . . . until today. This little bag—full of azure powder mixed by my daughter Ruth, according to a recipe I devised thirty-four years ago—holds the answer, and that answer is: We do not need to die! We do not need to suffer! Our loved ones may leave, but they will come back!"

He dug his fingers into the bag. A gust of wind blew the backstage curtain open. I flinched toward it. There was no one there.

Bully brought his hand back, then emptied his fist into the fire. The explosion cracked the night in half. Blue flames leapt higher than the cardboard cross, and smoke filled the stage. My eyes burned, and though I tried not to, I had to turn away. Just for a moment, my back was to the fire. I stared into the night, to the back of the stage, to the mountain of snow, and as my eyes felt the relief of the cool air, I saw Mary leap down from the ice.

She plunged into the smoke, faster than I knew she could. The Byrds were watching Bully; the lucky fifty were watching the fire, waiting for their loved ones to step out of it. No one saw her but me.

I reached out, but she brushed me off, throwing me against the red-hot brazier. It burned. I stumbled but did not let myself fall.

I was on one knee when she reached for the ax.

I was on my feet when she closed with Bully.

She swung her weapon. I lunged to knock him down.

I didn't get there quick enough to tackle him, but I brushed him, and he spun far enough for Mary's blow to bounce off.

She reared back for another try. Before she could bring it home, Ruth came to her daddy's defense and took the blow herself.

The ax caught her in the chin, knocking her head back and splitting her jaw in two. Her scarf fluttered away, revealing a mask of blood.

"Ruth," screamed Bully. "My girl Ruth! She killed her!"

It was another exaggeration, of course. She wasn't dead, but she was close.

I dragged the ax out of Mary's hands and threw it to the ground. Blood was splattered across her face and chest. I seized her by the shoulders, but she didn't even notice me. She looked wild and frightened and mad, but her madness was nothing next to that of the crowd.

They flooded over the rope barriers and climbed the stage. A gust of wind, cold and briny as the harbor, swept across, wrapping the scene in smoke. When it cleared, the Byrds were gone and so was the silver. There was nothing between us and the mob.

"Where did they go?" Mary said. "Where did that bastard *go*?"

I didn't answer. I just pulled, like a mother dragging a howling toddler out of a department store, hauling her to the back of the stage, away from the bloodthirsty crowd.

"We have to go back," she said. "We have to find them."

I shoved her off the stage.

She landed on her feet, more or less, stumbling backward onto the mountain of ice. I jumped after her, almost as gracefully, and pulled her up the slope. Below, the mob ripped the stage to bits.

Once Mary finally saw there was no going back, she stopped fighting and focused on the climb. It was awful going. The ice shredded our dresses and cut our hands, but we had panic in our hearts and a mob at our back, and we pressed on until we reached the top. Behind us was a riot. Before us, the endless black of the Thicket. The wind was fierce and we were numb.

"Why," Mary heaved, "why did you stop me?"

I couldn't talk. Fear pounded in my ears. My mouth felt dry and bloody. Mary looked pale, as weak as an invalid. She spoke without taking her eyes off the spot where Ruth had fallen.

"That poor girl," she said. "You got in my way. This is your fault, Miss Carr, this is all—"

I smacked her on the back of the head.

"Are you suicidal or just insane?" I said.

"I was aiming for Bully."

"That doesn't make it better."

"I was trying to do what's right. He killed Tom."

I grabbed her by the shoulders, wondering if she would give me a good reason not to hurl her back into the mob. My god, I was tired of her.

"Who the hell is Tom?" I said, but I think I already knew.

"My fiancé. My redheaded darling. You tried to hide him from me, but I'm not as dumb as you think."

The body in the snow, the dead man at the Electric Church, the corpse I had been running from this whole time. I'd been right to ignore him. He could have only led me here.

"How did it happen?" I said.

"I stepped out of that blue fire, stepped into that church doorway, and I saw the man I love dying in the snow and I saw that bastard in the white suit running away. He killed Tom. He had to pay."

The smoke was nearly clear. The stage was in shambles. The Byrds were nowhere in sight, but someone in the crowd spied Mary, and the more intrepid among them started to climb.

"But you don't remember that," I said. "You don't remember anything."

"Miss Carr, you must learn to stop underestimating me. I've remembered everything this whole time."

I pushed her closer to the edge, ready to drop her if she gave me cause. The first of the crowd was nearly at the top.

"Then, and for god's sake don't lie to me now," I said, "how did you get here? Where did you come from?"

From death. From my dreams. From some unknown hell. Every guess I had was wrong.

"Why, of course, I came from the past."

She smiled, almost as lovely as ever, and I wanted to throw her to the mob.

But she would answer my questions first.

TWELVE

The first hand shot over the ice. I stomped on it until it fell away.
Many more were coming.

"Let them," said Mary. "Let them rip us apart. Tom is dead. I
killed that woman. I have failed."

I didn't bother to contradict her. I was through wasting my
breath. I seized her collar and marched to the far side of the ice,
pulling hard enough that she had to scramble in order to escape being dragged. I pushed her to the edge.

"Climb," I said, "or I'll kick you off."

For the first time that week, she didn't argue. She climbed, and I
followed. As my head dipped below the ice, I saw the hungry hands
of the mob appear on the far side of the ledge. The climbers didn't
see me, but they would find our tracks and be on top of us soon.

It was a thirty-foot drop, and handholds were few. We had
adrenaline on our side, though, and the light of a generous moon,
and that put the impossible just within reach.

As my body worked its way down the ice, my mind formed
questions for her. It couldn't help it. *How did you come from the
past? What past was it? Have you met my father? Have you given
birth to me? And what happens if we don't get you home?*

Mary reached bottom first, and by the time I landed, the weakness and fear she'd shown on top of the ice had been tucked away.
She smoothed her bloody coat, clasped her hands, and smiled like
we were out for an evening walk.

"Don't smile at me," I said. "Not tonight."

I flipped my coat inside out, grateful I had never gotten around to replacing the forest green lining with Gilda Carr black. I tore Mary's coat off her shoulders, used it to wipe as much blood off her face as I could, and threw it into the Thicket, which swallowed it whole. In the heavy black dress, she looked more like me than I could bear.

"My mother gave me that coat," she said.

"Damn you, and damn your mother, too. Run."

Screams from the top of the ledge. We had been spotted. Once again, Mary no longer needed my encouragement. She picked her feet up and we ran up the border of the Thicket to the northeast corner of the Flat, where we smacked headfirst into the mob.

Having started running, she didn't want to stop, but I held her back and forced her to walk.

"Head down," I said. "Mouth shut."

The most bloodthirsty of the crowd had been left behind to rip the stage apart. These were the polite people, who were content to rage feebly as they slouched their way home.

"Goddamned disaster," said the man at my left, a gaunt fellow with his equally gaunt wife on his arm.

"A bitter disappointment," agreed his wife.

"Where do you think Bully went to?"

"The whole family was crushed. The stage collapsed, and they're right at the bottom of it."

"The stage didn't collapse. The people tore it down."

"That's not how I saw it."

"You didn't see a thing. You were running for the exit."

"What else would you have me do?"

"You could have gone with me to get our four bucks back."

"That money is gone, Herman."

"Then maybe I could have taken four bucks' worth of flesh out of that girl with the ax."

"That would have been nice. A girl who would hurt a man like Bully Byrd deserves to be strung up by her ankles and gutted like a fish."

Mary pressed herself against me. She was cold. I didn't care. I squeezed her wrist until I was sure it hurt. We walked on.

"Will you continue being cruel all night?" she whispered.

"I'm going to save your life, and you're going to tell me the truth or I'll kill you myself."

We kept with the crowd as it flowed north, grumbling like we were just another pair of disappointed mourners. When we reached Houston, I dragged her east, where the crowd was thinner and we could talk as we made our way home.

"Explain yourself," I said, "or I'll—"

"Yes, yes, you'll commit all sorts of horrible violence upon my person. I'm too cold to be threatened further. Stop posturing and let me talk."

"Go."

"Four days ago, it was 1888," she began. I was too angry to soak it in, too angry to do anything more than a bit of simple arithmetic. 1888. Four years before she married my father, five years before I was born. "But really it started the year before, when my father dropped dead at his easel while painting the boats. It took them three days to pull him from the river, and by then he was unrecognizable from bloat. Mother had to make the identification, and the sight of him broke her. He had been a beautiful man."

"What happened to her?" It was so hard to picture Anacostia Fall as anything but withered and indomitable and alone.

"Other women might have taken the opportunity to become hysterical. My mother did not cry. Instead, she went to church. First Sundays, then twice a week, then every day. She stopped sleeping. She stopped eating. She was dying from the inside out until she found the Electric Church."

"This was before the fire."

"Yes. It was '87, the year of Bully Byrd. Mother read about him in the papers and went to a service. The blasphemous passion, the fevered shouting, the leaping, dancing, writhing flesh, it transfixed her. She went back the next night, disguised by a mourning veil, and gave herself over to the electric word."

"Helen saw a widow."

"And that meant a target. She pulled the same scam she did on poor Stacey Tarbell. Why do you think that woman's stupidity made me so mad?"

The sidewalk ended in a deep ditch. I stepped onto the frozen street and forced myself to offer Mary my arm. She did not take it. We walked down the middle of Houston Street, stepping carefully on the packed ice, trapped in the past.

"What did Helen ask of your mother?" I said.

"Two thousand to buy a place in heaven for Pierrepont Fall. Mother didn't even haggle, a first for her. Helen and Bully treated her to a séance, just like the one they used to fool that pathetic Tarbell woman, and mother left feeling lighter than air."

"What changed?"

"Morning came, and she realized how stupid she had been. She confessed what had happened to my brother and me, and we forced her to go to the police."

"The NYPD sent a detective?" The image of young Virgil Carr stepping across the threshold of the Fall mansion made me dizzy. I locked my eyes on my feet, not sure if I was about to vomit or slip, and let Mary talk.

"If you could call him that."

"Did you meet him?"

"I was at the market when he came. But Mother said he was an utter wreck—cursing, belching, and quite likely drunk. Worse, he talked to her like she was a criminal. He made some half-hearted inquiries into the Byrds, but he was never serious about it. Informing the police was a waste of our time."

"What was his name?"

"I couldn't possibly recall."

She hadn't met him. He'd not even had the chance to make one of his hideous first impressions. No wonder she hadn't blinked when I introduced myself as Gilda Carr.

"What did you do next?"

"What any intelligent woman would do. I resolved to conduct

the investigation myself and find enough evidence not just to re-cover my mother's money, but to destroy the Byrds for good. You simply can't let people get away with this sort of thing."

"What was your approach?"

"Do you really care?"

"Intensely."

"You've shown so little interest in me the last few days, why should I bore you with this? I feel that a real detective would have pieced this together already, would have dragged it out of me bit by bit, but you've been so fixated on the Byrds that you hardly noticed me at all."

"You were my client. I trusted you."

"I'm a woman who broke into your house and thwapped you with a silver spoon. Why should you trust that?"

Before I could form a reply my feet found one of those patches of black ice, and my legs went out from under me. Mary caught me before I slammed into the ground. The way she laughed hurt worse than any fall might.

"What?" I said, jerking my arm out of hers.

"I'm just better at this than you. Better at walking on your awful Westside ice, and a sharper detective as well."

"You're an ill-mannered wretch and—"

Before I could finish my jab, the sidewalk reappeared. Mary hopped up on it and walked away. For what must have been the fiftieth time that week, I swallowed my pride.

"Tell me what happened next," I said.

"I turned bloodhound. I went to ceremonies at that ridiculous church, I lurked outside, I followed the Byrd children on their way to school. I cornered widows and demanded they tell me if Helen and Bully had offered to sell them a place in heaven for their dead."

"And they confirmed your mother's story?"

"Not one of them. But my mother told me what happened, and mothers don't lie."

"It doesn't sound like you were much of a detective at all."

"Don't be smug, Miss Carr—it suits you even worse than that awful dress. I didn't learn anything asking questions, but I hung around that church every day until spring, and that meant I was on hand for the fire. I saw a blue inferno zigzag up the building, I saw it swallow that church right down to the stone. When Bully got the children out, a cheer went up like nothing I'd ever heard, but then they did a count and saw four were missing, and I saw something on his face that no one else believed."

"What was it?"

"Guilt."

"You were raised in drawing rooms. I've spent my life mingling with killers and thieves. I assure you, a guilty man looks no different from any other."

"If that kind of observation is meant to impress me, you've failed again. Stop interrupting me or I'll stomp on your toe. I tell you that Bully had a look like a man who killed his own child, and I thought I could prove it."

"It would take quite a detective to prove arson."

"And I had the humility and good sense to go to the experts."

"The police?"

"Absolutely not. If that buffoonish detective had gone after the Byrds when my mother told him what they'd done, there would have been no fire, and those four children would still be alive today. I was finished with the NYPD, now and forever. I took it to Tom."

"Yes. Tom."

"You're annoyed at me for keeping him from you? I don't blame you. But he was the finest man this city has ever spit out, and you are coarse and cruel. You did not deserve to know his name."

It was a stupid, childish, incoherent sentiment. It was also exactly the sort of thing I would have said. We were at the corner of Washington Square, and Mary would walk no farther. The moon slid out from behind a cloud. Its light was nothing compared to the brightness in Mary's eyes when she spoke of Tom. Her speech was soft, matter-of-fact, and quick. I wanted to sympathize, but that night I just didn't care.

"Tom MacNaughton was the only man I've ever loved, the only man I ever will love," she said. "He was with the fire department—an assistant marshal specializing in arson."

"You met him after the fire?"

"Two years before. You don't get to know how. You don't need to know anything more than that he was more handsome than I thought possible for a Scotsman, that he was brilliant and kind, that I loved him, and that I saw him die."

The wind picked up, strong enough to cut through a coat that had stopped seeming warm enough hours before. My hands were numb, and my feet were, too, but somehow they hurt anyway. Over on Sixth Avenue, I saw torchlight and heard the remnants of Bully's crowd, angry still. I pulled Mary against the yellow brick of Father Lamb's church. Her skin was ice.

"What did you tell him about the fire?" I said.

"That I thought Bully had burned the church for the insurance money, and that it had gotten out of hand."

"Do you think he knew about the children in the basement?"

"I cannot say. It would take a monster to set a fire when he knew there were children downstairs, but that man is as close to a monster as I've ever seen."

"And did Tom believe you?"

"Of course he did." She forced a smile. "He loved me, and besides, I'm brilliant. Two nights after the fire, we were on the trail of Bully Byrd. We watched him walk the streets, all the light gone out of him, and followed him to the ruins of his church. The earth was still smoking. The bodies had not been removed. He knelt in that stone archway. He prayed. I was egging Tom to go ahead and arrest him already when the stone lit up blue."

"What do you mean?"

"A light came out of the archway where Bully knelt. First just a pinprick, but blinding, like a welder's torch, then bright enough that it might have been day. Turquoise light—same as the blue from the fire. It poured out of the archway, and I know it sounds lunatic, but I swear that light spoke Bully's name."

"And did he answer?"

"He just stepped through."

"And what did you do?"

"I grabbed Tom's hand and told him to stop whimpering and dragged him across the street and leapt in after."

"What did you see?"

"Nothing. It was too bright. I shut my eyes against the light and held on to Tom's hand until I felt it slip away. Then I was scrambling for him and gasping for air and when I opened my eyes, I saw Tom with his skull cracked open and Bully running away."

"You didn't see Enoch, or Judy or Helen or Ruth?"

"No one but Bully Byrd."

Sixth Avenue was dark again. I stepped away from the wall, toward the comparative warmth of home.

"Come on," I said.

"You still want me in your house?" It wasn't an apology, nor was it an admission of any kind of guilt. She looked amused by my anger, as she had been by everything I'd done that week. I wondered what it would take to make this woman take me seriously, and decided I didn't care enough to try.

"You need to warm up or you'll die," I said. "You pick."

She followed me down the sidewalk, rubbing the thin arms of her dress in a hopeless attempt to warm them up. Our brief stop had given the cold a chance to settle in, and we both moved like we were half-asleep.

"Why amnesia?" I said.

"I thought you would believe it. I wanted to kill Bully, to avenge Tom, and I didn't need you getting in my way."

"But you didn't just lie. You performed. You told me things were coming back. Every minute we were together, you were manipulating me."

She shrugged. Perhaps my numb mouth had not properly expressed how angry I was. More likely, she didn't care.

"I hired you, Miss Carr. I didn't adopt you. I'm surprised you think I owe you anything at all."

"Again, if nothing else, you owe me *money*."

"Really, the way you've fixated on that, it's absurd." She stopped me outside my gate. "And it's not as though you've been entirely honest with me."

"What haven't I told you?"

"I don't know. But you have a cunning face, and I can tell you lie. Now, since I've been so generous with the truth, is there anything you'd like to tell me?"

I looked at her, hated her, and told her no.

I built a fire in the kitchen and heated a pot of water to boiling. I carried it up the stairs, refusing Mary's help, walking slow enough that I didn't spill a drop, and drained the pot into the tub. I cut it with cold water—the only type that came out of my faucet—pouring in just enough that the water was steaming but would not burn.

"That's too hot for me," said Mary.

"Good."

I didn't bother asking her to get ready. I gripped her dress by the shoulders and ripped it open, then shoved her toward the water. She lowered herself in, wincing ostentatiously. I threw her a dishrag and soap.

"I suppose a touch of privacy would be too much to ask?" she said.

"Shut up and wash." She obliged. A trail of blood snaked through the water. There was a long cut down the side of her right arm.

"What's that?" I said.

"I cut it on the ice."

"Give it here."

I grabbed her arm and scrubbed the wound clean.

"That hurts," she said. I grunted and scrubbed harder.

"How old are you?" I said.

"Twenty."

"Funny. You look much older."

"But not nearly as old as you."

The cut was as clean as I could get it. I gave her back her arm. I stood and turned my back to her. I wasn't sure if it was for her benefit or mine. For a long time, there was quiet.

"That bath is probably cold by now," I said.

"Do you think Ruth is going to die?"

I looked at her again. With her hair slicked back against her head, she looked small, even girlish. I lacked the words or energy to give her the comfort she wanted. There were more important things at stake than life and death.

"Forget her," I said. "Our job is getting you home."

"And suppose I don't want to go?"

"You can't stay here. Every grieving soul on the Westside wants your hide."

"I have work to do."

"If you mean killing Bully, forget that, too."

"We don't know how I came here. How are we going to get me back?"

"Tomorrow, I'm going to show you how good a detective I am."

She wore a stiff smile, the same one I saw every day in my own mirror. It was the face of a woman who was going to do whatever she wanted and wouldn't let anyone get in her way.

I took the ruined dress and hung my least-mildewed towel across the sink.

"I'm suddenly quite tired," I said. It wasn't a lie. "Find your own way to bed."

That night, after Mary went to sleep, I took the heap of photos hidden beneath my bed—images of a mother and daughter at play, posed with family, posed with friends, sitting in front of backdrops of landscapes real and imagined, always smiling, drenched with a love that neither time nor death could spoil.

I carried them to the roof and I burned them all.

I woke around dawn, surprised by the unfamiliar sensations of a clear head, a settled stomach, and a mouth that wasn't sandpaper dry. I had been dreaming of dead women's fingers.

I lit a candle and felt that something was wrong. I tossed my quilts aside and tugged open the curtains to let in the dim, gray morning light, and saw that every stack of papers, every pile of tangled clothes, every forgotten bowl of food and red-stained empty glass—all was where it was meant to be. The only thing different was my closet door.

It was closed. I hadn't bothered to close that door in years.

I turned the knob and was greeted by my collection of black dresses in varying styles, of varying lengths, all varying degrees of unflattering. The dress I tore off Mary the night before had been my finest. Now the next-best was gone, too, and my spare coat along with it.

On my dresser, I saw that my wallet was thinner than normal. My meager supply of cash had been taken along with my papers.

I crashed out of my bedroom and met Hellida on the stairs.

"She's gone," said Hellida.

"She's gone. She took my identification. She'll have gone east."

I pulled on my coat as I stomped down the steps, getting the arms wrong twice and disregarding the buttons entirely. Hellida followed me out the door. As our eyes strained against the gloom, I told Mary's story.

"That stupid girl has made my life hell," I said. "I put her up, coax her through that ridiculous amnesiac's charade, risk my life and reputation and career and sanity to help her find answers. How does she repay me?"

"You look like you don't want me answering that question."

"By stepping on my toes. By ignoring me. By starting a riot and doing everything she can to get herself killed and make me look an idiot in the process."

We reached Fifth. I headed uptown.

"You're not going after her?" said Hellida.

"I can't. Not without my ID. That little slip of paper is the only truly valuable thing I own, and she took it without a word."

"What do you think she's doing?"

"I couldn't possibly care."

In one of the crumbling high-rises of lower Fifth, a door hung loose on its hinges. I kicked it shut as I passed, hard enough to make Hellida wince.

"My mother was a saint," I said. "My father put her through hell and she never bent, she never broke. She was as sturdy as an iron wall. She was not a giggling, impertinent little girl. She did not lie, and she did not run when things got tough."

"That's just how you remember her. That wasn't how she was."

"You have no idea. She was gracious, she was gentle, she was—"

"Putting on a show for her little girl. And don't pretend your father was the only one giving her hell. You were a rotten child from the night you drew your first breath. A skinny, screaming runt that grew into an impossible, disobedient girl. Mary was flesh, and no matter how cruelly you and your father jabbed at her, she never let you see her bleed."

We stood at the mouth of Washington Mews, where the wind was relentless. Hellida stared at me the way she had so often during my childhood, when I fell off a bench or tumbled headfirst down a flight of stairs. Her lips were tight; her eyes were cold. She was waiting for me to pick myself up and admit I was okay.

"What's going to happen to me?" I said.

"You mean what by that, exactly?"

"That woman is needed in the past. She needs to meet Virgil Carr, to fall into some kind of impossible love, to marry, to . . ."

"To have you."

"If I can't find her . . ."

"You will vanish into the mist. Or not. It will be like you never existed. Or not. How should I know?"

"Then you think I should let her go?"

"Good god, girl, you were stupid when I met you and you're stupid now. Why do you think I stay? You're irritable, you keep bad hours, you drink too much. You treat me like a servant and, worse, call me friend. You don't even pretend to do the dishes. But for this neighborhood, you're a good woman. The city needs more like you. What you did last fall? There's people alive because of you. One of them's me. If you were never born, then all them are dead. I call that not worth the risk."

Through the whole speech she stayed rooted to the pavement. It was on me to get my useless body moving. I did so, and she nodded, satisfied.

"So what do I do?" I said.

"What you'd do to any twenty-year-old nitwit who threatened your life. Put her in her place."

At last, she wrapped me in a hug that smelled of all the peculiar beauty products that were her cherished vice—creams and oint- ments scented with lilac, lavender, rosemary, eucalyptus, and god knows what else. It was a ridiculous smell, and I would have it on my collar for the rest of the day. A blessing.

She went home and I walked north, passing men huddled around a rare clear street corner, sharing a cigarette and talking about the excitement of the night before.

"I knew they was swindlers," said one, speaking with the dubi- ous authority of a man who is certain he is always right.

"They were honest," said a colleague, who had a square head and an even squarer beard. "It was that loon with the ax what ruined it."

"Doesn't matter. I'll string 'em all up if I don't get my two bucks back and fast."

"Why waste time with rope? If I don't get my money back today, I'll burn the whole city down."

I lowered my head and kept walking, always uphill, always into the wind.

THIRTEEN

At some point while Mary and I were bickering, the Portuguese woman gave birth to a slight but healthy baby girl. That was the report, anyway, from the midwife who answered the door at Ida Greene's labor palace.

"Mother and child rest happily," she said. "We'll send them home in a few days. A nice little baby."

"And Mrs. Greene?"

"She's at the plant on Morton Creek."

On the banks of the twisting waterway that swallowed Morton Street in 1915, Mrs. Greene had built herself a distillery. Slushy current turned a paddle wheel that crushed grain into white alcohol, which her half dozen employees dutifully stained beet red. With its wide gates bolted shut against the cold, the freshly painted maroon structure looked like it might once have been a barn—or a slaughterhouse. I let myself in through a side door and was walloped with the cloying stench of fermentation. It was like being drunk inside a loaf of bread.

The only distillery I'd ever seen had been Rotgut Barbarossa's underground bootlegging operation, where spilled liquor puddled on every rusty surface. Next to that, Mrs. Greene's barn was gleaming, orderly, and perfect. Four mammoth tanks nestled together in the center of the spotless floor, bubbling ceaselessly to provide the lubricant that kept the Lower West from shuddering itself apart.

The women who tended the stills were absent, but light burned in an office on the second floor.

Floating on the fumes, I climbed the steps and crossed a narrow catwalk where windows looked over the ice-choked creek. I did not bother knocking on the office door.

I was expecting Ida Greene, and I was expecting her angry. I was not prepared for the man himself. Glen-Richard Van Alen, benevolent dictator of the Upper West, leaned against the wall like a coat tossed in the corner, sipping tea. He looked hollow. His skin was nearly as white as the snow outside, his hair brittle and gray. A bullet to the stomach will do that to a man. I couldn't believe he had survived the trip downtown. He looked nearly as surprised to see me.

"What the hell gives you the idea that you have a free pass to bother me whenever you like?" said Mrs. Greene, not bothering to look up from the wad of papers in her hand.

"Gilda Carr means trouble," said Van Alen, a younger man's smile spreading across his face. "Trouble is something I've always enjoyed."

"I need passage to the Eastside," I said.

"I gave you that yesterday," said Mrs. Greene. "You brought nothing in return."

"I've come to report. Storrs Roebling is—"

"Immaterial."

"But I spoke to him. I saw the inside of his building, got a rundown of his entire operation from one of the senior staff. I—"

Mrs. Greene brushed me aside with a single well-dressed shoulder and handed the paper she'd been working on to Van Alen. He skimmed it and grunted.

"That'll work," he said.

I could have asked what they were talking about, but it was faster to snatch the paper out of his hand. It's so easy to take things from old men. The document was a brief accounting of every Van Alen asset on the Lower West—the distillery, the midwifery, the guards—with notes about how quickly they could be transferred north.

"What the hell is this?" I said. "You're leaving?"

"It hasn't worked, girl," said Van Alen. "When Barbie did the world a favor and dropped dead, I saw an opportunity to spread the empire of light below the Borderline. I'm a vain, silly old man, and I thought I could make the Westside whole. Alas . . ."

"You promised schools. Doctors. Markets. Street cleaning. Fire protection. Lights!"

"My guardsmen are spread thin as wax paper, and no matter how much we steal from the Eastside, it's nowhere near what we need to make the Lower West anything close to habitable. Last night sealed it. These people are unruly. If Roebling wanted to crack the Westside, he couldn't have picked a better chisel than Bully Byrd."

"So you're just going to give us up?"

"I can hardly afford to fight. My god, girl—"

"Don't call me girl."

"If you'd told me a year ago I'd be slopping out red liquor to keep Barbie's district docile, I'd have spit in your eye. I am too old to compromise."

I looked out the rippling glass window. A figure dragged its feet down the icy path. I couldn't tell if it was man or woman, young or old. It stopped for a moment, coughing horribly, then continued on its way.

Van Alen emptied his cup.

"You haven't done a goddamned thing," I said.

"Do not speak to him like that," said Mrs. Greene.

"I've saved his life and yours, too, and that spares me having to address him like he's a god. The empire of light—that's a stale joke."

"Girl, watch your tone," said Van Alen.

"I'm nobody's girl." He stepped back like I'd socked him in the nose. "You promised to save us. All you've done is sell us gin and watch us die. There's been no food, no firewood. Your men don't even clear the corpses from the streets. The Lower West was a business opportunity, and when it didn't pay off, you sold us out."

"I didn't come this far downtown to be yelled at," he said.

"Mrs. Greene, recall our guardsmen and shut down every facility below the Borderline. I want it all wound up before the lunatics tear it apart."

I was right on every count, but what did it matter? Without the guardsmen, the Lower West would drown in snow and blood. None who died would be comforted by the knowledge that as Van Alen abandoned them, Gilda Carr landed a parting blow.

I pushed past Mrs. Greene and followed Van Alen across the catwalk and down the iron steps. He moved glacially, shaking more the closer he got to the floor. I decided it was best to make my pitch quickly, in case he fell.

"What if I find the people who started the trouble?" I said.

"The Byrds are long gone, and the Westside's silver along with them," he said.

"Bully has no papers, and the family won't leave without him. They're trapped in the Lower West. I can bring them to you. Return the silver. Show the people—show Roebling—that you can still live up to your reputation."

"Mr. Van Alen's decision is final," said Ida Greene.

Van Alen reached the floor. He banged his hand on the nearest still and savored the clang.

"No decision is ever final," he said. "But why bother? Why fight for the Lower West? Every honest citizen of this district will find a home, heat, and food above the Borderline."

"And the dishonest?" I said. "The sick, old, drunk, mad, bizarre, useless? This is their home. It's my home, too."

"What's the soonest you can have everything shut down?" he said to Mrs. Greene.

"Tomorrow night."

"So we don't lose anything by giving her a day and a half. Perhaps I've been hasty. Perhaps a district that produces women this obstinate has some worth, after all."

Mrs. Greene opened the side door and we shielded our eyes against the sun. Van Alen cinched his scarf around his neck. In his greatcoat, he looked almost as big as he had a year before, but the skinny legs that stuck out from its hem gave him away.

"Before I start looking," I said, "I need one more favor."

"You always need one more favor," said Mrs. Greene.

"Let me use your tunnel to the Eastside, and I'll have the Byrds for you before Roebling makes his move."

"But you said yourself—the Byrds are on the Lower West," said Van Alen.

"Before I find them, I have to find Mary Fall."

"Fine," said Mrs. Greene. An unaccustomed thoughtfulness settled over Van Alen's brow.

"But that was your mother's name," he said.

"Was it now?" I said. "Say—do you recall how my parents met?"

"Of course," he said, and I felt the ground melt beneath my feet. "She was slumming in the Tenderloin. It was love at first sight."

"But how did he win her hand?"

"The hell should I know? I'm not one for living in the past."

He was smarter than he looked. Without another word, I turned my back on the old man and his fading empire and headed east.

On the Westside, no one bothered tracking the days of the week, but on the Eastside it was Saturday, which meant the foot traffic flowed slower than Morton Creek. Thousands battled up and down Broadway, emptying wallets and filling bags with junk they wanted badly and needed not at all. I struggled south, doing my best not to scream with impatience, and finally reached the Waverly Place nickelodeon, where a black-and-white cardboard cutout of a cowboy-hatted Sally Feeney begged me to come inside. The barker was at his post.

"The season's finest motion picture, 'Sally Out West,' ma'am, and I've got one seat left for a girl with a nickel to spare."

"Not today," I said. "Not ever, in fact. I'm not here for Sally. I'm looking for somebody else."

The barker leaned in to speak softly, like one used to being questioned by the police. A gold-uniformed usher stood in the doorway, lovingly smoking a cigarette, and leaned close, trying to hear.

"Who?" he said.

"A woman in a black dress. Thick brown hair, blue eyes. Never been to the pictures before."

"I'll tell you what I know if you pay me the goddamned nickel."

Mary had emptied my wallet but neglected the change scattered across the bottom of my endless bag. I dropped a nickel in the box.

"Where did she go?" I said.

"Haven't seen her," he said with a shrug. "Thanks for the nickel."

I might have punched him in the mouth, but it didn't seem worth the time. Instead I revenged myself against poor, defenseless Sally Feeney—decapitating the cutout with a single punch. The barker howled, following me a few doors down the street, demanding I pay him back. He finally gave up. I was at the corner when the usher tapped me on the shoulder.

"The way he's been staring at that cutout, I think he was in love," he said. "You did him a favor."

"Happy to help."

"I saw the girl. I was the one that dragged her out."

"She caused trouble?"

"As soon as the picture rolled, she started screaming—laughing so loud nobody could hear the piano. She didn't quit. Just laughed, louder and louder and louder until there was nothing I could do but haul her out to the street. I've heard of women getting hysterical. Didn't know that was real."

"She's a relic. Where did she go?"

"She asked for a cheap drunk."

"What did you tell her?"

"Nothing. I took the pledge. Strictly teetotal since 1914, and happier for it. She your sister?"

"My mother. Thanks for the help."

I left him shaking his head at the madness of women and went sniffing for gin. I have always had a talent for finding the worst bars the city has to offer. Even since Prohibition crashed down on the Eastside, I can root out a blind tiger or third-rate speak lurking behind the most innocent facade. It's not just that I love liquor—although there are days and years that my god, I do—but that I have a physical horror of fine things and seek out trash like a divining rod.

I spotted speakeasies hidden within a pet shop, a city office, a Hungarian cafe, and a corner store, but this was Broadway, where a drink couldn't be had without brass, marble, and mirrored glass. If Mary wanted cheap, she would walk east.

I picked my way up Fourth Avenue, where the sidewalks were crowded not with shoppers but families, mostly German, who spilled out of the tenements and shuffled from corner to corner, walking to forget the cold. Here I found gin joints that barely bothered to hide their purpose, where men nearly as hopeless as those on the Westside drank warm liquor and picked at mold-spackled free lunches. I visited six or seven such places, burning through my meager supply of nickels and putting together a respectable afternoon buzz, and was running out of ideas when a bartender cut me off.

She was a young black woman with thick braids and thicker glasses. She looked skeptical when I entered—besides the ceramic behind the bar, I was the whitest thing there—and even the grace with which I knocked back my gin failed to impress her.

"You're not here to drink," she said. "You're looking for someone. Who?"

"My mother. She's out on a drunk, and I know she's gone somewhere low, and—"

"And there's no place lower than a Negro saloon?"

"That wasn't what I meant."

"It's what you said."

"Yes. Hell. I'm sorry."

She took back my glass, spit in it, and scrubbed.

"You want to know where white people go to feel sorry for themselves?" she said. "There's a place on Stuyvesant a few doors before you get to the church. Looks like a shuttered spaghetti restaurant, but it's as nasty a pit as you or your mother could want. Have fun, and the next time you want to go slumming, stay the hell away from here."

I left, my gut churning with gin and my neck sweaty with shame. I would have to remember to tell Cherub about it—he so loved it when whites leaned into their natural inclination to make fools of themselves—but then I remembered that Cherub and I would not be speaking anytime soon, and I felt worse than I had all day.

The place she'd sent me was designed for feeling bad. The front room of the restaurant once known as Caminiti's was barren—the windows opaque with grime, the bar and few remaining tables covered with filthy sheets—but there was a door to the back, and the faintest noise came from inside. I knocked, and it cracked open.

"A woman," said the man on the other side, whose voice was as smooth as kid. "Hunh."

"You don't get many?"

"Most know better. Not a cop?"

"Not a cop."

The door swung. He jerked me inside and shut it quick. The ceiling was low, the room crowded. A bar had been built on the back wall out of empty crates. The bartender wore a striped uniform and the number 67. A smoked glass panel decorated the side wall. I felt I had been here before.

"Doesn't matter if you are a cop, really," said the doorman, who had a ready smile and almost impossibly beautiful eyes, and whose rating was a perilously low 57. He held a rolled newspaper in his hand, as lightly as a conductor wielding his baton. "You do any police work and I'm obligated to break your neck."

"This is a Roebling place."

"Are you here to drink or ask questions? Because asking questions is almost as dangerous as being a cop."

"Just one. Has another woman been here this morning—a pretty young girl with blue eyes and a rotten attitude?"

"That bitch defaced my paper. She took it, ripped out a page, and gave it back."

"Let's see."

He handed it over, and I flipped until I found the ragged remains of page fourteen. I handed it back to him.

"You're leaving," he said. I nodded. "That's probably the right move."

I thanked him and left, feeling light and full of cheap gin. That, I think, is when they started to follow me.

At a newsstand on Ninth Street and Third, I tore a fresh *Sentinel* off the rack.

"Careful with the merch!" shouted the vendor.

"It's all right," I said. "I'm not buying it."

I ignored his grumbling until I found page fourteen and saw the half-page ad that filled its right side. A delicate line drawing showed a row of women with curlers in their hair, smiling through the pain.

"That modern look," it promised. "You will find at Sarah Ovington's Beauty Palace." There, I prayed, I would also find Mary Fall.

The Beauty Palace was a three-story monster on the west side of Lafayette, just a few blocks south of the old opera house. Its grand entryway stank of lavender. Clamshell wall sconces spit unidentifiable mist. A woman with perfectly placed gray streaks and a suit that looked like it had been steamed onto her body took me by the elbow and guided me up the stairs.

"I think we'll have to shave it," she said. "That will be a start."

"I'm not here for a haircut."

"No. You're here for triage. Miss Sarah will provide."

"It's not Miss Sarah I want. I'm looking for a woman, a woman with hair lighter than mine, nearly as curly, who—"

"Say no more. I know her. I tried to help her, I assure you. We all tried to talk her out of it. But I fear, ma'am . . . I fear it is too late."

She guided me through a maze of strange pastel compartments, each occupied by a hairdresser and client, where oppressive floral scents were undercut by the acrid tang of the flat iron. At the end of a long, pink hallway, a clutch of employees peeked around a monumental doorway ornate enough that it might have been pilfered from St. Patrick's.

My guide tapped the shoulder of the nearest employee: a lumpy man who cradled a pair of scissors in his meaty hands as gently as a running back holding a football. He shook his head.

"Miss Sarah herself took charge," he said. "She tried. But even gods can fail."

"Oh lord, how bad could it be?" I said, and pushed through the pack. I should not have doubted the experts. Miss Sarah—a gray-haired matron with a barrel chest and an expression of pure fatigue—slumped in the corner, unable to look at what she had done. In a high, plush chair at the center of that sanctum sanctorum, my mother held a mirror and smiled at her new hair.

"That modern look," she said.

Her hair was my hair, so I knew how uncooperative it was, yet somehow they had applied enough steam and fire to iron it flat. They had hacked off a foot or more, and done their best to shape the rest into something that resembled a coiffure.

"What is it?" I said.

"The handbook would call it a bob," said the woman who led me there. "But I call it a war crime."

"I think it's rather nice," said Mary. "What do you think, Miss Carr?"

I simply did not know what to say.

Mary floated down the steps of Miss Ovington's esteemed institution, and when we reached the sidewalk she was so preoccupied with her reflection that she didn't notice how angry I was.

"Did you have a pleasant morning?" I said.

"Simply lovely. Once you get across the fence, 1922 is an altogether marvelous place."

I might have slammed her against a wall and explained the hell I endured to find her, but what was the point? If she hadn't learned manners by twenty, I couldn't teach them to her now.

"We're going back to the Westside," I said.

"Why? I'd much rather take in another motion picture. Have you ever seen one? They're a scream."

"For one, the money you stole from me won't last forever. For another, we have to find the Byrds. We have to get you home."

"You have to stop expecting me to listen to you. You're not my mother."

"No. I'm your victim. And I won't stand having you in my city for a minute longer than I must."

"Oh, pishposh. You've spent too long over there. You've gone snow-blind. There is a bright, wide, wonderful world right here, and you can't even see the lights."

"And your revenge on Bully Byrd?"

She stopped petting her hair long enough to look me in the eye. The haircut made her look thinner, almost starved.

"Oh, I'm going to find him," she said, "and I will give him what he deserves. But you're never going to get ahold of the Byrds by romping around the ice. We need a plan, and that's something you're dreadful at."

"And yours worked so well?"

"I enjoyed it."

"Fine. What's the plan?"

"First, I cut my hair. A disguise, and quite a becoming one, too. This should keep me safe from the Westside mob."

"Next?"

"If you want to find someone, Miss Carr, the first thing you need is their address."

"The Byrds live on Carmine Street, just past the Electric Church. They couldn't be foolish enough to hide there."

"Obviously. That's why we'll be looking wherever they lived before."

Beneath Lafayette Street, the IRT thundered south. The car was packed. The stench of sweat under winter coats, the clattering of the train, the gin in my stomach . . . If I had to vomit, I wondered, would I be able to part the throng and hurl the window open in time? Or would I simply make a mess across the people lucky enough to have found a spot on the rattan seats?

Mary was not concerned with such things. She hung on to the strap, her knees loose, rocking with every motion, squealing as we screamed around each corner.

"Good lord!" she cried. "With something like this in your city, why do you ever do anything else?"

I thought of the last time I'd endured the dark of a subway tunnel, walking north along a dead third rail in search of a cruel woman's corpse. It was not for me.

"It's not what I thought the future would be," she said, between squeals.

"What were you imagining?"

"I don't think I was imagining it at all. I lived in a city of gaudy lights and thick crowds. Or at least I thought I did—next to your Eastside, the New York of yesterday is as tame as an old house cat. I didn't think there could be so much color in the world."

She'd taken her gloves off to ride the train. I saw the spot on her finger where her engagement ring had been.

"You never told me what the ring looked like," I said.

"The stone was emerald green—not real emerald, of course, just colored glass, but emerald is my birthstone and this was close enough. The band was decorated with daisies. Awfully cheap, but as sweet as the man who bought it."

"Doesn't it hurt?"

"Doesn't what hurt?"

"Tom."

The subway bounced around another turn, and Mary's smile grew brighter.

"Mother taught us to push through black moods by standing up, dusting off, and pushing on. Tom's death has affected more than I care to share with you, but that's no reason to falter."

"That seems an unhealthy way to live."

"Maybe so. But it's a marvelous way to survive."

She swung on her strap, admiring the mustard yellows and mud browns of a cigarette advertisement. The passenger beneath her glanced up, then returned to his *Police Gazette*. For a moment, I was certain he was the man who had tried to kill us in Washington Square, or Storrs Roebling's private gunman.

But no. It was just another man with fat, flat eyes, unmoved by the engravings of obscene horror and lust that filled his newspaper. Could it be another of Roebling's Gray Boys? Or had the men of the city simply started to look the same?

Spotting him helped nothing. Like cockroaches in an apartment wall, there were thousands of them, all ready to sweep across the floor the instant I turned my back.

New York housed its records in an overwrought pile on Chambers Street, a building whose atrium was wrapped in Egyptian mosaics and lined with marble that glowed, gold and silent, like the nave of a Byzantine church. The staircases of that marvelous room swept toward the heavens, but the sleepy-eyed man at the front desk informed us that for the Westside we would need to head in the other direction.

In a cavern far beneath the main hall, we found a mess of overturned boxes and spilled files. I wanted to keep Mary close, but there was simply too much ground to cover, so when she suggested we divide our efforts I let her go.

I passed an hour digging through trash. I opened boxes of insurance claims, dogcatchers' time sheets, geological surveys, accounts of the digging of the subway tunnels, and lists of the employees of Trinity Church. I found myself in a vein of reports filed by social workers, twenty or thirty years prior, documenting in perfect schoolhouse cursive the horrid living conditions on the old Westside. No matter how far I ranged from where I started, I found more sick children, hungry children, children who died before I was born.

Once I had worked my way so far into the mire that I could no longer see the entrance, I kicked a filing cabinet and cursed as loud as I could. Its rotten wood cracked in half, and out tumbled city directories from the 1880s and '90s. I dug through the morass until I found what I wanted: 1888. Its pages were water-rotted, falling apart completely after the *E*'s, but I did not need to go that far. There were the Byrds as they had been on the first day of a lost year: Bulrush, Helen, Enoch, Abner, Judy, Ruth, and baby Barney, all living happily in a two-bedroom tenement apartment on 111 Spring, just west of Mercer, deep in the heart of the Thicket. Less than a mile from where I was standing, but a lifetime or more away.

"Miss Fall!" I shouted. "I found it."

There was no answer, save for three footsteps that sounded at the far end of the immense room—three footsteps that echoed and died. I walked toward them, the sheet torn from the directory clutched in my hand, as soft as an old man's skin.

"Mary?" I said.

I walked a narrow path between two piles of refuse and stopped at the first intersection, not sure where I'd come from or where I was going. I heard more footsteps, closer now, heavier than my mother's had ever been. I turned away, beginning to think about running.

Mary was right behind me.

"I called for you," I said.

"I didn't hear."

I led her out, feeling a powerful urge to sprint but holding it back for fear of—of what, precisely? Of looking foolish? Of seeming scared in front of a woman who appeared to fear nothing in this world or any other? How many people, I wondered, died from vanity each year?

When we reached the atrium, I realized I'd been holding my breath. My heart was racing, my forehead cold with drying sweat. If Mary noticed, she didn't mention it. She looked sick herself, her light dimmer than it had been before. Perhaps the haircut was catching up with her.

"I found the address," I said.

"I found more."

She handed me a faded red folder emblazoned with the seal

of the NYPD. Inside were a few sheets of paper in a sickeningly familiar hand.

"What is it?" I said.

"The city's investigation into the fire at the Electric Church. At the base of the walls, spaced evenly around the first floor, the investigator found drill holes just large enough for a slow fuse. A fine piece of detective work, especially considering he was forced to do without my help."

The verdict was written on the first page in block letters two inches high. Arson. No doubt. The report was signed with the illegible signature of Virgil Carr. Mary dropped it into my bag.

"Closing up now, ladies," said the man at the front desk.

We were nearly out the door when a voice called from the stairs: "You got one more!" The watchman turned around, his keys dangling from his fist, and waited for the straggler to cross the wide, immaculate hall. It was another gray man.

"Thanks," he said, pushing past us without even meeting my eye. But when we left, he watched us from across the street, and I knew he was not the only one.

FOURTEEN

Night in the Thicket was louder than it should have been. Unseen creatures crunched across snow and needles. Owls chanted unanswerable questions into the dark. We'd entered at Spring Street, through a gate in the fence whose hinges were rusted and whose keeper was half-mad with boredom. The asphalt melted into dirt; the storefronts vanished, and we were left on a faint path that wound into the trees. We did our best to walk west.

"I didn't see anyone come in behind us," I said. "But I've hardly seen these men all day. That doesn't mean they aren't there."

Mary was silent.

"Stick to me and keep your eyes open. I can't have you running off again."

Her silence persisted. It was the longest she'd gone without speaking since she exploded into my life. I was surprised to find it more grating than her chatter.

"What is it?" I said.

"Pardon?"

"You've had a hangdog look ever since we stepped out of the Hall of Records."

"I thought you'd prefer it. Earlier, you were so irritated at my good cheer."

We walked on, saying nothing, and the din of the woods grew louder and louder until I couldn't help but scream to keep it quiet.

"Goddamn it, what is bothering you?"

She stopped and laughed—not her normal laugh, which was as cool and clear as a creek in spring, but something cynical, alien.

"I'm so glad you're finally showing interest in how I feel," she said. "But it's too late."

"Why?"

"June 7, 1903."

"Should that date mean something to me?" I said, no longer able to look her in the eye.

"I shouldn't have gone looking for it, but I'm a curious woman. I suppose you know how troublesome that can be. While I was searching for the records of the fire, I found my death certificate, too."

"Oh."

"Funny that they call it a certificate. Like you've won a prize. I was thirty-six."

"I'm sorry."

"That's not enough time."

"No. No it's not."

She brushed her hands and clapped them together and tried to pull on that old, cheerful look. It didn't quite fit, but I acted like it fooled me and tried to match her smile.

"We're still on Spring Street?" she said.

"Near as I can guess."

"Well . . . quick quick."

We tried to hew to the remains of Spring, but the path wound and split impossibly. After we had wandered for some time, we saw the facade of an old apartment house, the worn brick wall swaying slightly against the wind. Somehow, the glass in the door was not only unbroken but spotless. Gold paint shone through the dark: "103 Spring."

"We're on the right side of the street," she said.

Ahead was a clearing, and beyond was another fragmentary building. We tried to walk toward it, keeping 103 fixed at our backs, our eyes always on the building up ahead. We were so fixated on it that we forgot to watch the darkness.

We did not notice the man step out of the night.

Here was another who might have been our archer, but who wasn't quite. He wore a long black coat and a slack expression, and he held a gleaming switchblade in each hand.

"From Mr. Roebling," he said, as he swung both knives at my throat.

I reared back and kicked him in the knee, knocking us both far enough off balance that his blow sailed wide.

"Run!" I shouted.

Mary obliged and I followed, sprinting away from the road, into the trees, running until my burning lungs expelled the frost. I fell to my knees—I didn't want to, but it happened anyway—and when I'd finished hacking I looked up and realized Mary was not there.

Far away, I heard a man scream. It was the desperate, choking cry of an animal caught in a trap, who feels hope bleeding out into the snow. I found my way back to the clearing. Our would-be killer was on the ground, one knife in his hand and the other stuck in his side. Mary stood over him, screaming, her face purple.

"I told you to stay back," she said. "I told you!"

He got a grip on a tree and started pulling up. Mary yanked out the knife. Red mist filled the air. She flipped the knife around so that the blade was pointed at his throat. I pulled her away.

"Don't," I said. "It won't help anything, and it will ruin your life. Trust me."

"We have to make them stop."

"But this won't do that. They'll send another one, and another one, and another."

"She's right," said the man, standing unassisted now, his left hand pressing against the wound, his fingers scrambling like he was trying to gather the blood back into his body. "I don't matter. But the company wants you dead."

"Why?" I said.

He shrugged, and Mary lunged at him. I tried to haul her back, but my fingers were numb and her arm was bloody, and I could not hold on. Mary raised her knife. The killer crouched, his blade pointed up, ready to catch Mary in the gut. I wanted to stop her, but they were a step too far away.

Then something fell from the sky—something orange, heavy, and hard enough that when it connected with the man's head, his neck snapped back and his body slumped into the snow. It's possible he was still alive.

"Oh," said Mary. "How odd."

She picked up the missile.

"What is it?" I said.

"A Bible," she answered, and Judy Byrd descended from the heavens.

She floated down from the trees above and landed as softly as a snowflake, her broom in hand.

"Thank you," said Mary. Or that's what she started to say, anyway. Before she could finish, Judy cracked her across the face and dropped a harness over her head.

"You killed my sister," she said.

I shook out of my shock and reached for Mary, grabbing her wrist tight. It wasn't tight enough. Judy snapped, and they were both yanked into the air, hauled by ropes that stretched down from someplace unseen. Mary's wrist snatched out of my hands. Her switchblade slipped from her grip and stabbed into the snow. I looked up and saw Mary and Judy disappear into the pines.

Up there, farther than I cared to contemplate, I saw lights. I took Mary's knife, wrenched the other from the broken man, and started to climb.

I slammed one knife into the wood, pulled myself up, and slammed the other in above it. Over and over I did that, dragging my aching body into the dark, thankful that in moments of panic, I tend to forget I am afraid of heights. It was agony from the first foot, but I kept on, never looking down, because I could not let that woman die.

It may have been the hardest thing I've ever done. It was certainly the most tedious. But every time my body howled at me to quit, I remembered that Portuguese woman at Mrs. Greene's, and I knew this was nothing.

I was halfway up when my hands began to slip. My palms were sweating, and even through my gloves it was impossible to maintain my grip. I wanted to let go, just with one hand, just for a moment, to dry my palm on my dress, but even a moment's pause would mean death for Mary, me, or both.

It was then that the piano gave me strength.

The music trickled out, soft and sentimental, through the frozen trees. It was a hymn, maybe, or the kind of love song that made people cry thirty or forty years before. It reminded me how polite the Byrds were, genteel in their poverty, respectable even when monstrous. It reminded me how much I hated them, and that let me finish the climb.

Stretched between six stout pines, I saw flickering light and the silhouette of what looked like a kind of platform. I dragged myself over its lip and collapsed on the floor. I tasted metal in my mouth and felt tile beneath my cheek. A raven screeched in my ear.

I opened my eyes and saw a toilet. A black-and-white checkerboard spread out, bleeding into the pines like the bathroom was just so much bark. A window hung from a higher branch, suspended where a wall used to be. I looked through it into the night. There was no sign of the stem, or the Eastside, or home. There was no light but the moon, nothing out there but pines, all the way down to the ground.

There was only one wall in my little hideaway. It held the bathroom door, on which little grooves had been cut, long ago, showing how tall the Byrd children were getting. The wall hid me from the rest of the apartment. From its far side came the chattering of the Byrds.

"We tie her up, we take her to the police," said Judy.

"I don't know," said Enoch. "Mam wants her dead."

"I'm not fond of either idea," said Mary.

"You don't get a vote," Judy snapped. "This family has committed enough crimes this week. We're not adding murder."

"Father will know what to do," said Enoch. "When he's finished praying—"

From farther up, a scream. It did not sound whole. I imagined it was Ruth. I hadn't expected her to still be alive. I doubted she would be for long.

A door opened. Someone, I supposed it was Helen, entered the room.

"She has an hour," she said. "Maybe less."

"Have faith," said Enoch.

"Shut up. What are we doing with this one?"

"In the morning we take her across the fence and have her arrested for attempted murder," said Judy.

"That's a fine idea. Here's a better one. I'll break her neck and let Ruth watch. Perhaps that will give my baby strength," Helen replied.

It was as good a cue as I was going to get. I opened the door and stepped into a candlelit parlor that wouldn't have been out of place in Mary's time. Samplers illustrated scenes from the Orient, and every surface was covered with a knickknack or doily. The walls were absent, save the windows, from which heavy velvet curtains dangled into space. In the corner of the room rose a flight of un-railed stairs.

Mary sat in an overstuffed chair, with Judy's hand pressing her back into the upholstery. Enoch was at the piano. Past him, another door led to a room I could not see. Helen was by the stairs. There was quite a lot of blood on her dress.

"You damned detectives are as stubborn as lice," she said. "I'd ask how you wormed your way into my bathroom but I don't particularly care. We're going to kill your cousin. Shall we kill you, too?"

"You're not going to kill her," I said.

"For once, I agree with Miss Carr," said Mary, unhelpful as ever.

"Why shouldn't I?" said Helen. "It's my house."

"If you kill her, I won't tell you the truth about Bully."

"There's never been an ounce of truth to that man. I've known that thirty years and more."

I walked around the edge of the room, straying as close to the lip as I dared, straightening gewgaws, hoping I was casual enough that they couldn't see me putting myself between Mary and Helen.

"Of course you know it," I said. "That's why even when he came back, even when his miracle came true, you made him sleep in an unheated office with nothing but cheap gin to keep him warm. You hated him, and you had good reason to, and I can prove that he's always been as bad as you think."

"My father's a saint," said Enoch.

"Nobody's father is a saint. They're all scum, of one kind or another. But your daddy is the worst."

"What do you mean?" said Judy.

"He takes advantage of weak people's faith. He's been doing that his whole life—first to the rooks of the Westside, and then to his own family. Where is he, anyway?"

Enoch pointed at the door on the far side of the room.

"Praying," he said.

"Or sleeping off a drunk," said Helen.

"How many of you really thought he came back from the dead?" I said. "Let's see a show of hands."

"He *did* come back," said Judy.

"He came back, certainly, but not from death. He stepped through a hole in time—that he cut, that somebody else cut for him—and landed here. Luckiest break he ever had, because he was on the run."

"From what?" said Helen—another perfect cue. From my bag, which I knew I'd lugged up that tree for a reason, I pulled the file Mary had found in the Hall of Records. I threw it on the coffee table.

"From that. Ironclad proof, straight out of the city vaults, that Bully lit the fire in the Electric Church, that it was always supposed to get out of hand, that it burned just like he wanted. The investigator's theory is that he planned to fake his own death or make a fast grab for the insurance money. He didn't know about the children in the basement."

"I'm fully aware of the city's opinion," said Helen. "It's that awful file that ensured I didn't collect a cent of the insurance money that was rightfully ours. Not for the church, and not for my husband's life."

"And nothing for Barney," said Judy, staring at the file like she was waiting for a grenade to explode. "Why didn't you tell us?"

"Because it's a lie! Cooked up by the insurance men, bolstered by the city, to save them having to pay. Why would I tell my children something as ugly as that?"

"Because you knew it was true," said Mary.

"Bully was rotten from the day you met," I said, "but he was a handy way to make a buck. He didn't ask you about the fire. He just did it, and when it went wrong, he ran away with every penny you had."

"It's a fake," said Enoch.

"Why not take a look," said Mary, "and make up your own mind?"

"I did. A long time ago. I was *in* the basement when that fire started. I smelled the smoke, choked on it. I was about to give up when my father stormed down those stairs and got us out. He saved my life, and he would have saved Barney's, too."

Judy leaned on the window, which swayed under her weight. She stared out at the snow-covered branches that twisted out into the dark. She said, to no one in particular: "He didn't kill himself. He wasn't called up to heaven."

"He ran as far as he could go," said Mary.

"He ran here."

Helen jerked Mary out of her chair and pulled her close. She wasn't threatening her, not quite, but they were awfully close to the drop.

"What does that do for my daughter?" said Helen. "What does it do for Ruth?"

"Nothing," said Mary, like she wished she knew how to say sorry. I approached Helen, slowly, lest I startle her, and inched Mary away from the ledge.

"What happened to Ruth wasn't Mary's fault," I said. "It was Bully's . . . and it was mine."

Helen pulled, harder than I thought possible, wrenching Mary away from me. Mary stumbled, tripping on a bit of frayed carpet, but Helen did not let Mary fall. Stretching her arm out straight, Helen held Mary right against the edge of that impossible room.

"Prove it," Helen said. "Prove it beyond doubt, or this one dies."

"She can't prove it," said Enoch, smashing something porcelain against the floor, "because it isn't true."

"Miss Carr," said Mary, "perhaps the time for rhetoric has passed."

I walked up to Helen, and she squeezed Mary tighter. I walked right past them, right to the door to Bully's room. It was locked. I kicked it open. It was empty.

"Here's your proof," I said. "Bully is gone."

Helen hurled Mary into one of the armchairs and pushed past me to confirm what she'd already known was true. She looked around the room.

"And the silver, too," she said.

"Where the hell did he go?" said Judy.

"Nowhere," said Enoch. He rushed into the empty room to search every barren corner. "He can't have left again."

I felt sorry for Enoch, who wanted his daddy as much as he wanted the miracle. But the latter didn't exist, and on the Westside, the former was just as hard to hang on to.

There was another scream from upstairs. It didn't seem to touch them. Helen circled the empty bedroom, flipping stray bits of furniture over the edge into the dark. Judy entered the bedroom and inspected the harnesses and winch she'd used to spirit Mary into the sky. One harness was missing. She wrapped the other around her waist and called her mother back.

"Lower me, Mam, and don't be shy about it," she said. "That

bastard. The minute he staggered into the church, I knew, I knew, I knew."

Enoch sobbed softly. Another howl from upstairs. Helen nodded to Judy, who stepped backward into space. The winch spun and caught, and Helen slowly lowered her down. A third scream from upstairs, rough and bloody.

"I can't take that," said Mary.

"Me either," I said, but there were things I had to know before Ruth died. On leaden feet, we mounted the stairs. They seemed to float between the trees. At the top, nestled against a smooth white pine, a doorway opened onto what might have been called a bedroom, but which was really just a platform, where a cast-iron bed sat by a burning lantern, raked by ceaseless wind. It looked a lonely place to die.

I sat in a hard chair at the head of the bed, pulling it as far as possible from the edge. It was quiet enough that I could hear my heart pounding and feel the cold sweat on my palms. I wasn't sure if it was vertigo or fear of the woman buried under the heap of wool blankets.

Her right hand was exposed, and her face, too. They'd cleaned most of the blood and found a way to slow the bleeding, but her neck and dress were streaked with dried gore. Her face was loosely bandaged in a torn muslin gown that was soaked through with crimson and needed changing soon. It showed part of her mangled jaw, where her ragged, burnt lips framed what remained of her mouth.

Her eyes were open, and she must have recognized me, because she peered over the bandages with as much hate as I had ever seen.

"Ruth," I said. I meant to apologize, somehow, to say that even though I thought her crooked I'd never meant for her to come to this kind of harm, but before I could say anything, she groaned, as deep and rough as an iron door sliding over stone. No apology could touch that pain. There were heavy steps on the stairs. I looked down and saw Enoch bounding up from the room below. Mary locked the door and pressed herself against it.

"Did you bring your father back?" I said. She shook her head, barely, side to side. "Who did?" She shook her head again.

"Hurry up," said Mary.

"That's my sister in there!" shouted Enoch. "You can't keep us out."

He banged hard enough to shake the trees. Blood pooled on Ruth's neck. She squirmed under the quilts.

"Hot," she said. "Hot."

The talking shook her bandages loose and started the bleeding anew. I peeled off quilt after quilt until she was exposed to the air, her bloodied dress clinging to her clammy skin, her sweat starting to freeze. She breathed a little easier as the cold embraced her, and she croaked something that might have been thanks.

I touched her forehead, expecting it to scorch my hand, but her skin was cold and getting colder. Her fingers dug into the sheets; her mouth twisted, and the last of the bandages fell away. She groaned again, as fiercely as the women laboring in Mrs. Greene's birthing center, but without the hope.

"Goddamn it, Gilda," shouted Enoch. The door started to splinter. "Mam!"

Ruth gurgled, then spit out the blood streaming into her mouth and grunted some kind of sound. She said it again.

It sounded like, "Róisín."

"Did you take the finger?" I said. She swayed her head. "Who did?"

The door burst open, knocking Mary to the ground. Enoch came halfway through and stopped, frozen and pale. Helen was a few steps behind him, hurtling up the stairs. They hung there, fixed in space like the steps that dangled from the trees, and paused for a long moment before Ruth finished her final sermon.

"Him," she said.

Helen slammed me out of the way. I hit the floor hard but did not feel it. She dragged the blankets back onto her daughter. She knelt at her side and tried to kiss the life back into her face, but Ruth was gone.

I thought Helen was going to explode. She did not. She straightened the blankets, tucking them down tight on the side of the bed, then dabbed some of the blood away from Ruth's mouth. She took her place in the chair and held her daughter's hand.

"Mrs. Byrd," said Mary, but there were no words after that. I took Mary's hand and led her back to the stairs.

"Not now," I said. "Not ever."

We found Enoch in the downstairs bedroom, fumbling with the winch, trying to get one of the harnesses back up so that he could escape us, too. We dragged him back into the parlor. I slammed him into the hardest chair.

"Where's the finger?" I said.

"I don't know," he said. "That's why we hired you."

From the coffee table, Mary picked up a handsomely printed Enoch Byrd Bible. I didn't think much of it. I was focused on Enoch—sweet, honest Enoch—wondering how someone so gentle could lie.

I took the NYPD report off the table.

"You were how old when this happened?" I said.

"Ten."

"When your father disappeared, where did you think he went?"

"Mam said he'd been called back to heaven. I wasn't stupid. I'd seen his eyes when he realized he couldn't go back for Barney, and I wasn't surprised when he chose to die."

"Only now you know that he didn't die. He came here."

"That's not possible."

"And resurrection is?"

"Why shouldn't it be?" he said, almost shouting. He pushed his hand through his hair, trying to smooth back some of the strands that his passion had sprung free. "We've built airships to cross oceans, machines to talk to people on the other side of the globe, telescopes to stare into the deepest reaches of space. Why can't we conquer death?"

"You sound like you've been asking yourself that for a long time."

From the pocket of his jacket he pulled a yellow notebook whose front cover was peeling apart. He tossed it onto the table.

"My inheritance," he said. "Every sermon my pap ever wrote. Not a word in there that isn't a lie—until you get to the last page."

The book's spine was cracked such that it opened right to Bully's final testimony—a few lines of pure gibberish, followed by a recipe for blue fire.

"Why do you say this is true?" I said.

"Because it's Latin. It's real. Bully preached in English—the common tongue. If he needed some Latin, he made it up."

"So that means it can raise the dead?"

Enoch shrugged.

"Did you ever try it?" I said.

"Hundreds of times. I mixed the blue powder. I burned it over a cedar fire. I said the words, every way I could think."

"And it doesn't work."

"I couldn't get it there. I was too weak."

The Bible cracked shut, loud as a bull whip, and Mary dropped it on the table. "Second Kings, chapter thirteen, verse twenty-one!" she shouted. "He's lying, Gilda. He took the finger. The Bible says so."

"What are you talking about?" I said.

"I knew it. Sure as I know that this bob makes me look stupendous, I knew I'd heard this story before."

"Don't you dare use that book against me," said Enoch. "I printed it myself."

"And a very fine job you did, too, but that doesn't change Second Kings: 'And it came to pass, as they were burying a man, that, behold, they spied a band of men; and they cast the man into the sepulchre of Elisha: and when the man was let down, and touched the bones of Elisha, he revived, and stood up on his feet.'"

"The bones of Elisha," I said.

"Or failing him, a saint. Just the thing to put a little kick in Enoch Byrd's patented resurrection powder."

"You stole it. You ground it into dust. Am I wrong?"

"No," he whispered. From his pocket he took a little snuffbox monogrammed *E. B.* He opened it, and I saw blue powder flecked with gray.

"You went to the old church," I said. "You performed the ceremony. No one in your family knew what you were doing."

"I didn't think it was going to work. It never had before. I felt so guilty, I didn't even put any feeling into the words, but as soon as that powder hit the cedar—"

"A turquoise gate opened in the threshold," said Mary.

"How did you know?"

"I'm a woman. I know all sorts of things. Bully came through the gate, followed hot on his heels by the most handsome, doomed man the fire department ever spit out. What happened next?"

"I don't know."

"Did Bully kill Tom?"

"I swear to you—"

"Did you kill him?"

"No!"

"Then what happened?"

She held the arms of his chair in her hands, looking ready to fling him into the night. I steadied her. She shook me off.

"I never saw anybody come out of that gate," he said. He guided my hand to the back of his skull, where I found a lump like a chunk of coal. "Whoever killed your friend knocked me out first. I woke an hour later. It took three days for the headache to subside. I didn't see him till everyone else did, when he showed up at the church."

"So you thought you'd brought him back from death?" I said.

"And for a day or two, I felt the relief that comes from feeling like your life hasn't been a waste, after all."

He lifted his head and stared up with wet, red eyes. If he wanted sympathy, I was past giving it.

"What was the plan for the resurrection ceremony?" I said.

"Get the silver, perform the rite, and get the hell out of there before the crowd saw that it wasn't going to work."

"It was Bully's plan?"

"And Ruth's. They built a trapdoor in the stage. I didn't like it—"

"But you went along with it."

"He was my father. What else was I supposed to do?"

"Did Bully disappoint you?"

"In what way?"

"The greed. The lying. The truth. Did it break your heart? Or were you just happy to have him home?"

"Yes. Both of those things, all at once."

There was no point telling him, but I understood.

A boot crunched on a branch overhead, sending a little flurry down onto the carpet. A Gladstone bag dropped from the tree, thudding onto the floor, and was followed by Bully Byrd, his hair wild, his hat missing, his collar no longer spotlessly white. He landed easily, strode across the floor, and placed his hand on Enoch's shoulder.

"That was a lovely story," he said, "and before you girls waste any more time arguing, I'll confirm it's true."

"Then you killed Tom," said Mary.

"I didn't, but I know you don't believe me and I don't particularly care. I've never been much for murder."

"Just arson," I said. "Let the fire do your killing for you." His smile dulled.

"That was an accident."

"Tell that to Barney. Or Ruth, for that matter. You are really hell on this family, you know that?"

"I love my children, and that's the most any man can do."

"Quit your lies," said Enoch, not looking his young father in the eye. Bully knelt before him and took his hands.

"Please, son," said Bully. "You think I don't love you? I remember the minute you were born. I can still feel the weight of you on my chest, the touch of those little fists, the look of those midnight blue eyes. I feel like it happened this morning. How could I ever stop loving that sweet little boy?"

Bully hugged Enoch, and for just a moment, Enoch's face relaxed. Then Bully jerked away, the snuffbox in his hand. I reached to snatch it, but he was quicker than me. He pulled back, and I lost my balance, falling over the table just in time to see him grab the yellow notebook, throw his Gladstone over his shoulder, and start for the winch. Helen was waiting for him, though, her face like a corpse frozen in ash.

"Stop," she said. "You've hurt us enough."

Bully didn't answer, and he didn't break stride. He threw the Gladstone bag right at her chest. The weight of that silver knocked her backward, just half a step.

And then she was in midair.

And then she was gone.

FIFTEEN

Bully leapt for the line that led to Judy's harness. He slid down in an instant. The moon was gone and the night was dark, and I did not see where Bully had gone. I was steeling myself for the jump when Enoch grabbed my shoulder and said, "We're taking the stairs."

They led down to a broad branch that stretched across the void into a half-ruined building. After just a moment's deference to my terror, I raced across it, trusting the luck of idiots to carry me over the span.

When my feet hit hard, sensible tile, I allowed myself a breath for the first time in an hour or more. Mary and Enoch touched down beside me. Mary clapped a hand on my shoulder hard enough to make me flinch.

"I had no idea you could move so fast," she said, panting.

"Where did he go?" said Enoch.

"The church," I said. "It could only be the church."

"Follow me," he said. "I can find the way."

He ran to the far side of the empty building. The floors were inconsistent—in some places solid tile, in others wood, in others open entirely to show the branches below. A match revealed flickering, dancing shapes that on closer inspection turned out to be dressmaker's models, padded flesh rotted away to expose their bent steel bones. Ever a gentleman, Enoch held open the fire door and we passed into the stairwell, which wound around a pair of skinny pines.

After a long walk down, we found ourselves on solid ground. I could have kissed the snow. The shadowy landscape of trees and brick was alien to Mary and me, but Enoch hadn't lied—he knew the path. He led us down one twisting street overrun with spindly little pines and up an alleyway formed in the gaps between two fallen buildings. We ran hard enough to drive the breath from our lungs. At the end of the path was a clearing, and through the clearing burned a fire.

Bully stood before the stone arch of his ruined church, his shadow fifty feet tall on the trees across the street, holding the notebook and screaming in Latin. His other hand held a fistful of blue powder, flecked with the dust of the saint's bones, ready to hurl it into the flames.

He was too enchanted by the sound of his own voice to hear us approach. Just as his speech climaxed, I tried to grab the notebook out of his hand. He spun away with a jackal's grin and hurled the powder into the flames.

I felt the explosion before I heard it. The force knocked me onto my back, crushing the wind from my chest and leaving me blinded.

Blue flames snaked along the frozen ground, split, and raced up the archway. The fire burned up, sideways, and down, filling the doorway with an irresistible turquoise glow. When the flames were at their highest, Bully leapt through headfirst. Enoch went after him. They did not emerge from the other side.

I prepared to jump, but Mary hung back. I looked at her. She shook her head.

I crossed the ground between us in one long stride. I took her by the hand.

"I can't go back," she said. "I'll die there."

"I know," I said, and pulled us in.

The light was brighter than any I'd ever known. Even when I shut my eyes, it burned through the lids. For a long time, I felt nothing, heard nothing, but then my legs collapsed, and I knew I was falling to the earth. I opened my eyes and still could not see—there was only the afterimage of that awful turquoise—but I heard someone moving in the grass.

I twisted, crawled backward, and blinked furiously until my eyes cleared. At last I could see just well enough to recognize Mary, gaslight shadows dancing over an expression of purest rage, in the instant before her palm cracked across my cheek, stopping my reverie and sending vibrations through my head like my skull was a gong.

I vomited horribly, each convulsion sending arcs of pain shooting through my poor, tortured brow, and was not quite finished when Mary pulled me to my feet and slapped me again.

"Why?" she said, and threw me down. "*Why?*"

I rubbed my eyes and was trying not to retch when I decided there was really no point in being modest. When my stomach had at last stopped spasming, I looked up and saw the Electric Church, freshly ruined. Bully was gone, and Enoch, too, vanished into a city that seemed neither fully dark nor fully light. We were on a deserted side street, where two neat brown rows of town houses ran down immaculate sidewalks, presenting a picture of such perfect symmetry that it made me reel. Faint yellow flickered from the occasional streetlights, as soft as butter. As my eyes adjusted, I realized I no longer felt cold. The numbness in my hands, the shooting pains in my feet, all the other symptoms of near frostbite that had kept me company since the death of autumn were suddenly gone.

"Where's the snow?" I said. "How did they clear all the snow?"

"Don't make me hit you again. I'm afraid I'm starting to enjoy it."

I raised a hand. She did not pull me up, so I managed to get up on my own. I swayed against a light post, pressing my face on the cool iron, hoping that would make the world stand still.

Mary intruded on my vision. Her skin looked like chalk, her hair was a mess, and little deltas of sweat pooled around her eyes. She still looked stronger than me.

"Don't you care if I die?" she said.

"You died a long time ago."

"No more past tense. We're in my time now, and I'll be dead in fifteen years if I don't get back out. Why did you pull me through?"

"Because I need you here."

"You haven't needed me for an instant. All you've done since I hired you is insult me, patronize me, and try to push me out of the way."

"No. All I've done is absorb your abuse. I've been trying to *protect* you."

"Then you should have left me behind." She grabbed me by the shoulder. It was more than I could bear. "What is it you're not telling me, Miss Carr? Why have you been so intent on frustrating my every step? Why did you drag me here to die?"

"Because you're my mother."

She let me go. She stepped back and looked me over, like a sculptor trying to decide whether to keep his latest work or throw it in the bin. She had heard the truth at last, and she answered from the heart.

"But you're so old."

I started walking, not sure where I was going, certain I didn't care. I just couldn't stand to look at that perfect, youthful face for another moment. She ran after, jabbering.

"It's not your age, Miss Carr—"

"My name is Gilda, just call me Gilda—"

"It's not your age, but your soul. You're a grim, angry, pessimistic woman. You're misery in a black dress. Not even thirty and already waiting for death."

"Then you believe me?"

"I do. I do, and it sickens me. What happened here? How could I . . ."

I stopped, and she nearly ran into me.

"How could you what?" I said.

"How could I produce a daughter so . . . so vile?"

I felt like I'd been holding my breath all night, all week. I sucked down a mouthful of cool night air, and she waited, taller than me, prouder than me, for my answer.

"His name," I said, "was Virgil Carr."

"How am I meant to procreate with someone I've never heard of?"

"And the cop who took your mother's statement when she complained about the Byrds."

"She called him a thug."

"He softened, ever so slightly, over time."

"When did we marry?"

"About four years after—about four years from now."

"And how am I supposed to have met him?"

"Nobody ever bothered to tell me. By all accounts, you loved him well."

Far down the block, a horse-drawn hack stopped, and a man in a top hat stepped from it like it was the most natural gesture in the world. Between her bob and her dress, Mary did not look part of this time. She sat on a stoop and kicked her heels against the stone.

"What sort of man was he?" she said.

"When you met him? He was a half-reformed brawler, hedonistic and corrupt, who wore a badge because it gave him license to crack skulls. The last time I saw him? He was an addled old drunk with a head full of mad theories who rarely found the initiative to get off the couch. In between he had a few shining moments, when inspiration touched him and he was able to loose the brilliance and love that I truly believe existed in his heart. He was my father and I loved him terribly, but he was an awful man."

"For that you would let me die."

"I need you here. I need you to meet Virgil. Otherwise, what will happen to me?"

"Have I done anything to give you the impression that I care?"

"That's why I didn't tell you. I knew you were too stupid to make this decision on your own."

She stood and shoved me hard enough that I stumbled backward into the street.

"I am not some idiot child," she said, jabbing me in the shoulder. "I am an intelligent, useful young woman, and I will not be condescended to by filthy, derelict trash."

"You're just like any bratty girl with a bad haircut. You think you own the world, but you haven't the faintest idea what it is to live in it."

"At least I leave my house. You're walling yourself in with newspapers—it's a wonder you haven't burned to death."

"If you have nothing better to do than attack my housekeeping, I'll leave you here."

I climbed back onto the sidewalk and walked away. With each step, my feet felt heavier.

"Is this how you wanted it?" she shouted. "You must have spent all those years dreaming of your poor, lost, noble mother. Is this how you wanted to meet her again?"

I kept walking.

"I am a lovely person, you know," she called. "Everyone says so. Amusing, witty, smart! A bright light on a bright island."

"So what?" I said, without turning around.

"So why do you hate me?"

I stopped, and she caught up to me. I couldn't tell if her chest was heaving from the chase or the tears.

"Is it really because I'm young? Because I'm silly? Because I have too much wit to follow your orders? Or is it because I had the gall to die, oh so selfishly, when you needed me most?"

All of that was a little bit right, but none was the whole truth. I was tired now, and still dizzy enough from our trip that there was no use being anything but honest.

"It's because you're not her," I said.

"And how could I ever be?"

"I've spent my whole life trying to live up to her. The parts of me that are what I remember of my mother? Those are the only parts I like. But if she wasn't what I remember, if she wasn't perfect, if she was just some stupid girl, then what the hell am I?"

"None of that is my fault."

"That doesn't mean I'm not angry."

"That's still not a reason to condemn me to die."

I walked east, uneasy at the unfamiliar feel of asphalt beneath my feet, and she followed. I was used to a quiet city, but the silence of the Westside is crypt-like, suffocating. This city was silent the way I imagine the country was, its icy clear air pure enough to carry sounds from a mile away. Horses snorted, milk bottles clinked, voices echoed from men's clubs, a policeman's baton clicked along a cast-iron fence, and far away, a trolley screamed as it rounded a tight turn. I had never known a city neither crowded nor dangerous, and because of that it hardly felt like a city at all.

"How many people have to die?" she said.

"What?"

"You talk so much about how you love the Westside. The weirdness. The quiet. Thousands died to make it that way. And now you want me to die for you."

"Those years were not so bad. We had fun, you and me. We had fun every day."

"If you leave, if you escape this quiet hell, I am coming with you."

I didn't answer. There was no polite way to say that I would keep her here because otherwise I was certain I would die. In any case, there was no time. Van Alen had given me thirty-six hours. I'd wasted most of a day. If I couldn't bring him Bully Byrd by tomorrow night, I didn't think Van Alen would accept falling through a hole in time as an excuse. The Lower West would be finished.

I walked a little faster. It was then that it started raining: a cold, hard downpour that washed away the scent of lemon verbena and filled the night with noise. The temperature fell with the rain. We were quickly soaked.

"I hate cold rain," Mary muttered. "Cuts right through me."

"It's worse than snow. Snow you can shrug off."

"There's something we agree on."

"Yes."

"And there's another thing, too."

"What?"

"Neither of us is getting out of here without the notebook and the powder nestled in Bully Byrd's pocket. We have to find him."

It wasn't a suggestion. It was a statement of fact. We'd both known it as soon as we hit that Victorian pavement, and even while we fought we had been walking toward the only place Bully could run: his once-and-future home.

Spring Street was in better condition that year than it would be in 1922. The buildings were solid and wholly free of the vegetation that would one day overtake them. No vines crept up the cast iron and marble; no grass sprouted through the pavement. At 111 Spring, lights glowed in every window, pushing feebly through the rain, but the lobby was dark, as damp and foul as a wet dog.

"What story, do you think?" said Mary as we shook out the damp. "It was hard to guess through the trees."

"We've had no luck so far. It has to be the top floor."

On the sixth floor, where a single light cast inky shadows along the warped hall, black crepe dangled over an apartment door. I didn't knock. I was through asking this family for permission.

The door opened onto a hallway, where two boys in crumb-flecked suits dozed against the wall. They were both around ten. One was thick, the kind of child that would grow up to be either strong or simply fat. This must be Abner. The other woke as we entered and gazed up at me with Enoch's puzzled squint.

"Papa?" he said.

"No," I answered.

He curled up against his brother and went back to sleep. We stepped over them and walked down the hall, which was littered with torn newspaper and well-loved toys. The parlor was just as crowded with trinkets and lace as it would be in three decades' time, but the dust was thinner and every wall was in its right place. Dust collected on a spread of cold cuts and flowers rotted on the piano. Judy leaned against the window, watching raindrops race along the glass. She looked thirsty. Crying will do that. Ruth, her head bandaged as thick as a swaddled newborn, sat at the table, flipping through a ladies' magazine. What I could see of her face was peeling red. She winced every time she turned a page.

Helen stood in the doorway to the kitchen, a glass of cloudy water in her hand. I wasn't sure how long she'd been there. She had the face of a woman who had been happy not too long ago and did not intend to ever be so again. She spoke with none of the grave polish she would affect later in life. Her accent was pure Westside trash.

"If you're bringing more flowers," said Helen, "we don't need 'em. If you've got news of my husband, you can tell him to rot."

"Did we miss the funeral?" I said.

"The undertaker has the body," said Judy in a sweet, singsong voice.

Ruth turned another page. "We won't bury brother until Papa comes home."

"If he comes home at all," said Helen. Her face was as hard and gray as slate.

Young Ruth took Mary by the hand. Mary flinched as if she had been bitten.

"Yes?" she said, twenty years of good breeding working to hide her horror. No etiquette course prepares you for an encounter with a woman you have so recently killed.

"What's wrong with your hair?" said Ruth, her croaking voice muffled by the bandages.

"It's the modern style," said Mary, softly.

"Your dress is all wrong, too. Here. I'll show you. I have magazines."

The girl led Mary to the table. I would let Mary confront her own ghosts. I was having enough trouble with mine.

"I don't know you from the church," said Helen. "What are you doing here?"

"I'm searching for the finger of Saint Róisín."

"I don't know her, either. Get out, why don't you?"

"You're going to talk to me, and you're going to tell me everything you know." My voice was shaky. My hands, too. The paper of the police report fluttered as I drew it from my bag. "Or I'll tell your brood what started that fire."

"If you have any decency . . ."

"That's not something I've ever been burdened with. You talk, or I will."

She didn't react. She just walked out, like I'd never been there. I followed her into the kitchen, where a cracked window looked onto the black of an airshaft. Rain crept in along the seam in the glass. Helen stood beside it, staring at nothing, her face as convincing a mask of grief as I had ever seen. But this was a woman who swindled widows for a living. She would know how to play the part.

I took the glass from her hand and tossed the water down the drain.

"Where is Bully?" I said.

She twisted a rag between hands so thin that every bone shone through the skin. She looked strong enough to rip it in half.

"After the fire he was . . . broken," she said. "Couldn't sleep. Could hardly talk. Looked at me like he didn't know me. I'd never seen a man go so cold, so fast. When he didn't come home, I wanted to think he was out on a bender, but I knew."

"Knew what?"

"Bully was always clever, but he was never strong. I figure he laid down in front of a trolley car, but then the body didn't turn up, so now I guess he threw himself in the river. We can't afford another funeral. I don't know what to tell the kids."

"Tell them you're sorry for marrying such a bastard. Tell them you're sorry you lied."

"We are in mourning! Don't you have any respect for that?"

"Don't," I said. "I can tolerate deception, because it's exactly what I expected, but the indignation stops here. You're a cheat, and I'm sick of you acting wounded."

"Who the hell are you?"

I grabbed her by the collar and yanked her away from the sink. Up close, her teeth were yellow. Her skin was puffy. She looked even worse than me.

"You've seen him," I said. "I know."

Helen spit a wet yellow glob that hit me on the cheek. I pushed her back against the counter. Mary pulled me away. Ruth and Judy watched from the doorway.

"She could be telling the truth," said Mary.

"It hasn't happened yet." I rapped the folder with my left hand. "You know what he did. Even without reading a word, you know. There's a child's bed that's empty because of Bully Byrd, and you're protecting him."

Helen looked at her daughters. She glanced to where her sons were sleeping in the hall. She was on the verge of breaking, I thought, either telling me the truth or reaching for something to draw my blood. Either would have been progress, but progress was denied.

"We're leaving," said Mary. "We're sorry for your loss. Ruth, thank you for the advice about my hair."

"Your coiffure is how you say hello to the world," said Ruth. "It's God's own truth."

The girls took their place on either side of their mother. Helen rubbed Ruth's hair and kissed her head. The moment had passed. She would never break again.

I let Mary lead me out. She shut the door gently, so as not to wake the sleeping boys. I could not look her in the eye.

"She knows where he is," I said.

"Possibly."

"I could have gotten her to talk."

"There was no need to be so cruel, not in front of the girls."

"She deserves it."

"Thirty years from now, maybe. But not tonight."

I started down the stairs, almost smiling. Mary was wrong. The Byrds were monsters from start to finish, and we would stop them only by calling on someone worse. I had dreamed of it my entire life. It was finally time to watch Mary Fall meet Virgil Carr.

Broadway, free of the fence, lit by electric lights instead of gas, looked impossibly clean and beautiful. A horse-drawn streetcar took us north, giving us a chance to dry off and warm up. As the rattling crate swayed uptown, rain hammered the roof. Outside the window, I saw people struggling with umbrellas, fighting wind and rain to get someplace warm.

"Where now?" said Mary.

"Lasko's Twenty-Seven. Virgil Carr's favorite dive."

"All right."

"You're not afraid?"

"I may be well-groomed and exceedingly polite, but I am not afraid of a jaunt into this city's darker quarters."

"Not of the dance hall. Of Virgil. Aren't you worried you might fall in love?"

She laughed hard enough to shake the rain from her dress.

"Oh, oh my, Gilda," she said, "I don't think so. But the horse is slow and Broadway is long. Make your pitch."

And so, as we lurched up the avenue, I shared the legend of Virgil Carr: the six-foot tower of fire who burned a path of destructive justice up and down old New York. I had seen pictures of him from those days, I had heard stories from his friends, and I sold him as hard as I could, describing a man as fearless, as eccentric, as dangerous as Mary herself.

"He was the NYPD's first great detective," I said. "He was the greatest brawler Sixth Avenue ever spit out. He was a marvelous dancer and he could eat his weight in beefsteak."

"I suspect he smells."

"Why?"

"From what you've said—he just sounds like the sort of man who smells."

"All men smell."

"Some better than others."

"Perhaps I could be clearer. There was never a man like Virgil Carr. He was—"

"Worth dying for?"

I had no answer for that.

"Do you know what I loved about Tom?" she said. "Of course you don't. You never asked a thing about him. I loved him because he was tender. He put me first. He didn't always know what I wanted, but he was always trying to figure it out. Virgil Carr was your father, and you can't be blamed for loving him, although it does suggest deficient taste. But tell me—did he ever in his life put someone else first?"

"No."

"And that's why I'm not afraid."

We rode on quietly, through a city as peaceful as purgatory, and I thought about how Virgil Carr smelled. He was an awful father and an indifferent man, but even three years after his death, I could remember the sharp mixture of smoke and grease that clung to him like his own skin. It was not a pleasant smell, but it was irresistible. I knew that if she met him, if she saw him at the best he had ever been, she would learn to love that, too.

And if that was a death sentence, I was still too cold and too damp to care.

SIXTEEN

Twenty-Fourth Street divided the New York of 1888 as sharply as the fence did Westside from East. On crossing that unassuming side street, Sixth Avenue transformed into a hellish circus. Despite the weather, the electric lights were bright and the crowds were thick enough that our streetcar slowed to a crawl. At Twenty-Seventh, it stopped altogether.

A slat opened and the driver peered inside. Water dripped from his sopping curls.

"Twenty-Seventh!" he said. "You ladies sure you want out?"

"We fear no sinner, and we fear no sin," said Mary, stepping lightly into the rain.

"Your funeral, ma'am."

Music tumbled from dance halls, saloons, brothels, and dives—crude, jangling music that joined into a nauseating roar. Packs of men staggered down the sidewalk, scanning each establishment in search of the cheapest fun. Street preachers with none of Judy Byrd's wit failed to compete with the din, while women moved in pairs—either soliciting business or seeking amusement of their own. They dressed in blacks and grays, wearing bell-shaped dresses and coats whose shoulders puffed out like a gouty leg. Corsets cinched every waist tight enough for me to wrap my hands around and hoisted their busts to the sky. Next to them, we were wearing nightgowns. Even the prostitutes looked scandalized.

Just off Broadway we found Lasko's, a three-story tower of sin whose lights lit up every drop of falling rain. It was nastier than I had dared imagine. There was no door, no bouncer—just a wide flight of steps that swept us off the sidewalk into a little patch of hell.

Oil lanterns and dancing gas cast a yellow pall over the gawking toughs who milled around the thrust stage, craning dirty necks to get a glimpse up the dancers' many skirts. The favorite was a thick-legged brunette with a lush, venomous smile; her exposed breasts thrashed like a rough sea, and her legs lifted higher than seemed healthy. Three stories of box seats ringed the stage, curtained to give the inhabitants privacy for deeds best not imagined, and a long, raised bar gave a view of the whole scene.

We leaned on the brass rail and nursed cups of watery whiskey, grateful to abuse our throats with something other than red gin. Mary pulled her coat tight and said nothing. Despite her bravado in the streetcar, she had the look of someone who wasn't sure if she should fear more for her purse or her life. At last, I thought, we have found someplace where I feel more at ease.

As the dance climaxed and the musicians ground every last note from their tortured instruments, I caught the bartender's eye and asked for Virgil Carr.

"Haven't seen him," he said. "Not tonight."

The stage show finished. The band launched into a violent waltz, and couples seeped onto the dance floor. After a few minutes, the bar was deserted, save for a lithe blonde with yellow skin and teeth to match. She was one of the cancan dancers, out from backstage in search of a drink, and the bartender would not meet her gaze.

"Just a cup!" she called. "Come on—I'm frozen from my ass to my elbows. Just a cup!"

"I told you, Viv, if you don't got a nickel I haven't a damned thing for you."

Viv. Vivian Pretzker, founding member of the Seven Bloody Fists, a dancer who would one day be murdered on the floor where I stood, cut down by Angie Barbarossa for the sin of looking at Virgil Carr.

I put my hand on her clammy shoulder and tried not to picture her corpse. She looked at me, cheerful as a rabid dog.

"What?" she said.

"Miss Pretzker, you dance beautifully."

"Shut the hell up. I dance like a cow."

She went back to sulking at the bar. I fumbled in my bag until I found something useful—a quarter, which I slid across the wood. Viv looked at it like it was a star falling from heaven. She stared at me with a smile that was ungainly but not unpleasant, picked up the quarter, and pelted it at the man behind the bar.

"What?" he said, rubbing the back of his neck.

"I want two bits' worth of so-so whiskey, plus glasses for me and my friends."

"I never saw a quarter like this before."

"It's good," I said. Either I was convincing, or he simply didn't care—silver was silver. He dropped it in the box and smacked the bottle onto the bar. With shaking hands, Viv sloshed liquor into our glasses and raised a toast.

"Here's to quarters," she said, and sucked her drink down. Relief poured over her, and she draped a thankful hand across my shoulder. "Say—you're soaked, ain't you?"

"It's nasty out," I said.

"Nasty in here, too. Come back and get dry."

She took the bottle, ignoring the bartender's protest, and led us backstage. The dressing room held enough chiffon and gaudy lace to open a fabric shop, and quite a bit of exposed flesh as well. There was a fire in the corner, and the inviting smell of perfume, women, and sweat put both Mary and me at ease. We stripped off our boots at the bootjack and laid our coats before the fire.

"No wonder you're shivering," said Viv, who had been shivering herself not too long before. "Those dresses are positively indecent. Let's find you something sensible to wear."

She hitched up my dress. I smacked her hand away.

"This dress is mine," I said.

"And it's nothing to be proud of," said Mary. "We are grateful for your hospitality, Miss Pretzker. What do you have that we might wear?"

Viv confiscated our clothes and bound me in an unforgiving satin corset, lined with embroidered diamonds in blue and black. It swallowed my torso, squeezing parts of my body that had not been held tightly in far too long. I tried not to think about the last time I was fitted for a corset, by a grim businesswoman whom I soon saw die. I scowled at my reflection in the warped green glass. I looked like a girl's doll made up in the image of Gilda Carr.

"You're lucky it's not five years prior," said Mary, as Viv crushed out the last of my breath. "We wore them so much tighter then."

The corset was ridiculous, but the dress was as heavy as cast iron, and the warmth was welcome. I twisted as best I could, trying to get a feel for what movement, if any, it would allow. Viv poured another round.

"You look much more respectable now," she said. "Can't imagine two women with your kind of breeding out in the rain without a corset. Are you whores, or do you just like to look the part?"

"We are detectives," said Mary, more comfortable in her new clothes than seemed possible.

"We are looking for Virgil Carr," I said, and Viv's hands started shaking again.

"Don't say that name," she hissed, but it was already too late.

A heavy hand fell on my shoulder. It belonged to the woman who had led the dancers on the stage. She was still half-naked, still beautiful and mean, but now that we were closer I saw through the makeup and recognized the face that would one day grow fat, jolly, and dead. Starlight Angie Barbarossa, my father's once-and-future lover, who held his body and his heart long after he married my mother, had the floor.

"What do you want with that man of mine?" she said.

Although I was inconveniently shorter than she was, I squared my shoulders and put all the rage of the Westside into my response.

"Tell us where he is or I will rip your face off with my hands,"

I said. I thought it was an awfully good threat, but Barbarossa was not impressed. With as much effort as one might swat a fly, she whipped her right fist into my chin, knocking me backward over the bench.

I hit the floor hard enough to rattle my teeth. The corset did little to cushion my fall. I wanted to pop up, to cripple her, but Mary held me down.

"Perhaps you're better off on your back," she said. Barbie loomed over Mary, an ogre ready to swallow her whole.

"You make threats, too," she said, "or you just run?"

"Neither," said Mary, drawing on all her society experience to sound as rich as she possibly could. "I apologize for the ill manners of my colleague. The temptations of the Tenderloin proved too much for her. She is drunk, and when she is drunk, she is worse than useless."

"Can't take a punch, neither."

"She is an embarrassment to our movement."

"And what movement is that?" said Barbie, pulling back her shoulder blades to crack her spine.

"We are representatives of the Women's Safety Committee. We distribute pamphlets advising young ladies which streets are safe and which are not, how to recognize a man who cannot be trusted, and how to behave when threatened."

"So far I'm not seeing much know-how."

"There are areas in which we are deficient, and so we are searching for Virgil Carr. We're told he's an expert in violence of all kinds."

"That he is," said Barbie, looking proud. I buried my face in the floor.

"We're hoping to engage him to give a lecture," said Mary, "to prevent unfortunate cases like my associate here from embarrassing themselves in the future."

Barbie gave me a thoughtful kick in the side. I rolled under the bench.

"Yeah," she said. "You could use the help. I haven't seen him tonight, and if he ain't here he's usually at a place on Twenty-Fifth, right west of Sixth."

"And the name of this establishment?"

"It doesn't really have one. Take a look and see where you get. I gotta warn you, though—on a night like this, he won't want to talk to anybody. He's not as social as me."

She punctuated her warning by giving me one last kick. The music groaned back to life. Barbie straightened, clapped Viv on the shoulder, and dragged her back to the stage. Mary offered a hand. I tried not to take it, but the corset made it impossible to stand on my own. I took a last belt from Viv's bottle.

"That worked out rather well!" said Mary.

"Yours was the right approach," I said, trying to choose between rubbing my jaw or my ribs.

"I put her in her place, didn't I? I can't think she'll be bothering either of us again."

I decided not to puncture her rather naive optimism. Time was ticking, here and in 1922.

At the stage door, we braced for another shellacking by the rain, but when we stepped onto Twenty-Seventh, we found it had turned to snow.

"Our luck has turned!" said Mary. "Snow at last."

It fell hard, sweeping out of the dark and into our faces like it was meant just for us. For a few minutes, it was beautiful. Sixth Avenue, that wonderful strip of vice, took on the aspect of a Christmas wonderland, and even the most desperate of its thrill-seekers took a moment to stare up at the reddening sky.

We stepped down Twenty-Fifth, where there were no lights and few people, and into a nameless dive that made the Basement Club look like the Hyperion Hotel. Fires blazed on both walls. The bar was full and the air was hot enough that the dirt floor had melted into mud, which squelched up our still-damp boots as we searched for Virgil Carr.

"We don't need to buy a drink, do we?" said Mary.

"Not if we can find him before the bartender notices us," I said. I didn't think that would be a problem. The bartender, a shrunken woman with stringy hair and jagged teeth, was half-asleep against the back wall, serving no one and looking nowhere. Patrons who wanted drinks simply leaned behind the bar and took what they wanted, leaving a pittance as thanks.

"He isn't here," said Mary, when we'd walked the length of the place.

"No."

"Then we'll press on alone. I'm not convinced he would have been any help, anyway, and—"

That was when I heard it. A rumble like artillery, far away but growing closer, powerful enough to shake the walls of that wretched dive. It came from a bench by the front door, a narrow slat of wood where a drunk was draped, half on and half off, squeezed against the wall. It was the sound that had often lulled me to sleep, and it was just as obnoxious and beautiful as I remembered. It was my father's snore.

I left Mary and stood over him, alone for a moment, seeing him as I never had. His coat had fallen off his magnificently whiskered face. His skin was clear, showing broad cheekbones that seemed less like the ruin of some great structure than simply part of his face, and his brows were softened by sleep. His hair was as thick as summer grass.

Mary prodded him with her toe. He did not stir. When Virgil Carr was this drunk, only an expert could rouse him.

With two fingers, I reached under his collarbone and pressed as hard as I could. He shot up like a firework, eyes still shut.

"Whiskey, damn it, hot as hell," he shouted, straight at the wall.

"Behind you, detective," said Mary. He turned around and sneezed in her face. He staggered toward the bar. Mary looked seasick.

"And when does he sweep me off my feet?" she said.

"He grows on you."

"So does a tumor."

Virgil hurled his empty cup at the bartender's head, missing by a few calculated inches. At last she roused. She pulled a bottle from a high shelf, tumbled some of it into a cup, and warmed it with a ladle of hot water from a burner in the back. Virgil had it nearly at his lips when I took it, downed it, and slammed it onto the wood. At last, I'd caught his eye.

"The good stuff," I said. "No fire in the world burns as pretty as Boulton's Rye."

"True," he said, "which is why I break the neck of any whelp with the nerve to drink mine."

I poured myself another. It really was fine.

"I thought I knew every madwoman in this city," he said, "but I never met one quite like you. What's your name?"

"Gilda Stern."

"And you live up to it. Is there something you need, or are you just going to keep stealing my whiskey until I cut your throat?"

"I'm here to introduce you to Mary Fall."

I stepped aside, and he saw her at last. If I expected lightning to strike, I was disappointed. He nodded, wrenched his cup out of my hand, and turned back to his bottle. Mary shook her head.

"We're looking for Bully Byrd," she said.

"The preacher?" he said.

"The preacher, the grifter, the killer, the thief," I said. "In the last week, he's set a fire that killed four children, stolen thousands of dollars in silver, killed one woman, maybe more."

"That has the sound of a police matter," said Virgil. "You don't look police."

"I'm a private detective investigating a private matter. But *you* are a cop, and you're going to help me find him."

"Byrd's church is downtown, isn't it? That's far past my turf. You want the"—he burped a thoughtful burp—"Eighth Precinct."

"The Eighth is all lightweights, and you know it. They lack the necessary vigor. I need a quick man who isn't afraid to crack skulls."

On his hip a polished club brushed against the shining knee

of his pants. He bounced it on his leg, smiling at the memory of bloodshed.

"Tonight I'm drinking," he said, "not working."

"And what of the four dead children?" I said.

"Not my children. Not my concern."

"If you're playing on his honor," said the bartender, "you've picked the wrong cop."

"You were fun when I met you, Miss Stern," said Virgil, turning his back, "but you got dull quick. If you ever drink my liquor again, I'll throw you out myself."

Mary shoved me aside and slapped the fire report on the bar.

"What sin did I commit this morning," he said, "that I must spend my night being tortured by short women?"

"Open it," said Mary. "Assuming you can read."

"I said I'm not working," he said, so she flipped it open herself. He was looking for the appropriate way to tell her to go to hell when his eyes snagged on the paper. "That's my handwriting."

"If you can call it that," she said.

He turned around, as confused and angry as a wounded bear, moving faster than I'd known my father could. Before I could duck he had me by the throat. With his free hand he grabbed my elbow and lifted me off the ground.

"Explain the joke," he said.

"A good comic never does," I said. He didn't think that was very funny. He squeezed tighter.

"I didn't write those words. So who did?"

"Just read them," I said, kicking my legs and prying at his fingers with my loose hand. It did no good, but he dropped me to the floor anyway, downed his drink, and flipped through the file. I tried not to rub my neck.

Or my ribs.

Or my jaw.

"I couldn't tell you the meaning of half these words," he said, "but yeah, it sounds like arson."

"You could take it to a judge and have Bully arrested tonight," said Mary.

"I could at that, if it weren't a clear forgery. It's dated three months from now."

"It's not a forgery," I said. "It's a mystery, and doesn't that draw you in? Aren't you tempted by the inexplicable, the strange?"

"I believe in what I can touch, taste, and kill. Worrying about any more than that will make a man dyspeptic or dead."

It was sound advice. I wished I could tell him to have those words embroidered on all his clothing, that he might remember them two decades hence, when an obsession over the biggest mysteries the city had to offer would drive him to his death. But he was swaying, and his eyes were drooping, which meant our audience was nearly at an end.

"I thought you were supposed to be a great detective," I said.

"And just who told you that?"

You.

I couldn't say it, though. I could barely even think it. Here he was, as aggravated and useless as I remembered. The grief I had buried, the grief I thought I had put behind me, swept back up and swallowed me, and I fell into the trap that had consumed so much of my life: of wishing that just for a moment he would be as great as I wanted him to be.

Mary had no such frailty. She reached into his shirt and grabbed hold of the carpet of hair half-hidden beneath the cloth. She twisted hard, pulling him close, until both of us saw that she had been right—this man smelled like a corpse.

"Find him for us," she said.

"Or what?"

"Or so help me god, I will marry you, and that will destroy us both."

For a moment, she seemed bigger than him. Virgil was frozen. I recognized those glassy eyes and slack jaw from my childhood—the look of a man so forcefully put in his place that he was physically dazed.

"I'll get word to Mulberry Street at dawn," he said, his voice shaking with a little fear and a little love.

"Now," said Mary.

"I've got a chest cold that'd kill a weaker man," he said. "Stepping into the rain would be suicide."

"Lucky you. It's turned to snow."

Grumbling incoherent curses, Virgil pulled a massive nickel-plated flask from his pocket. He filled it with Boulton's and headed for the nearest precinct house. Mary strolled after him, serene as glass, and as I saw her silhouetted against the snow, I thought for the first time that she looked like my mother.

SEVENTEEN

We walked east. I might have marveled at the uncanny sight of streets I knew in an era I didn't or the bizarre sensation of crossing Broadway without having to show my papers, but the snow had become impossible.

It whipped sideways, slashing our faces, carried by wind so strong we could hardly walk. That evening's rain had turned to ice, and the sidewalks were as rough as any on the Westside. We had not gone more than a block when the electric streetlights died. Aside from the gas flickering out of the saloons, the city was dark. The streets emptied. By the time we reached Fifth Avenue, we were alone in the world.

It was just a few more blocks to the precinct house, but they were longer than any I'd ever known. Blinded by the snow, we were frozen past the point of reason. The short walk seemed to go on forever. I thought the winter of 1922 had been brutal, but this was a frozen hell.

Something whipped through the air, quick as an arrow and right past my face. I stopped, and snow welled up in the collar of my coat as I reminded myself how to breathe.

"What was that?" I said.

"Telegraph," said Mary. She picked up the fallen wire. The wind had snapped it in half.

"Does this sort of thing happen often in your city?" I said.

"Not that I've ever noticed."

"I'm beginning to think I'd prefer cold rain."

"I'm beginning to think I'd prefer having never met you," Virgil muttered.

"Don't say that," Mary said sweetly. "We're on an adventure."

Virgil scowled at her and I did, too. I couldn't tell which of us disliked her more.

We pressed on. There was little else to do. I tucked my chin against my chest and buried my hands in my pockets, walking almost parallel to the ground in order to push against the wind. Virgil was beside me, tilting like a dead oak.

I was unsure how much farther I could go when he grabbed me by the wrist and pulled me through a door. We crashed into a drafty old station house where policemen dozed and rats scuttled around the corners. I slumped against a wall, my eyes burning, every part of me cold or wet or both, my mouth too numb to speak.

"Thorne!" said Virgil.

A head popped out from around the corner, and I saw the stupid, surprisingly handsome face of Eddie Thorne.

"Eddie can get you whatever you need," said Virgil. "He's an idiot, but he listens, which is more than I can say for most of the scum that make up this department. I'm going to see about a god-damned cup of coffee."

Virgil stomped off, scattering snow everywhere, and Eddie waited for me to boss him around. Just a few months prior, it seemed to me, he had been responsible for the deaths of thousands, children mostly. What good would it do, I wondered, to snatch the pistol off his hip and shoot him through the eye? Would it save those dead boys? Would it snap the universe in half? Such questions remained beyond me. I left his pistol where it was, partly because I was too cold for gun-grabbing, and partly from my characteristic certainty that nothing I did could ever improve the world.

"We need everything you have on the Byrds," I said, forcing the words through lips stiff with cold. My mouth felt stupid. "Their preaching, their movement, the fire."

He flitted off. Mary leaned on the sergeant's desk, not even rubbing her arms, just staring frozen into space. A prod beneath the collarbone roused the nearest sleeping cop, who was gentleman enough to let us collapse onto his bench. We sat, sensation creeping back into dead limbs, and watched as refugees from the storm staggered inside, each entering with some variation on "That snow is a goddamned bastard!" A consensus formed: New York had never seen anything like this, and it showed no signs of slowing down.

"They're shutting down the elevateds," said a lean, older cop between attempts to claw the ice from his beard. "Streetcars are frozen in their tracks. Horses won't go more than a step. Horses are smarter than me."

Quietly, citizens and police gathered blankets and pulled them tight. They filled their pockets with food, and watched the gaslights nervously, fearful they might go the way of their electric cousins. They were preparing for a siege. As usual, I didn't care.

"It's that finger," I said, suddenly enough to startle Mary.

"The world is ending, and you're stuck on that?"

"It isn't ending. It can't. We have seen it, decades from now. Ice melts. Snow blows away. New York rebounds. But that finger . . ."

"What?"

"Kings whatever-it-was inspired Enoch to grind up a saint's finger and use it in his father's rite. He hoped it would bring back the dead, and it worked."

"That's no more insane than anything else that has happened to me this week. Why shouldn't it have?"

"Because it *didn't*. The Bible verse suggested a prophet's bones might bring a dead man back to life. Enoch had the supposed finger of a saint—not a prophet, but a saint—and even if one believes in magical holy skeletons, it is staggeringly unlikely that what the Byrds called a relic was truly the thirteen-hundred-year-old finger of Saint Róisín. And even if it *were* her finger, it brought no one back to life, did it? It simply opened a gate through time."

"Simply?"

Her skepticism was justified, and so I ignored it. "If it wasn't poor, martyred Róisín's finger, then whose was it? And why did that specific finger, combined with the rite and the fire and all the other hokum, connect 1922 with today?"

"I don't care, so long as it gets me away from here."

I leaned back and let the frigid wall suck away the last of my body heat. I looked around that dim room and thought about the brute who'd led us here. I couldn't believe I'd thought the sight of him might convince her to stay.

"You're still set on leaving?" I said.

"I used to love my city in the snow. But after seeing your East-side, my New York feels stale. I should like to taste something new."

"But Virgil—" I said.

"Please. I've seen rats more likely to inspire love at first sight."

My father raised me to believe in lost causes, but even I had to admit this one was particularly dire. Mary closed her eyes, and I let her pretend to sleep.

Virgil returned with coffee, spiked with enough whiskey to make my eyes water, and Thorne came in his wake. As he delivered his report, Thorne kept his eyes locked on Virgil, searching his hero's face for any glimmer of approval. It didn't come.

"A fire department arson investigator named, ah, Tom Mac-Naughton informed us last week that he considered the fire at the Byrds' church suspicious. The next day, he disappeared. We've had a man keeping watch on the Byrd apartment for the last few days, looking for some sign of Bully. They haven't seen him."

Tom's name sent a spike of pain through Mary that pierced the cold. I wanted to hold her hand. I didn't think she would let me.

"Did your man call in tonight?" I said.

"He did. Two women came to see Helen—ladies in whores' dresses with strange haircuts who . . . oh. That was you."

"Yes. After we left?"

"No more visitors, but Helen went for a walk at . . . nine fifteen."

"Where?"

"To a funeral parlor on Mulberry Street. It's where they've got the body of her boy."

"Then Bully's coming home."

"How can you be sure?" said Virgil, still not convinced he cared.

"Because they won't bury that boy until he does," said Mary.

"How far do you think it is to Mulberry?" I said.

"Two miles downtown," said Thorne. "But how will you get there?"

"I'm a New Yorker. I'll walk."

"It's the apocalypse out there."

"Then I should be right at home," I said, looking around for something to smash. "Have any of you got an ax?"

"Can't we at least wait till morning?" said Virgil.

"I'm not staying in this city one minute longer than I have to," said Mary. "If Gilda wants an ax, fetch it."

"I don't think we—" Thorne started, but I was finished waiting. I brought my foot down onto the bench we'd been sitting on, as hard as I could, hoping to smash it into bits. It barely groaned. Virgil let out a rare, beautiful laugh, and elbowed me aside.

"This is my sort of police work," he said, and crushed the bench beneath his feet. Every head in that dim, cold room turned, then looked away when they saw that it was simply Detective Carr in one of his destructive moods. "Now, why did I just do that?"

"Snowshoes," I said.

"Isn't she clever?" said Mary.

I pulled a blanket off the nearest supine cop, tore it into strips, and lashed a pair of boards to my feet. Virgil and Mary did the same. Thorne brought a rope, and we tied it around our waists to create a chain: Virgil, to Mary, to me.

"Thorne, your gun," said Virgil. Eddie obliged. "I want every scarf, every blanket, every coat in this room. I'm taking two ladies for a walk, and they're going to be warm."

There was grumbling, and then there was Virgil scouring the crowd with his hand on his club, and then there was a pile of blankets and jackets. We cocooned ourselves in as much fabric as we could pack on, until we were nothing but three pairs of eyes peeking out above the cloth. Between the corset and the coats, I could hardly move, and I was so hot under those layers that every part of me sprang out in sweat before we took a step. It didn't matter. The Carrs were together at last.

Snow, dry and hard, blew from every direction, shredding my inch of exposed skin like a shower of broken glass. A foot or more had fallen, and it surged across sidewalk and street like a rolling white wave. The snowshoes helped, but not much. Within a few minutes, the cold had cut through all my layers. My sweat began to freeze.

At the head of our procession, Virgil kept himself going with a furiously profane song about a prostitute named Anne Marie Foddan's "notorious bottom." How, I wondered, could this man be responsible for me?

I had known him when he was broken by failure and grief. Knowing he had once been a violent, overgrown boy had let me look at him with something other than sadness. It had helped keep my love for him alive. Seeing that boy in the flesh, I realized that Virgil Carr did not wait until old age to become pathetic, and I hated him as much as I ever had, even as I yearned to have him back in my life.

The wind picked up when we crossed Twenty-Eighth Street, blowing hard enough that I could do nothing but curse and stand still.

"Pick it up!" cried Virgil. The rope around my waist jerked, and I stumbled forward until the street was passed. A snowdrift, seeming to move on its own, roared toward me. I pulled my legs high, my muscles burning, and got out of the way.

My eyes stung so badly that I could hardly keep them open, much less look straight ahead. Not that there was anything to see. The rope disappeared into the white. There were moments where I could see Mary's silhouette, but as we stumbled south those moments grew rarer. Her figure was gray, small, indistinct. She looked like the ghost I had always imagined.

Feeling seeped out of my toes, then my feet, then my legs, and the snowshoes became dead weight. I kept on.

The wind's screaming was pierced by something—a thump?

A whoosh?—that forced my head up. Through the gloom, I saw a shadow tumbling through the air. I pulled on the rope, jerking Mary sideways. She fell into the street, and the pile of falling snow landed where she had stood.

I fought my way forward and helped her up. The scarf around her face had slipped. Her skin was gray. She looked too cold to be afraid.

"It is bad out here," she said.

"Are you all right?"

"No."

I wrapped her scarf tight. The rope jerked, and we pressed on. Over my right shoulder, I saw the vast, swirling black of Madison Square, unshielded by the skyscrapers and hotels that would gird it in my own time, where the wind whipped the snow into shapes too terrible to contemplate. We staggered onto Broadway, and I thought of summer. I thought of spring. I thought of Cherub Stevens, a decade from being born, leaping from branch to branch in one of the towering oaks of Washington Square, with a laugh that could beat back any snow.

The rope went slack. I wondered, numbly, if Virgil had died. I kept walking, gathering it in my hands until I reached Mary, who said nothing. We found Virgil leaning on a carriage that sat askew, half on the sidewalk, its horse and driver long vanished, the snow piled nearly to its windows. Virgil drained his flask and hurled it into the night. It landed silent and unseen.

"I need a break," he said.

"Where?" I said.

"Here."

He pulled open the carriage and was halfway inside when someone cried, "It's taken!" Virgil dragged the occupant out by his hair, hurling him backward into the snow. He turned, a savage smile on his lips, and offered his hand.

"Ladies?"

Mary climbed in and I followed. Before I shut the door, I looked back for the man Virgil had possibly sent to his death. He had vanished into the snow.

Virgil filled the rear bench. Mary and I pressed against each other on the front. We sat for some time, saying nothing, too tired to shiver, and waited for feeling to come back. Every time I looked at Virgil, he was staring at Mary with all the admiration of a puppy just meeting its master. At last, he remembered he was a detective.

"Where did you come from, with hair like that?" he said.

"Philadelphia," said Mary.

"Oh, aye. They're strange there. And what's got you set against the Byrds?"

"They swindled my mother. You met her."

"I did? I did! The tough old bitch with the funny name. She was steel, that one. Scared the hell out of me."

"Fall women have that effect," I said.

"I like a woman who scares me," said Virgil. There was no polite answer to that, and so for some time, we were quiet again. I may have slept, or the snow outside may simply have achieved the power of nightmare.

"How far have we gone?" said Mary.

"We just crossed Twentieth," I said.

"No," said Virgil. "That was Twenty-First. Twentieth is next, then Union Square, then god knows how much more. Better to just stay here."

"We'll freeze."

"You might. I probably won't."

He closed his eyes. I kicked his bench. He did not stir. Mary laughed and leaned her head on my shoulder. It was not unwelcome.

"I expected he would be better," I said. "I was wrong."

"How could you know?" said Mary.

"We can go on without him."

"What's the point? I thought we'd gone farther. Halfway, maybe more. How long have we been walking?"

"I don't know."

"It's tough going out there, Gilda. It's very, very tough."

"Then we'll just have to be tougher."

I kicked open the door, and the snow howled in—a few inches in an instant.

"Would you close that goddamned door?" said Virgil, his eyes still shut. I smashed my elbow through one window, then another, then the last. I was so thoroughly padded that I didn't even feel it. Our little pocket of warmth popped. Virgil looked mad.

I hopped out, and Mary followed. We gripped the rope through gloved hands and pulled until Virgil flopped out of the ruined carriage and started to walk again. He didn't sing anymore.

The next part was worse. There was no more distraction, no more feeling, no more hope. I simply put one foot in front of the other, struggling to keep my shoes level on the shifting snow, each uneven movement sending spikes of pain through my otherwise numb legs. The wraps around my head fell away, and my gloved fingers were too clumsy to put them back. Spit froze on my face. Ice filled my hair. I kept walking.

I stopped looking at the street signs. They told me nothing I wanted to know. My legs were heavy and my steps were slow.

Mary, utterly invisible through the snow, was moving faster, driven by reserves I did not know a person could possess. I could not keep up. The rope drew taut, digging into my back, pulling tighter and tighter until the knot slipped and the line snaked away. I reached for it, but I was moving so slowly, I had no chance. It was already gone.

"Mary! Virgil, you bastard, stop!"

My voice was no match for the wind.

I was a woman overboard, and the ship that had dropped me was out of sight. I strode forward, already lost, not caring at all. I did not need them. They had died before, and I had pressed on. I had seen things they could not imagine. I had passed through death. I had saved the Westside. Girls like that have no use for parents.

I came to a corner. I couldn't read the street sign, but it looked like letters, not numbers. Perhaps I'd passed Houston. Perhaps I was close. But I was just so unfathomably cold.

Around the corner, I heard voices. I followed them—just a step, just a few steps. I saw a beam of light, thick as a finger and bright as the sun, shining through the falling snow. Using all the strength I had left, I pushed open the door.

I stumbled into a saloon lit by gas and candlelight, its walls lined with wood and floors softened by deep crimson carpet. I didn't know where I was, but I knew it was warm. A few dozen were scattered at tables and booths, and the air was laced with sounds of conversation and laughter and clinking glass.

"The door!" called a voice from the back, too happy to be angry. A woman hopped up from her table and helped me close it tight.

"You look like hell," she said. Before I could tell her what I needed, she guided me toward the bar. The bartender smiled like he'd been waiting his whole life for me to walk through the door.

"A triple whiskey and a bowl of chowder hot enough to burn," I said. He poured a pint glass full of whiskey. I drank as much of it as I could stand. It didn't even tickle my throat.

"Is this whiskey," I asked, "or rusty water?"

"It's the finest we've got, ma'am. Perhaps you're not used to the good stuff."

He topped up my glass, and I drank it dry.

"Where's the soup?" I said, and looked at him for the first time. He had a broad nose and coarse hair, fat suspenders and a shirt striped in black and green. His rating was 64. His name was Abner Byrd.

"Oh hell," I said.

"If you want to call it that," he said, and his skin split along the veins in his face, drying and spluttering as blue fire burned out from inside him and charred him to black. His crumbling hand reached out for me. I threw myself backward but did not move. He took me by the throat.

The world went black. The cold returned. My neck felt ready to burst. The next thing I saw was Mary's face. She pulled me out of the snowbank by my scarf, dragged me to my knees, and smacked me until I could stand. She shook the loose end of the rope in my face.

"Where the hell did you go?" she said, as panicked as if she were really my mother, and I were really her lost child. "Good lord, Gilda. Good lord."

"What happened?"

"I felt the rope go slack. I screamed and you didn't answer. Virgil refused to stop. I untied myself and came back to find you. You'd fallen into a snowbank. Buried in an instant. Nothing sticking out but those big black boots."

"Thank you."

"Shut up and walk," said Mary. "Let the rope go."

We walked on, hand in hand. We found Virgil a block or two south. Our snowshoes came loose and we abandoned them. The going was too uneven now, and they were more harm than good. We shed our excess layers, reasoning that numb is numb, and moved faster without them. The sun came up and the snow did not stop, but neither did we, the three of us together, bulldozing downtown, then east until a sign, at last, said Mulberry Street, and the longest walk of my life was at an end.

Brandyce Funeral Parlor was a sagging building, a relic from early in the century sustained by the convenient fact that even the poor need to die. Out front was a hearse buried nearly to the driver's seat in snow. A foolishly handsome youth hacked at the mess with a shovel, but every gust undid his work. His curses were carried our way by the wind.

I started toward him, but Virgil pulled me back. He waved a heavy paw at the building across the street.

"You gotta eat, don't you?" he said. "You gotta get warm?"

"I wouldn't fight it," I said.

"We're so close," Mary said.

"But in no state to fight."

"Up here," Virgil said with a nod. "I know a guy."

We clambered over the snow and lurched through the front door of an anonymous tenement. Virgil bounded up to the third floor, his legs full of a bounce that seemed impossible, and banged on the front apartment. The door cracked open.

"Vanish, detective," said a voice from the other side.

"If it were a raid, I'd have brought friends," said Virgil. "Tell Brass we just want a seat by the fire."

The apartment was bare save for a few unfinished benches and chairs and a pair of tables where men in coats and gloves shot dice. Felt curtains blocked out the light. The room was deliciously hot. The floor was wet with melted snow.

Mary and I fell into chairs by the front windows. I cracked the curtain and saw the undertaker's across the street.

"Close that curtain!" cried one of the gamblers.

"Why?" I said, with venom enough to let him know that I was not in the mood for an argument.

"The police might see."

"The police are already here, idiot."

That satisfied him enough to leave me alone. Across the room, Virgil spoke to a slight young man in a green suit so well-tailored and so old-fashioned that I could only think of it as something a dead man would wear. He headed our way while Virgil took a spot at one of the tables, brushing the shooter aside and seizing the dice. As he tested their weight, he stared at Mary.

"Brass Aiken," said the man in the green suit, sitting down with us. "Proprietor. You got an appetite?"

"Like a newborn," said Mary.

Brass waved his hand and somewhere, I assumed, the process began of getting us something to eat.

"Which of you is the one Clubber's set on marrying?" he said.

"Pardon?" I said.

"You look more his type. Bitter, worn, a little rough."

"Thanks. I do try."

He looked at Mary. "I can't imagine someone as sweet as you going near him, though."

"Over my dead body," said Mary, laughing hard enough that Brass had to laugh, too. A waiter in an incongruous tuxedo set steaming black tea and tin plates of baked beans on the table. It was barely edible, and it tasted sublime.

Brass left us to eat and gaze out the window, where the boy with the shovel finally gave up his fight. We watched the drifts grow higher and the wind blow stronger, as Virgil lost what little money he had, until I was ready to say the thing I had realized while I was dying in the snow.

"You can't stay here," I said. Mary set down her tea. It may have been the first time I had managed a surprise.

"Gilda Carr, giving in," she said. "I never thought I'd see it."

I pointed a thumb at the policeman sulking in the corner, cursing rigged dice, demanding Brass stake him for another throw.

"I knew he'd be rotten," I said. "He's worse than I imagined. I cannot abandon you to him, to this city, to death."

"What changed your mind?"

"You pulled me out of the snow."

"So?"

"It wasn't that you saved my life. It was . . . it was the way I felt when I came out of that dream and saw your face. I lost it a long time ago, and then it came back to me, and I knew that I would be a fool to let it go again."

"And if that means you die?"

"I don't think I will. Something about being with you—it's made me think that maybe things can change, that a bit of stubbornness and good cheer are enough to rewrite history."

I don't think she bought it. I didn't, either, but we were both willing to pretend.

She embraced me, and I laughed with her, enjoying it more than I ever thought I could, but there was something cold inside my gut. I felt quite close to death, or something worse—to having never existed at all. But it didn't matter. She was the sun made flesh, and her life would mean more to this city than mine ever could.

EIGHTEEN

Two hours and several welcome plates of beans later, a figure trudged up Mulberry toward the undertaker's. She hunched low, moving slowly but with irresistible purpose. When she climbed the steps to the battered old house, I was certain it was Helen Byrd.

We were halfway to the stairwell when I remembered my father. Virgil had sweet-talked, or possibly threatened, Brass into giving him another stake, and he had made it last. He gazed down on a pile of coins and crumpled banknotes like a proud father and looked surprised to see that we wanted to leave.

"Are you coming?" I said. He looked at Mary and looked at the dice, showing equal affection for both, but I knew where his decision would lie.

"Not while I'm winning," he said.

We were already on our way out. We raced down those dark, slick marble stairs and threw open the door to outside. A fresh wave of snow roared across the threshold. It was like a white hurricane. Mary gave a mad grin.

"Well," I said.

"Quick quick."

We leapt into the street. The fragile warmth we had built over the last hours was erased by the time we got across. Once again, it was impossible to imagine anything but cold.

The drooping porch dipped beneath our feet. A hand-scrawled sign informed us that Brandyce's was closed, due to the storm. The door was locked to drive the point home, but the lock was as old as the house and just as ready to give up. It opened in an instant, and we stepped into a parlor where black curtains hung from every surface. Even the stairs were draped in dark velvet. The ceilings were low and the air was close, swollen by heat from an unseen fire and polluted with the tang of formaldehyde. Steep steps led up to the second floor.

The first doorway opened onto a reception room. A chalkboard welcomed guests to their final viewing of Barnabas Byrd, 1885–1888. At the front of the room, before a dozen neatly arranged chairs, a platform as small as a boy waited for the coffin.

"Poor bastard," I said.

"Yes," said Mary.

Voices drifted from a door at the end of the room: a woman and a man. We crept along the wall, our steps muffled by mildewed carpet, and listened as best we could. The chemical stench took hold. We were near where the magic was done.

"I want the body out before noon," said Helen.

"But with the funeral tomorrow—"

"The funeral doesn't matter."

"What will we have for the viewing?"

"Show them an empty casket. Keep the lid closed. Nobody wants to see that . . . thing anyway. Can you move the body today?"

"We can try. Some of the ferries are running, I've heard, and there may still be a way across the bridge."

"Go. I'd like to be alone with my boy."

Silence from the embalming room. We crept closer. Through the half-open door, we saw Helen, and we saw her child.

I could tell it had been human, but not much more than that. The body was tiny, fragile, charred. The face was a brittle husk. She brushed her lips across its forehead, and then she reached for the undertaker's tools. She wiped the bone saw on her leg, shaking loose some of the rust, and applied the saw to what remained of her son's hand.

She was a strong woman, and she worked with purpose. Back once, forward once, and the smallest finger dropped off the boy's fist to her palm. She lowered it into a small jar, filled it with murky liquid, and set it aside. Here, at last, was one mystery solved: the finger of Saint Róisín. A false relic, but holy all the same. Religion remained an impotent farce, but there were miracles in a child's hands.

"Should we fetch Virgil?" I whispered.

Mary shook her head. She took my hand in hers, and we stepped into the embalming room together. It was a long, narrow passage with marble tables in the middle and a door to the backyard on the far end. A bank of grimy windows filled one wall. The others were a jumble of toxic chemicals, saws, hammers, and knives. Helen whipped around at the sound of us. She leaned back, blocking our view of her son's body. Her hand inched toward the saw.

"Don't try to hide it," I said. "I saw you cut him. Why?"

"I can't let him go. Not yet. Not ever. And your question yesterday, about the finger of—who was it?"

"Róisín."

"With Bully gone, we'll need something to draw people to the church. I've always wanted a relic, and yours was as good an idea as any."

"But Bully isn't really gone, is he?" said Mary.

"He certainly isn't here. Why are you two so stuck on him?"

I walked closer. I wondered if I was near enough to snatch that saw before she could get a grip on it. I didn't trust my own speed. I had been numb too long.

"You're a smart woman," I said, "and many decades my elder, so I'm going to do the respectful thing and tell you the truth. I suspect you know most of it anyway. After the fire, Bully returned to the church. A gate opened there—a gate through time, created by Enoch in the year 1922, because he wanted his daddy home."

"That's insane."

"Isn't it though?" said Mary.

"Bully stepped through that gate and wreaked havoc upon my city," I said. "He stole thousands in silver, he killed, and he came back here."

"Who did he kill?" said Helen, raising the saw. She was a calculating woman, cynical and deceitful and cruel, but I remembered what it had done to Mary to learn about her own death. No one needs to know how they die.

"No one important to you," I said, and I think she believed me. "I followed him back here, and I want to find him—"

"And what? Bring him to justice?"

"Is that such a joke?"

"Some men are beyond its reach. Dead men, madmen, and those who simply do not have a soul. Bully is gutter-grade filth. He will tell any lie, he will break any law—man-made or otherwise—to get what he wants."

"And what does he want?"

"An easy life. To do whatever he wants, whenever he wants it, and to have the world cheer him on."

"Then why have you kept him around?"

"He was useful. He could pull money out of thin air, amuse the children, swindle suckers so that we could eat. I never let him too close to the kids; I never let him into my heart. I thought I had him under control."

"What changed?" said Mary.

She didn't answer. Something came over her that I hadn't seen before. Tired. She was as tired as any woman I had ever met.

"It was the fire," I said. She nodded. "You knew it was going to happen. What was the plan?"

"The church was bankrupt. We didn't have nothing but the building and our flock, and you can't hock faith. The church was insured. A fire was the only thing for it."

"And the kids?" said Mary.

"Knew they wasn't supposed to play in the basement. Children don't listen."

"How is Ruth?"

"What do you care?"

Mary stared out into the swirling snow, ignoring Helen, ignoring me, and seeing only the face of the woman she would kill. I might have told her that now was not the time, but guilt is fiercely impatient.

"I liked her," said Mary, "when I met her yesterday. She seemed such a terribly normal child."

"Not anymore," said Helen. "I spent the last bit we had on the doctor, and he was a butcher. Her face is mangled; she misses her brother, she misses her daddy, too."

"Just tell her, when she gets older—tell her to forget New York. Tell her to go far away."

"I think it's time both of you leave my family the hell alone."

Mary had Helen's full attention. I was sick of this room, of the corpse at the center of it, and of Helen and Bully Byrd most of all. Deciding it was one of those days where it was a mistake to turn your back on me, I crossed the floor, snatched a particularly long knife off the wall, and pressed it to Helen's back.

"Oh," said Helen.

"Yes," I answered.

Mary took the bone saw out of her hand.

"It's time to give Bully up," I said.

"I'll say it again," said Helen, "the bastard's not here!"

My knife pierced her mourning dress and nestled against the lacing of her corset. The blood drained from the back of her neck. She looked at Mary, asking if I meant it, and Mary nodded.

"She's a true Westside brute," she said, with honest pride in her voice.

"If he's not here," I said, "where is he?"

Helen didn't answer. I twisted the hilt. Her blood oozed. One, two, three drops fell to the sawdust on the floor. She shook her head, then banged hard on the nearest window.

"Goddamn it!" she shouted. "It's finished. Come inside!"

The door swung open, letting in a swirl of snow and a blast of cold and the grinning, half-frozen figure of Bully Byrd. He wore a stolen coat that stopped two inches short of his wrists; his once-gleaming white suit was wrinkled and stained. His face was red, his hair matted with ice. His cheeks and fingers were frostbitten black. At last he looked as evil as I knew him to be. His smile faltered somewhat when Mary pushed the bone saw to his throat.

"That's it," he said. "Just who the hell *are* you two?"

"The daughter of Anacostia Fall," said Mary. "You took her money. You humiliated her. That was a stupid thing to do."

Bully tried to step back. Mary pressed the saw closer. He froze.

"I just want to pull something out of the cabinet," he said. Mary nodded, and followed him with the saw close to his neck. He opened the tall white cabinet doors and withdrew the bloody Gladstone bag. He dropped it on the counter. It rattled with stolen silver.

"You want money?" he said. "Take it."

"That's not why we're here," I said.

"Then what do I have to do to get you women to leave me alone?"

He said "women" the way I'd have expected, like it was the nastiest slur he could reach for. I didn't like men who talk that way. I was finished with this one.

"There is nothing you can do," I said, "but give us the notebook, give us the powder, and say the words that send us home."

"And what do I get?" he said.

"An audience at the feet of Glen-Richard Van Alen, lord of the Westside. A chance to beg for your life."

He tried to argue. Mary wasn't having it. She darted the bone saw closer and, miracle of miracles, Bully Byrd shut up.

I turned to Helen, who stood guard over the body of her boy. Soon we would be gone, and she would be left alone to bury Barney and wait for the man who killed him to reappear. When Bully made his appearance in 1922, she would pretend she didn't know what had happened, hoping to wring one last bundle out of him before he came back here. She hated him so much. To hide that, I thought, she must have talents I'd never imagined.

"You were going to smuggle him out in the hearse," I said. "To where?"

"There are plenty cemeteries on Long Island," said Helen. "I was gonna drop him and let him go. I'd keep the silver. I'd be free."

"Free," laughed Bully. "It's no joy to be free of the best thing that's ever happened to you."

"Shut up, pig."

"She calls me immoral. But burning the church, that was her idea. Checking the basement was her job. She lit the fuses while I did the sermon. And the powder? She mixed it, tripled the explosive dose without giving me fair warning. She hoped I'd die in the fire."

"I could never be so lucky," said Helen.

The wind picked up another screaming notch. The back door swung open, slamming into the wall and causing all of us to flinch. Bully laughed.

"I'm the most innocent person here, really," said Bully. He stared down the saw at Mary, acknowledging her for the first time since he pulled down the bag. "You tell her what you did to our Ruth?"

"Shut up or I'll cut your throat," said Mary.

"Oh, go ahead."

He smirked, and when she didn't cut him, he knocked her arm away. She kept her grip on the saw. He backed her toward the door. I pressed the knife harder against Helen's back, feeling terribly distant from where I wanted to be.

"What did she do?" said Helen, stepping away from Barney's body for the first time.

"It was an accident," said Mary.

"It was a goddamned massacre," said Bully. "Swung an ax like it was a golf club, caught poor Ruthie right on the chin. Split her face like a coconut. Took our girl a whole day to die."

"And last night you looked her in the eye!" said Helen. She tried to charge at Mary. I grabbed her with my free hand, trying to hold her back, but she slipped out of my grip. My knife cut her deeply, but she didn't care. She ran down the long, grim galley. I ran, too.

Mary swiped at Bully with the saw. He grabbed her wrist and squeezed. The saw dropped from her hand. He dropped to his knees, trying to grab it. Mary kicked him in the face, and then

Helen was on top of Mary, clawing at her, choking her. I raised the knife, trying to pretend I was ready to kill.

Helen slammed Mary back into the counter. Mary grabbed the closest heavy thing—an apothecary bottle filled with some unknown elixir—and brought it down on Helen's head. The bottle didn't break. Neither did her skull. But she reeled, half-conscious. I dropped the knife, grabbed her by the hair, and slammed her into the floor. She tried to sit up, and I stomped her face back into the tile. She stopped trying to move.

"Good god," said Mary.

"I'm finished with this family," I said.

The door to the backyard crashed shut. The silver was gone. So was Bully. So was my long knife. Through the filthy windows, we saw him struggling to hang on to the Gladstone. We pushed our way outside just as he abandoned the bag, littering the snow with coins from another time, and bolted across the yard faster than I thought possible. We followed, but the snow was deep and our legs were tired. He ran into the shed. We were almost at its doors when they exploded open, and Bully burst forth, riding bareback on what I suppose must have been the undertaker's horse. It was a towering gray animal, frightened of the driving snow and terrified of the man on its back.

The horse snorted, a terrible choking sound, and Bully kicked its flanks until it got up to speed. It charged down the alley. We ran after. By the time we reached the sidewalk, he was gone.

"Goddamn it," I shouted, stamping uselessly in the snow.

"Patience, patience. He's a friendless, coatless man riding a stolen horse through a hellish storm. Where could he possibly run?"

"He'll try to get off the island."

"He can't count on a ferry. It will have to be the bridge."

For a moment, I wondered which one she meant, but then I remembered where I was—a city with only one bridge worth a damn. When we turned onto Mulberry, Virgil called, from the steps of Brass's tenement: "Hullo!" We didn't stop. We just ran, or tried to, and he ran alongside.

After that, we didn't talk anymore. The storm had not slowed, and sunlight had done nothing to soften the snow, much less melt it. It was as tough a trip as our odyssey the night before, and the only thing that kept me moving was the knowledge that we had much less far to go.

We crossed Canal, hurling ourselves over snowbanks and raw ice, drawing stares from the few people foolish enough to be outside on this dismal morning. Another long block and we rounded the corner into Five Points. The doors of the ramshackle buildings that huddled around that famous slum were bolted shut, the streets emptier than they had ever been. Across the snow, we ran, we ran, we ran. This time I was in front, and this time I did not slow down.

As we neared the river, the wind blew fiercer than it had the night before, assaulting us with the stench of freezing salt water. At the edge of City Hall Park, Bully's horse lay broken and abandoned, its breath steaming through the snow. We ran past the poor beast and saw the bridge, whose span rose into the white. Not even the first tower could be seen.

On the approach to the bridge, the trolley waited for passengers that would not come. Past it a policeman leaned on the edge of the promenade, black uniform stained with blood, with his head tilted back and his hand clutching his nose. At the sound of Virgil's heavy footsteps, he lowered his head and recognized a brother officer.

"Where is he?" said Virgil.

"Ran east, sir, just bashed me in the face and ran."

Mary and I didn't break stride. We weren't running anymore; we were dragging our bodies up that glorious bridge, which had never seemed so steep or so new. The wood was lighter than I had ever known it, the stone less worn.

"Stop," shouted the policeman, his voice wet with blood. "In that wind, it's suicide!"

We didn't care. We were over the water now, where the gale came from every side, pelting us with snow and ice, threatening to hurl us into the river. We could not see the water, but I heard ice cracking against the boats like the snapping of faraway bones.

Manhattan was gone and Brooklyn impossibly far away. The whole world was white, screaming pain, but Mary was close by.

"Don't stop," she said, her arm wrapped tight around mine.

"I never would."

The first tower rose out of the swirl like a ship cutting through the fog. Its stone was as solid as the earth, its cables hardly twitching in the wind. In the whole city, here was the one thing the storm could not touch. And here we found Bully Byrd.

He slumped against the stone, pressing his face into the tower in a feeble attempt to escape the wind. He whimpered like a dying rat.

We stood over him. He looked small. I liked him that way.

"Get up," said Mary. "It's done."

I offered my hand—I'm not sure why, perhaps I'm kinder than I thought—and Bully took it. He squeezed tighter than he needed to. I was trying to wrench free when I remembered the knife.

It shone dully in the feeble light, clutched at his side in his red, gloveless hand. He swung it at me, a low, lazy haymaker, and Mary screamed, and I was too numb to get out of the way.

That long knife split my coat and split my dress, and would have split my side if it were still 1922. But this was the Gilded Age, when gaslight flickered and horseshoes echoed on cobblestones, and women were encased in whalebone or steel.

The knife bounced off my corset. Mary's fist smashed into Bully's wrist, and the blade fell from his hand, skipped off the promenade onto the trolley tracks, and then down to the invisible river.

"Damn," said Bully. "That was my last ace."

He smiled that cheeky smile, and I punched him in the mouth hard enough to make my knuckles rattle. It didn't accomplish anything in particular, but I was too numb for it to hurt.

The bridge rumbled. Out of the frost, the trolley ground its way along the icy tracks, making for Brooklyn at something slower than a walking pace. Far to the east, we heard its twin attempting to make the reverse trip.

"That's a lesson in patience," said Bully. "If I'd hid on the trolley, I'd be free now."

The promenade vibrated as Virgil Carr, late as ever, bounded up to the tower.

"Jesus goddamned Christ," he shouted. "This snow!"

"You have a marvelous grasp of the obvious," said Mary.

"I try. This the fellow?"

"Bulrush Byrd," said Bully. "Pleased to meet you."

"You've got blood on your face. Which one of them put it there?"

"I did," I said.

"Classy work," said Virgil. He wrenched Bully's arms behind his back and applied the handcuffs, then marched the preacher down the bridge, his pistol nestled against Bully's spine.

As we turned toward shore, the adrenaline seeped out. Mary slumped against me. Each step we took, we took together. We were nearly off the bridge when we saw a figure standing in the middle of the promenade, unbent by the snow. I assumed it was the cop. I think we all did. But it wasn't—it was the forgotten man.

"Father," said Enoch Byrd, standing in our way, dirtier than I believe he had ever been in his life. Where had he been for this last, long day, I wondered. What had he done to pass the storm? What had led him here, to this place? I didn't know, and I didn't ask. I lacked the strength, and anyway, this was not my moment.

Virgil shoved Bully toward him. Enoch, still looking at Bully like a wet-eyed boy who didn't understand why his father treated him so rough, took Bully's face in his hands. I thought he was going to speak, to unload a lifetime of misery and disappointment and betrayal. But perhaps he was cold, too. As the bridge rumbled with the weight of the trolley's twin rolling down from Brooklyn, Enoch pulled Bully to him and sobbed.

I looked at Mary. For that moment the sight of her was free of the pain that had clouded the last week. For that moment, she was simply my mother—younger than she should have been, of course, but back in my life in a truly miraculous way. And then the moment ended as her eyes went wide. She had seen Enoch's gun.

It was a small pistol, but dangerous enough. He pressed it against Bully's neck.

"Son," said Bully, hopeful, smiling again.

"I believed in you," said Enoch. "You killed her."

Enoch drew back the hammer, and he was about to fire when Bully smashed his forehead into his son's nose, once, twice. That was all it took.

Enoch staggered backward and the pistol fell, onto the tracks, down to the river. Enoch sagged against the wall of the promenade, and then he fell too, landing squarely in front of the Manhattan-bound trolley.

Its engines were powerful enough to fight back the storm. No matter how strong Enoch's faith, it could not stop that terrible machine. It ground over him, not pausing, not even shuddering, leaving something too broken to be called a man.

NINETEEN

It took us hours to reach the Electric Church, during a walk as snow-blind and painful as the one the night before, but far more pleasant because Mary was beside me, because in the moments I could forget the horror of what had happened to Enoch, it almost felt like we had won.

As we walked, Virgil alternated between abusing Bully and making increasingly desperate attempts to impress Mary Fall. He failed to make an impression on either. Bully was catatonic, a walking corpse, and Mary had eyes for the future alone.

"I should like a little apartment," she said, "something desperately small, even depressing, but every inch my own."

"You could live with me," I said. "As long as you want. I have the room."

"Oh, Gilda, we'd kill each other within a week. And I'll need a job. Women in your city can get jobs, can't they?"

"If they're lucky, pretty, or smart."

"And I'm all three."

"No chance of enticing you to join me at my work?"

"One tiny mystery nearly killed me. I don't think I can stand much more. But don't look so gloomy, Gilda dear! I may not be your mother, precisely, but I will always be your friend."

Her voice was as warm and welcome as a coal fire. It wasn't what I'd always wanted, but it was better than I could have hoped. And it would all be mine—assuming I survived.

We were crossing Broadway when something that had been troubling Mary finally bubbled up.

"You said you knew from experience," she said, "you said you knew about killing."

"Yes."

"How?"

"Last fall I killed two people, a man and a woman."

"Did they deserve it?"

"If anyone ever can. But that didn't make it easier, and it didn't make it right."

"How did you move past it?"

"I didn't."

"Well, you're going to have to. We'll both have to. We are too young and too pretty, Miss Carr, to let guilt weigh us down."

Even through countless inches of snow, the Electric Church stank of burned wood and charred flesh. When we reached it, Virgil gave Bully a final shove toward the archway, which was half buried in the snow. I reached into his vest and pulled out the notebook and the snuffbox.

"Is there enough powder for the ritual?" I said.

"Should be enough for one more go."

"You open the gate. We step through, and you come with."

"What if I refuse?"

Mary took the pistol out of Virgil's hand. She pointed it, straight and steady, at Bully's heart.

"In that case," said Bully, "we'll need a fire."

"There's plenty of wood under the snow," I said. "Dig."

Virgil uncuffed him, and Bully knocked the snow away with his hands, scrambling to collect the shards of old pews before the driving wind buried them again. Mary kept the pistol trained on him the whole time. Virgil stared at her unashamedly, chuckling occasionally, waiting for someone to notice him. We both did our best not to. Finally, he couldn't stand it anymore.

"So what's it all about?" he said. "I'm a patient man, I've tried not to press or pester. But you two act like you're about to vanish for good, and for the life of me, I can't figure out where."

"He'll light a fire," said Mary. "He'll talk. He'll toss a handful of that powder and a gate will open that she and I will step through."

"To where?"

"1922."

"That must be the silliest thing I ever heard." Mary shrugged, and Virgil settled back into his unwilling silence. After a few seconds, he broke it again. "Really, though . . . 1922?"

"1922."

"You both came from there?"

"Gilda did. I didn't."

"But you're going back there, to stay forever?"

"I am."

He rapped a knuckle against his club, searching for the words that would make her stay. Finally, he hit on his best attempt.

"Now I'll ask you," he said, "what's 1922 got that we can't give you right here?"

"Everything."

"Everything. A fella can hardly compete with that." Another long pause. "Say—can I come too?"

"I don't think the future could hold you."

"Well! I've been rejected by women before—not often, but enough to recognize it—and I must say this is the firmest refusal I've ever heard. Go with my compliments. May you live to see the new millennium."

He tipped his hat, bowing low enough to make her smile. I smiled, too. It was something Cherub would have done.

Bully tossed a final chunk of wood onto the snowbound base of the arch. He shaped the pile into a rough pyramid.

"You call that a fire?" said Virgil. He pushed Bully aside and finished preparing it himself. Boys. Whatever century, good god they are predictable. "There. That'll burn like hell itself."

Virgil lit the fire with as much masculine swagger as he could muster. Once it flickered to life, he leaned back on his heels and watched it pop and crackle.

"I spent my whole life selling suckers on life after death," said Bully. I wasn't sure if he was talking to me, to himself, or to his dead. "When I finally hit on a real miracle, things got too twisted up for me to use it. I could have made a million."

"Where did the ritual come from?" I said.

"My pa. He said he'd gotten it from his daddy, who claimed to have been told it in a dream, whispered by Satan himself. He was a bad drunk and a relentless liar, though, so . . . y'know. My old man was too yellow to ever use it. I stayed away from it, too, until I was desperate. As you can see, it didn't quite work out."

Virgil placed his club on Bully's shoulder, as gentle as a mother's touch, and said, "Shut up and get started."

Bully brushed the club off and opened his notebook.

"Quiet, detective," he said. "I have one last sermon to preach."

He planted his feet above the fire and started in on the Latin. I'd only ever heard it mumbled before, but this time he belted it out, his mouth tearing its way around the awkward corners of words unknown, forming syllables ugly enough that they did not sound of this earth. When the flames were at their highest and the liturgy most unbearable, I handed him the snuffbox.

I had not planned it, but I took Mary's hand. She looked at me, almost giddy, a girl about to go on a trip she had waited for her entire life. I squeezed her tight, and we stepped in front of the archway.

His eyes closed, Bully emptied the snuffbox into his palm. I had just enough time to think that it looked like quite a lot of the stuff when he threw it into the fire and the world exploded blue.

My skin felt hot and tight, like I'd been in the sun too long, and for a moment I worried my eyebrows had been burned away. I opened my eyes—or had they been open the whole time?—and saw Virgil step to Bully, swinging his club over his head. Bully ducked the blow, picked up a log from the fire, and swung a flaming blue arc at Virgil's chest. It caught Virgil on the flank, spreading like termites across his heavy black coat. He twisted, trying to smack the flames dead, then stepped into thin air and fell backward into the snow.

Mary fired the gun twice, but her eyes were squinting and her balance was off and the bullets went far wide. Bully swung his flaming log. Mary jumped back, and I kicked him in the side of the leg. He stumbled, dropping his timber, then swept his hand up and seized Mary's wrist. I tried to loose his grip, but he twisted Mary's arm until the pistol dropped into his hand.

That's when everything stopped.

This is what I loathe about firearms. A swung fist, a broken bottle, a hurled rock, a chain twisted around your opponent's neck—these are weapons that ask questions. Am I stronger? Am I faster? Did I throw it hard enough? Am I mad enough to pull this until you stop thrashing and I have won? But a pistol doesn't ask questions. It answers them, and its decision is always final. Guns are ugly. They are dull. They are a perfect match for men like Bully Byrd.

Behind him, the fire opened and reached across the archway like spreading vines. It filled the gap in the wall with that hypnotizing turquoise glow.

"Step back," he said. "Don't try to follow me. Or it's a bullet in your throat."

"Even without us," said Mary, "you're dead in this century or any other."

"If there's one thing I've proved this month, it's that I'm smarter than death."

He pressed the gun to Mary's neck.

"Back," he said.

"Gilda—" said Mary.

"No," I answered. "We do not give in to him. We are getting you away from here."

The turquoise light dimmed. The screaming wind that flowed through the gate dropped to a whisper.

"What will it be?" said Bully.

Mary took a long step back.

"Thank you, ma'am," he said. "But I'd still feel better if you were both dead."

He swung the pistol toward her face.

I jabbed my elbow to the right, catching Mary in the temple and knocking her out of the way just before the gun went off.

Bully twisted, falling toward the gate, and fixed the gun on Mary. This time, he wouldn't miss.

I didn't have time to look at her. I don't know if she was afraid or resigned. I've tried many times to picture her expression, but there is no version of it that stills the guilt in my heart.

I flung myself at Bully as he squeezed the trigger. We tumbled across the threshold and were gone.

On my first trip across the decades, I had closed my eyes to the blinding light. This time, I forced them open and saw the dead.

They were not as I had seen them before. These were not sightless ghouls with arms of smoke, nor were they corpses rotting in the street, nor bodies burned far past the point of looking human. As I fell back toward the twentieth century, I saw the dead as they had been in life—as real, as boring as you or me.

I watched Mary stagger off the burning platform, rubbing her head with her hand, and haul Virgil out of the snow. She dragged him to the street and they leaned on a snowdrift. He patted his pockets and scowled when he remembered he had thrown away his flask. I couldn't hear what they said, but I saw her swallow her anger and force herself to laugh. Watching this was harder than I could stand. I turned away, and I never saw her again.

I saw Helen Byrd, warped by grief, dragging that satchel of stolen silver back to her apartment through the snow, using it to give her children the best life she could provide. I saw them hang their father's picture on the wall.

I watched Judy and Ruth learn to preach, each aping their father in their own way, and I saw Abner rebel against his family, striking out on his own and finding that life in the church had prepared him admirably for life among thieves. I was there when Enoch talked his way into an apprenticeship at a print shop and found that rows of hard type responded to his obsession with order in a way the real world never could.

Over my shoulder I found every life ever lived. Bowery boys watched the sun rise over Five Points. Runaway slaves escaped through Manhattan. British soldiers gambled in the back rooms of old pubs. Dutch traders carved geese and served it to their families. Lenape women looked out at the river, sipping drinks and telling jokes. Millions of people walked this island, their lives so typical, so real to them, now gone so thoroughly cold.

We crashed out of time just as the trigger clicked and the hammer hit home. But this was my Westside, where guns did not fire.

I may have smiled as I punched him in the face. I had nothing to be happy about, lord knows, but there was satisfaction in knowing that he was just as ruined as I. My fist connected with his nose like I was pounding wet dough. He screamed and kicked, and knocked me onto my side.

We got up and attempted to fight. Our limbs were heavy and our vision blurred. We moved like we were underwater. My feet tangled up in themselves and every step I took forward was followed by two back, but I landed a few soft blows, and I did not quit. I knew that soon my head would clear and my muscles would awaken and I would be able to end him.

I have killed before. I had expected the misery of it to fade, but five months later, the feeling felt more sour every time it returned to me—and it returned more often than I can say. I felt I did not know myself anymore, that something vital had been lost from me, and all I wanted when I thought of the corpses I had made was to never kill again.

But as I fought through the fog and tried to get my feet to straighten, all I could think was that this man had stolen my mother from me, and for that he deserved to die.

I was ready to crush his skull with my bare hands. If I'd gotten a grip on him, I certainly would have tried. I'd like to think that I would have eventually beaten him down. He was injured and weary from too many days on the run, and I had fury on my side. In a fair fight, I'd have had him, but every fight on the Westside is a little bit fixed. I did not get my shot.

"It's done," I mumbled.

"Naw," said Bully, and then his mouth fell open in a bloody smile. I turned to see what he was looking at, and before I got my head all the way around, something heavy cracked over my skull. My legs went out from under me, and before I knew it, I was falling through the air, to land on a pile of packed snow.

Oh, I thought. Snow. I'm so tired of snow.

My eyes were closing again, and this time I could not fight them for long. But before my vision fuzzed into black, I saw whoever it was that had clubbed me senseless stride toward Bully Byrd.

"Hello, friend," said Bully. "Have you heard the gospel of the electric resurrection?"

The figure answered by bringing a club down hard on Bully's face, once, twice, and again and again until the preacher didn't have a face anymore.

I slept longer than I should have. God knows I needed it. When I woke, our assailant was gone, the sun was low, and there was frost on Bully's dead sneer. I dug my arms beneath his shoulders and tried to do what I should have done for Tom MacNaughton the day I found him, to get him out of this shadowy, wooded hell. But Bully, who had danced so nimbly across life, was far too heavy for me to move.

I forced one foot in front of the other, following twisted paths that had become almost familiar until I broke onto Sixth Avenue. A few blocks north, I recognized the multicolored uniforms of Van Alen's guards as they prepared that night's candles. If I couldn't get that body to Ida Greene before the sun was gone, those feeble, invaluable lights would never burn again.

I screamed for them, leaping and stomping and waving numb arms, but the wind was against me. If they heard, they didn't care. They turned their backs and were gone.

"Sons of bitches," said a voice at my back. "Rainbow silks. A stupid joke."

I turned and saw a weather-beaten Senegalese man with an improbable hairline and a gut as round as a cannonball. He was a sailor, or used to be. I knew him from Berk's, Lamb's, and a few of my other favorite unsavory dives. His name, I think, was Malik. I had not seen him that winter and, though I hadn't thought of it, I'd assumed he was dead. I wondered if he'd assumed the same for me.

"Gilda, right?" he said. "You need help?"

"Only every day. Were you at the Flat the other night?"

"Aye. The things I did to scrounge up two bucks in silver. Bastards."

"How'd you like to see the corpse of the man who stole it from you?"

A vicious smile lit up his face. I pointed toward the Thicket and led him into the dark. When we found Bully, Malik prodded the corpse and grunted approval. His face fell when I told him what I needed next.

"Can you help me lug him out of here?" I said.

"Like hell."

"Would you do it for a jug of gin?"

He didn't say anything. He just bent down and started to drag.

I don't know how long it took us to wrestle Bully's corpse through the woods. Rocks and sticks and shards of ice tore his suit and his flesh until his backside was a mess of bloody fabric. No matter how rough the going, though, I made sure to protect his face.

The trip was tough on our bodies, too, and by the time we made it back to the street we could hardly stand upright. We kept moving, though, sliding the corpse up the ice as best we could. At the first intersection, three passing drunks saw us, and recognized the tortured corpse, and volunteered to help without us having to ask.

"I'd have liked to burn this bastard alive," said one of them, a woman of indeterminate age whose hair, face, and clothes were all the same coarse gray. "This is the next best thing."

They carried him on their shoulders. I was too short to join in, but they told me to save my strength. I did not argue. Black was creeping in at the sides of my vision. I wanted so badly to sleep.

We moved faster now. At every corner, others joined our procession: one or two more of my lunatics, addicts, poets, highwaymen, killers, black sheep, and prodigal daughters. By the time we got to Morton Creek, there were fifty of us—not a bad crowd for a cold afternoon on the Lower West—and we were singing too loudly to be ignored.

I banged on the great barn doors. High above, the office window shot open. Ida Greene's quizzical face peered down at the assemblage below.

"Hmph," she said. "Come in, Miss Carr. The corpse you may leave outside."

Inside, the machines were quiet and the tang of yeast was gone. Crates were stacked halfway to the ceiling. The aproned gin maids leaned against their silenced stills, admiring the frost on their breath and the smoke that curled from their cigarettes. They watched me stumble across the floor and offered no help as I started up those steep stairs. I didn't complain. I'd gotten more help today than I'd ever hoped for.

Mrs. Greene stepped out of her office and watched me fight against the stairs. When I was halfway, she called down, "Your time is nearly up. Are you sure you don't want to walk just a bit faster?"

I expended what was left of my energy and got across the catwalk as quickly as I could. I tried not to let her see how hard I breathed.

"I've got him," I said. "I brought him in time. You don't have to leave."

"Is he as dead as he looks?"

"Yes."

"Who killed him?" She stared down her nose, almost smiling. I think she wanted to hear that it was me.

"I'm still sorting that out."

"It doesn't really matter."

"Tell your workers to start unpacking and get those machines bubbling again. The crowd outside deserves a drink."

"I'll do just that. But first, why don't you come inside the office? It's a bit warmer there."

If it was, I didn't feel it. Everything was boxed up, save for the pen and paper in the middle of Mrs. Greene's desk. Even the chairs were gone. Van Alen wasn't there, but there were three men standing in the corner he'd occupied the last time I'd come. Three men with the thick necks, soft faces, and dead eyes of Roebling's finest. They stood in a line against the far wall, their hands buried in black coats, staring at nothing.

"What are they doing here?" I said.

"You've arrived just in time for a historic event. The signing of a truce between Westside and East, between the empire of light and the Roebling Company."

I didn't swoon. I didn't scream. I'd taken so many blows to my spirit and my body over the last few days. This one hurt worse than most, but it wasn't going to knock me down.

"You're giving them the Lower West," I said.

"Hardly."

"The company has no interest in holding territory," said the tallest gray man. I was certain I'd seen him before, but lord, it was hard to tell. "The Lower West is a business opportunity, nothing more."

"What's the business?" I said, too angry to move, to think, to do anything but stare at him and hope my look was sharp enough to pierce his heart. "Drugs? Liquor? Early death?"

"Those are services we offer, yes, and much, much more."

Mrs. Greene picked up the paper and read it one more time, rolling her pen between her lips.

"Are you going to try to justify this to me," I said, "or shall I ask my mob to storm the building?"

"There will be no need for such theatrics," she said. "The Basement Club was an experiment—an attempt to see if the Roebling Company's product could find an audience on this side of the fence. As you saw yourself, it did. Mr. Van Alen has found the Lower West to be a financial and spiritual drain. He is a humanitarian, not a gin slinger. And so we're selling the distillery and giving Roebling permission to develop a few blocks of disused waterfront property—a stretch of docklands not far from here."

"That's a hell of a stupid mistake for a smart woman to make. This company is a cancer. They spread fast. They can't be controlled."

"Thank you for your concern."

"And what does Van Alen get out of it?"

"Money. Lots of it. Enough to buy beds for laboring women, heat for those miserable souls huddled in the bottom of St. Vincent's, and food for all the hungry people assembled outside. It's a good deal, Miss Carr, and you can't stop it."

"We had a deal, too. I brought you Bully Byrd before the sun went down."

"Well done. Someday, you'll have to tell me how. For now, be happy that you are getting what you want. Van Alen's flag still flies above the Lower Westside. It's just . . . going to have some company. Now get home before your legs fall out from under you. I have papers to sign."

I left the office and waited outside, hidden in the shadows to the right of the door. After a bit of silence, the gray men emerged. I waited until they were halfway across the catwalk to slip behind the last one, the tallest one, kick him in the back of the knee, and push him face-first over the edge. I held him by the belt, but not very tight. His fellows watched, as still as death.

"Kill me if you want," said the dangling man. "The company won't care."

"But you will. I don't care about this crooked deal. All I want to know is, am I right?"

"About what?"

"You were the one with the arrows. The one in the trees."

"What does it matter?" I moved my hand forward. Another inch, and he would fall. "Yeah. Yeah, it was me."

"Who sent you?"

"I gotta check my book."

I pulled him back. He sat down and reached a shaking hand into the inside pocket of his coat, to pull out a little leather book printed in immaculate Roebling ink. He flipped back a few days and showed me the entry: "Kill Gilda Carr (Washington Sq. West/Westside/NO GUNS)."

"Who ordered it?" I said.

"The man at the top," he answered, and pointed to the signature that proved it.

At the other end of the catwalk, Mrs. Greene slammed her office door.

"You are a terrible disruption," she said. I thanked her for the compliment, pushed past the gray men, and stepped down the stairs as fast as my trembling legs would allow. When I got outside, Malik and the crowd were waiting for me with Bully's body still held aloft.

"Did it work?" he asked.

"Break down the doors and take as much liquor as you want," I said. "That's the best I can give you today."

"What do we do with the body?"

I tugged Enoch's snuffbox from Bully's gnarled fingers and said, "I don't care what you do with the rest of him." As I walked away, they chucked him in the creek—another corpse to bob between the hunks of Westside ice.

TWENTY

After two or three days of heavy sleep, I invaded a room that stank of money, leather, and all the liniments and creams required to keep brittle old skin from cracking. Tightly drawn blinds shut out the morning sun. The air was thick enough to swim in.

Eight men sat around a titanic wooden table, listening to a murmuring report of, I realized after a few moments, heroin sales, building by building in a block on Mott Street. Storrs Roebling sat at the side of the table. He was the youngest there, and the most awake. He etched notes on a pad of paper, staring intently at the man reading the report, who was working very hard not to meet his boss's eye.

No one looked at me when I entered the room. No one turned when I rapped on the corner of the table, or when I spoke up, as clearly as my mother taught me, to say "Roebling." Money was talking, and money had to be heard.

A side table held four carafes of water and a platter of disheartening sandwiches. I stretched out my arm and walked its length, sweeping its contents onto the floor. The carafes shattered. The carpet flooded. The sandwiches were put out of their misery.

The murmuring stopped as the men at the table jumped into their chairs to save their shoeshines. Only Storrs stayed put. The doors opened, and the guards I had dodged in the hall appeared, pointing semiautomatic pistols at my skull.

"I have business with the Roebling Company," I said.

"Making a mess is no way to get a meeting, Miss Carr," said Storrs, still not looking up. He rapped his pen like a marching band drummer. "Your report, Carver."

"But sir," said the man who had so lovingly detailed the wildfire spread of opiates across his territory. "The rug."

"We are on a schedule."

Carver, shaking, lowered his feet into the puddle beneath his chair and read the last few lines of his report.

"Fine," said Roebling. "We're twenty-eight seconds behind. Make a note in the minutes, Carlisle. It will come out of lunch. Next we have Monroe detailing his penetration of the Eighth Precinct using blackmail and simple graft. Monroe?"

"No," I said, before Monroe could get started. "I have to speak to the boss."

"A truly observant detective would see that I am engaged."

"I didn't mean you," I said. I walked across the room, to the black glass panel that occupied the far wall. From my pocket I took the snuffbox, monogrammed *E. B.* I held it up to the glass.

A little door opened and a little old man stepped out, cane first.

"Jerome," I said.

"Miss Carr. I do think it would be profitable to have a word."

We left that rich, damp room. Before the door shut behind us, another timekeeper stepped into the compartment, and the meeting recommenced.

Men with guns tried to follow us, but Jerome waved them away. The hallway ended at a small terrace where all the furniture had been stacked in the corner and covered for winter. Broadway was a dull noise, seventy feet below. The buildings around blocked out the morning sun, and there was nothing to see but the snow-clogged Westside, where only the shocking green of the Thicket provided any relief from the gray.

"I'm disappointed I didn't recognize you before," I said.

"It's amazing what thirty-four years will do to a man. How did you work it out?"

"You died under that trolley."

"Almost. The cop and the motorman peeled me off the tracks, got me warm, saved my life. Born again."

"And so you named yourself after the Roeblings, the men who built the bridge."

"I've always admired people whose work stands the test of time."

"It clicked for me the other night while I was falling asleep in the snow, wondering if I was going to die. The other day one of your gray men confirmed it. The order in his book that put a target on my back was signed J. Roebling. Storrs really had no idea."

Overhead, a pair of seagulls screamed at each other. The old man turned and watched them wheel around the perfect, cloudless sky.

"How, Enoch? How did that sweet, dull printer turn into you?"

"I spent quite a long time in the hospital. If you've never been on the receiving end of nineteenth century medical care, I don't recommend it. Simply grisly, but I survived. I got back on my feet, and while I was trying to remember how to walk I looked at a newspaper, and read the date—December 1888—and I thought how long I had to go before I was back to the world I knew. I couldn't stand the weight of time. If I was stuck repeating the worst years humanity has ever faced, I wanted to get rich along the way."

"Why drugs? Why violence?"

"I spent half a lifetime doing God's work. My reward was three decades and more in an inescapable prison. Once I reckoned with that, I saw no reason to stay on my old path."

"And who is Storrs?"

"My son. He is not a good man."

He tilted his head back, and beneath the age and the moustache, just for a moment, I saw the man he'd been when we met, pushing beautifully printed tracts to drunks who wanted anything but to hear the word of God.

"You were at the church when I came back," I said. He nodded. "You killed your father when he stepped through the gate."

"I failed on the bridge. I spent thirty-four years promising I would not miss again."

"But you did, didn't you? Because this was not your first attempt."

"Correct."

"You tried to kill him when he came through the gate the first time. What happened?"

"I remembered from my life as Enoch that he would be brought back on March sixth. I didn't remember what time. I spent hours in the cold, waiting for my younger self to perform that damned ritual, waiting for the gate to open, waiting to bash simple, stupid Enoch on the head. When Bully stepped through—I don't know if I was numb or nervous or scared, but I made a mistake."

"You killed Tom instead."

"One swing of my cane, and he fell."

"That's an awfully casual way to describe the death of a good man."

"What do you know about him? What do you care?"

"I knew someone to whom he was very dear."

"In the dark, they looked the same. My eyes were weak from waiting, and anyway, I knew I was going to fail."

"Why?"

He flicked his eyes at the Thicket, at Spring Street, at a floating apartment littered with useless memories where no one would ever go again.

"You don't know what it is to be trapped in history," he said. "The vanishings. The war. The influenza. I lived through it all once, and when you left me on that bridge, you condemned me to see it all again."

"I didn't know."

He shrugged. "I wrote letters, you know. I warned Franz Ferdinand to stay out of Sarajevo. I cautioned the captain of the *Titanic* to watch for icebergs. Every tragedy I could recall, I warned the principals against, but they sailed into them anyway. The closer I got to my father's return, the more I was certain I would not be able to break the pattern I had lived through before. He would survive his transit through the gate. He would reappear at the banquet hall; he would escape the blow of Mary's ax. He would make it back to

'88, and he would get the better of a young, incompetent Enoch Byrd. He would kill my mother."

"But once Enoch was left behind, you didn't know what was going to happen next."

"And I was free to act."

Then Mary was wrong. History cannot change. No one can be saved. She had been doomed from the moment she stepped through the gate, and no struggle could have saved her. That tragedy was not Enoch's fault, but it pitched my anger just a little bit higher. For the first time, I noticed how close he was standing to the terrace's edge.

"The Basement Club," I said.

"I rigged the raffle machine. I set the fire."

"Why?"

"In hopes of killing you. I remembered the heroic way you knocked Mary aside at the ceremony, deflecting her blow onto Ruth. Things would have been easier with you out of the way. And I admit, the idea of taking revenge on the woman who left me behind all those years ago had a certain appeal."

"But Abner . . ."

"I sent him a letter, too. He ignored it. They all do. And anyway, he died for me a long time ago."

He tugged a small gold watch from the pocket of his vest. He said nothing, but I could tell he was running out of time.

"You knocked me out at the church," I said. "Why didn't you kill me?"

"Oh, I was planning on it. I stood over your body. I held my cane over your head. But a funny thing happens when a man finally succeeds in murdering his father. I felt so terribly free. I've spent so long trapped repeating patterns. At that moment, I knew I could do whatever I wanted. And anyway, I always liked you, Gilda. You found my blue ink."

He leaned back onto the lifeless ivy and let his elbows dangle off the wall.

"Do you need a push?" I said.

"I need to know I gave you the choice, but no—I don't want to fall. I've spent two whole lifetimes stuck in this awful winter. This is the part I've been waiting for. I want very badly to see the coming spring."

"Someone has to pay for Tom MacNaughton."

"What would you have me do?"

"Go to the police. Confess."

"They wouldn't believe a word. If you want me to pay, you'll have to take my blood yourself."

The seagulls screamed. I shook my head. Jerome walked away from the edge.

"I don't believe myself fit to dispense that kind of justice," I said. "I'm going to refer your case to a higher court."

"That's fine. I should get back to my work. But that reminds me—I owe you thirty-four years' interest on several months of work."

He tugged a fat wallet from inside his coat and withdrew an obscene wad of cash. That money was made from blood and misery, but I had a hole in the front of my house, and I saw no reason to turn it down. As we walked down the hallway, he asked a final question, one that would cost me sleep for the rest of the year, for the rest of my life.

"At the ceremony," he said, "what color was Mary's dress?"

"Black."

"Not yellow?"

"She had a yellow one, but she spilled wine on it. Why?"

"That is going to gnaw at me," he said as the elevator doors opened. "The first time it happened, I'd swear on every Bible I ever printed that she was wearing yellow."

The doors shut, and I rode down alone, left to decide for myself if an old man's memory had betrayed him, or if a switch in dress meant that everything could have changed.

On the facade of an old Italian banquet hall on Carmine Street, Judy Byrd wrote a list of names. She scrawled them out in chalk, in long columns not quite as neat as Enoch would have managed, writing from the cornice all the way to the ground. I looked close. I did not recognize a single one.

"Who are they?" I said.

"The vanished. Thousands that we know about, probably quite a few more. I always thought there should be a memorial. Now there is."

"Why chalk?"

"I don't have room for a tenth of them. When it rains, I start over. This will keep me busy as long as I need."

I tossed her an offering from the Eastside: two pounds of Carolina tobacco, smelling of summer right through the canvas bag. She sat, opened one, breathed deep, and rolled herself a cigarette.

"I found your saint's finger."

"I don't want it back. That church is going to stay dead."

"Do you want to know where I found it? What happened to it? Whose finger it really was?"

She crossed her legs, leaned her wrist on her knee, and ashed. I remembered Ruth doing the same thing. She thought for a long time.

"Will I feel better if I know any of that?" she said.

"I don't think so."

"Will you feel better for telling me?"

Yes. Yes, my god, yes, did I want to lay this burden down. But that's not what I told her.

"A client hires me to find something," I said. "I find it. If they don't want it back, don't want to know where it went, that's their business, not mine."

"Would you be surprised to hear that I can't afford to pay you for the work?"

"I took this job because I thought your family could give me— and I am very embarrassed even using this word—absolution. If I get nothing at all, that's what I deserve for being such a fool."

"There's gotta be something I can do."

"If you ever find me passed out on a snowbank, stand me up and smack me and tell me to go home."

"With pleasure."

There was something else. There was always something else. I chitchatted with her until her cigarette was finished, and then I told her to roll another one, looking grave enough that she did so without hesitation.

"I didn't think it was the finger that brought you by here," she said. She closed her eyes and took a hard drag.

"Enoch is alive."

"Oh?"

It may have been the first time I ever saw Judy Byrd look pleasantly surprised. She held the look even as I told her where Enoch was, how he'd survived, and all that he had done. When I was finished, she asked, "Why are you telling me?"

"He killed a man, a stranger, for no reason at all. He killed your father, too."

"My father was not worth mourning."

"Still. That might demand justice. I don't know one way or the other, but—"

"You wanted to make it my problem?"

"You are a determined woman, and the last one living who might care to avenge those crimes. If you wanted him dead, I'm sure you could see your way to make it happen."

She sat until her cigarette was smoked down to nothing, then flicked the butt in the street. She picked up her chalk and returned to her wall.

"I don't kill people," she said. "I may be the only person in my family who understood this, but murder is a sin."

"Then you really do believe."

"It's how I was raised. My parents may have been frauds, but I bought the lie. Now it's all I have."

I thanked her again, as deeply as I could. I set a donation on the banquet hall steps—half the money that Jerome had given me—and left her to her work. The city was frozen, and she glided across it with enviable ease. She had faith. The rest of us were not so lucky. We had to stumble forward, falling and busting our lips and getting up again, not sure where we were going, certain only that we had to keep moving, because to stop meant an end that could not be escaped.

I spent the rest of that winter in the Hall of Records, looking for some trace of the Mary I left behind. I wanted to find a Mary Fall who broke with destiny, who walked away from Virgil Carr to find a shabby rooming house and make her own life. No matter how deep I looked, I only found "Mary Fall, b. May 5, 1867, d. June 7, 1903." No matter how badly I wanted it to be otherwise, thirty-six years is never enough.

When the earth softened, I found Cherub Stevens and proposed something romantic: a walk in the woods.

"Bring a shovel," I said, and he was game enough not to ask why.

At the ruins of the Electric Church, a body waited on holy ground. We took turns digging, and before night came to the Thicket, we had given Tom MacNaughton a proper grave.

"Though there's a certain gothic appeal to burying a body at a ruined church," he said, "this was not the date I had in mind."

"Have a better idea?"

"I've been thinking of getting a boat. Something trim, easy to handle. Probably stolen. If I do, would you let me take you out on the river some fine spring afternoon?"

"I would like that."

He had the sense not to kiss me, but I rather wish he had. As we were walking away, the light caught on something half buried in a muddy patch of melted snow. A fake emerald ring, its band decorated with daisies. I put it on my right hand, beside the finger that wears my father's heavy band. I felt lighter for wearing it home.

As winter faded, the wreckage that filled my house became repellant. Every crowded table, every heap of paper, every cabinet filled with cloudy glasses I had never drunk out of and never would—it all reminded me too strongly of Anacostia Fall's mansion of junk. On the first warm day, I threw open my doors and windows, and launched as much stuff onto the sidewalk as my arms could stand to hurl. I smashed trinkets, broke glasses, destroyed furniture, and shattered plates. I made a bonfire of the crumbling newspapers that filled my parlor—though of course I rescued the box scores, and spent a happy weekend pasting them into a dozen sturdy albums.

When my sidewalk was cluttered and my house shockingly bare, I turned at last to the room that frightened me most. My parents' bedroom was almost impenetrable with dust—I did not blame Mary for turning up her nose—and I attacked every surface with a damp rag. I scrubbed like I was in a fever, wiping and coughing around the room, until I reached the battleship of a dresser that still held her old clothes.

I opened the window, sucked down some clean April air, and tossed her dresses out. They fluttered to the tall grass like waving flags, and I felt a little bit free.

I scrubbed the outside of the dresser and the inside, too. I was running my blackened rag beneath the bottom drawer when it caught on something. I reached under, pulled at the obstruction, and a letter came free in my hand.

"Gilda," it read. "If you ever stop moping long enough to pick up a duster, perhaps you will discover this little note."

> *I thought you deserved to know what happened. At the close of our adventure, I spent a week or two in the Gilda Carr mode, sulking about my mother's house, failing to scrub the blood from my hands, wondering what might have been. Once my hair grew long enough that I might appear in public, I went back to Lasko's and grabbed ahold of Det. Carr. (Starlight Angie did not look pleased with this, but we put her in her place—I think I've seen the last of her.) It took some time to quell my nausea, but we were finally married earlier this year.*
>
> *He's not an easy man to live with, but I'm working on breaking his spirit. He seems physically terrified of the fact that I am with child, and there's something almost sweet in how determined he is to do his part. I was up early this morning*

doing a bit of vomiting, and in between retches he suggested—quite unprompted—that if the baby's a girl we name her after that bizarre woman, Gilda, whom he credits with saving our lives the night of the blizzard of '88. I did not disagree.

The nausea has done its part to distract me from what I did to Ruth, and what must come on June 7, 1903. Those black thoughts intrude every so often—no more than ten or fifteen times a minute, I assure you—but it's getting easier to beat them back. Thank you for all you did for me. I'm sorry we didn't manage it, but I'm glad we had our try. I've got more than a decade to come to terms with what will happen, and I intend to make it count. Dying young is no tragedy if it means ten years with a child as remarkable as Gilda Carr.

I shall be, apparently,
Your mother.

I wiped my tears off the letter before they could stain it too badly. I didn't believe her, not all the way. Mary Fall lived life too well to let it go. But god I loved her for the lie.

ACKNOWLEDGMENTS

I must give supreme thanks to the magnificent, incomparable, other-worldly Sharon Pelletier, and equal gratitude to David Pomerico, Mireya Chiriboga, Camille Collins, Angela Craft, Paula Szafranski, Owen Corrigan, and everyone else possessed of the talent and grace necessary to work at Harper Voyager.

Closer to home, I owe an overwhelming debt to my wife, Yvonne, who spent huge chunks of her maternity leave watching both kids so that I could hammer out this book's first draft. Thanks as well to my parents; my brother, Caldwell; and my children, Dash and August, since if they weren't good sleepers I would never get anything done at all.

ABOUT THE AUTHOR

W. M. Akers is an award-winning playwright, the author of *Westside,* and the creator of the bestselling games *Deadball: Baseball with Dice* and *Comrades: A Revolutionary RPG.* He lives in Philadelphia.